SWEARING AT A SEA MONSTER

FOLK HAVEN BOOK THREE

LAUREN CONNOLLY

For the monsters who are not monstrous.

 Created with Vellum

CONTENT WARNINGS

This book contains scenes with discrimination, violence, captivity, and attempted assault. In addition, there are discussions of manipulative relationships and past hate crimes.

1
———

MOIRA

WHEN I PUSH through the front doors of Town Hall, I'm ready to go to battle. My territory is under attack.

Sort of. No one has shown up on the shores in Viking boats, attempting to pillage my village, or convinced me to wheel a giant wooden horse behind my protective walls.

This assault is subtler but an attack all the same.

Despite my simmering anger, I keep a professionally pleasant smile on my face as I walk through the grandest building in Folk Haven. Not that there's much competition. Tucked away in the forests of northeastern Georgia, this small town boasts few impressive buildings, tending to tilt toward quaint. But Town Hall tries to put on airs with its towering ceilings and ornate molding and polished marble floors. Wood would have suited the space fine, but the founders of Folk Haven had a point to prove.

To whom? I'm still not sure.

"Heya, Moira. Council meeting today?" The greeting comes as I pass by a cracked door.

I pause long enough to peek my head in, meeting the kind eyes of Samantha, police chief and mermaid. That second fact makes her one of my constituents.

"It is. We're having two petitioners come to speak at nine thirty. If they accidentally wander in here, can you point them our way?"

"Will do. Do I know them?" Normally, the question would be laughable. With a town this small, it's hard not to know everyone, especially when you work in a public office.

But this meeting is odd for more than one reason.

"Not sure. Two witches from out of town. They haven't been here long. Names are Morgana and Amethyst." My eyes flit down to the meeting agenda I hastily printed this morning, immediately regretting the glance when I re-read the last-minute add-on.

"Witch names if I ever heard them." The mermaid snorts as she absentmindedly drags her fingers through inch-long blonde strands. A habit she's had since grade school, although back then, her tresses grew past her waist. I can still remember how her milk-pale skin would flush a blotchy red when our classmates called her Rapunzel. No one is brave enough to do so now that she's got a gun hooked to her belt. "I'll keep an eye out. I'm on the desk till the rest of the slackers show up."

The rest referring to the three other police officers Folk Haven has. A tiny force for a tiny town.

Not that I'm complaining.

Less police means less people to catch me after I murder Levi Abadi for sticking my business on The Council agenda.

"Thanks." I manage to keep my renewed anger out of my voice as I head farther into the building to the room reserved the first Monday of each month for the Folk Haven Mythic Council meeting.

When I push the door open and find the space empty, I silently thank my brother Seamus for grabbing me a latte this morning, so I didn't have to delay with a side trip to Coffee & Claws.

Now, I can pick a power position. One more tool in my arsenal against the coming attack. I'm debating if my back should be to the windows when Trayvon, the mayor's assistant, shuffles in, carrying a tray with water and glasses.

"You're early," he chirps, friendly smile solidly in place, even as his armful wobbles.

"Here. I can get that." I pluck the tray from his arms and carefully place the load on the conference table.

"Thank you." He uses his empty hand to push a set of curls even tighter than mine off his forehead. "I forgot there was a reason I never tried waiting tables." He grins, flashing a set of slightly-crooked-in-a-charming-way white teeth. "Do you know, I've spilled at least three drinks on Mayor Nightson, and she still hasn't fired me? People have to think I'm blackmailing her to keep my job."

If anyone thinks that, they're obtuse. Trayvon graduated with a 4.0 GPA in political science and could easily have gotten a job in a larger town or a city like Atlanta. And since he's a human, no one would have blamed him for leaving this town built primarily for mythical creatures. But he came home, and Belinda Nightson knows the importance of keeping talent in Folk Haven. She immediately took the young man under her wing. Literally and figuratively, seeing as how the woman is a griffin.

We go through the normal small talk as I settle in the best chair at the table. Trayvon's upbeat conversation abruptly ends with the next arrival.

Juan Greymark, beta of the Folk Haven wolf pack and council member representing Of the Claw mythics, meanders into the room.

Trayvon gives the shifter a tight smile, polite nod, and then beats a quick retreat. Juan and I exchange a silent look, both knowing what the other is thinking.

He's going to need to get over that if he ever wants to become mayor.

Tray's friendly nature shuts off around the wolves. Not out of fear. The exact opposite. Greymark's daughter broke the human boy's heart when she decided to go to college in Canada and stay there.

One more piece of the gossip foundation that supports a small town. I'm convinced the entirety of Folk Haven would crumble without all the little dramas that fill townsfolk's lives.

But that doesn't mean I'm going to give a slight against me a free pass.

As Juan pulls out a chair that has him facing the door, another council member arrives.

"Hello, Georgiana," I offer the greeting as I arrange my items, trying to smooth the wrinkles out of the agenda I scrunched up in anger after reading it the first time. Despite the itchy annoyance still coursing through my veins, I cannot abide the cluttered appearance. If I'm going to win the upcoming showdown, I need to be an utter professional. Not a petulant child.

Tomorrow is the dark moon, I remind myself. *I'll get to swim for the whole night in my selkie form. Slip into the cool water and finally be free from all responsibility for a time.* The thought helps me calm myself and pull on my usual unflappable boss-bitch armor.

"Moira," the siren responds with a beauty-pageant smile. The expression sits perfectly on her Southern belle face.

I never trust that kind of smile. That's the expression the senators wore before knifing Caesar in the back—I'm sure of it.

Not that I would ever call the woman on it. Georgiana is a master at twisting words to her benefit, which helped her win the council spot reserved for an Of the Wing mythic. Still, I get the sense that the majority viewpoints of her constituents are shifting from traditional to progressive, and the siren might not come out the next election with a victory. Will be interesting to watch next year.

My own council seat race was laughably easy. I would have relished a true competition. My only challenger was a merman who made promises like he was running for student body president.

Later noise curfews on the lake! First choice for fishing spots! Free boats for every voter!

That last one, which I'm sure he thought was his clincher, shot him in the fin. People knew an empty promise when they heard it, and my practice of visiting every water mythic to discuss their needs and concerns garnered me over eighty percent of the votes. Maybe next time, someone will give me an actual fight.

"I am awake before noon. I hope you all are happy." The whip of a voice comes from the doorway as the witch council member enters. Selena strolls to the first open chair and collapses into the thing like a sulky teenager rather than the sixty-year-old woman she is.

Even though Selena's views and voting practices are unpredictable, I've reached the conclusion that I like the witch. Like me, she takes no shit and is up front about the fact.

"So sorry to have disturbed your beauty rest," Georgiana offers with the exact amount of sweetener required to convey her contempt for the witch.

"Not all of us can naturally look this gorgeous. Goddess knows I can't." Selena rubs strong hands over onyx cheeks with the smoothness of a woman thirty years her junior. "Thank the elements for healing witches and their cosmetic spells. Of course, you wouldn't know anything about those, Georgiana, would you?"

The blow lands. The siren must be approaching fifty, and

she has yet to show a wrinkle in her ivory skin. With the amount of judgmental eye-squinting she does, there should at least be the hint of crow's-feet. Even at thirty-five, I'm starting to spot creases when I look in the mirror.

Georgiana doesn't say a word, but a flash of fury in her eyes, there and gone, is plenty revealing.

Seems like today has everyone on edge.

I should focus more on playing peacekeeper than revving up for my own fight. The Council is supposed to act as an example for the residents of the town. To show how mythics can coexist and work together.

We have in the past. There are even times we all unanimously agree on an issue. Rare, but it has happened. At the core, I do believe we all have the good of Folk Haven driving our decisions. The definition of *good* is what causes problems.

At one time, The Council only had to deal with four differing views. In those days, the mayor acted as a deciding vote in the event of a tie. But in the original bylaws, The Council creators stated a new seat could be added if a faction of forty or more mythics, gathered under a similar grouping, petitioned for a space. Hence the addition made a year ago.

Monsters—aka today's pain in my ass.

As if summoned by my silent seething, the door opens one final time to reveal my nemesis.

Levi Abadi.

2

———

MOIRA

My pulse does *not* quicken at the sight of Council Member Abadi. And if it does, dislike is the fuel for the rapid rhythm.

The monster is all midnight-black hair, framing a strong face that complements his prominent nose. His skin is in a constant love affair with the sun until he practically glows golden. Not a truly supernatural color, but a hypnotizing one nonetheless.

There was a time when we first met that I briefly … might have … not intending to … flirted a little bit. But that was when I just knew his name and that he was a monster. I didn't know who Levi Abadi truly *was*. Now that I'm aware of his lineage, I will never let the monster's devastating good looks sway me in any manner. Especially not today.

Pretending not to watch the arrogant man straighten his shirt cuffs, I let my fury boil quietly, as hot as Georgia's summer sun is outside.

I bet he'll sweat through that dress shirt by midday and have to walk around with pit stains. The thought soothes me enough to pay attention to Georgiana as she starts the meeting.

"All who approve of last month's minutes, say I."

They'd better. I was the scribe, and I wrote down every line precisely as it was spoken. There's a chorus of agreement, and Juan taps away on his laptop, scribe for this meeting. The responsibility passes to a new council member each month, just as the lead of the meeting does. All in the name of fairness.

"As I'm sure you all know, Galen's Gauntlet will take place in two weeks," Georgiana begins on the first topic on the agenda.

I want to skip down to the last-minute addition and start laying into Levi, who hasn't met my eyes a single time since entering the room. But I refuse to turn this meeting into a spectacle. That's no way to get members on my side if I need them there. I sit back and let them talk.

"Competitors are allowed to enter up until an hour before the competition. The same goes for spectators purchasing tickets, so we won't have final numbers on the profits until the day after. However, the earnings are already promising. As in years past, a fourth will be kept by the sirens, a fourth to the witches as payment for their services"—despite their earlier sniping, Georgiana and Selena share a nod of understanding—"a fourth to the winner, and a fourth to this council to be used for public programing or to finance improvements to Folk Haven. Juan, please add discussion of usage of the Gauntlet funds to our next meeting's agenda," Georgiana says.

He grunts in acknowledgment.

The siren continues relating the necessary information about the Gauntlet. As nothing seems to have changed from the years before, my mind wanders back to the pissed off thoughts that have occupied my focus since I looked into the shared council file this morning and saw the update.

Did he think I wouldn't notice the change? That I'd be so thrown off guard that I'd let him walk all over me today?

The world might think selkies have an easygoing nature, and many of us do.

But I am a barracuda.

We review two more items that take less than five minutes each. Then, finally, we arrive at the last-minute addition, stuck into the list above the final discussion item so I can't even try to run out the clock on it.

"Council Member Abadi has requested we discuss issues surrounding plot 236." Georgiana waves toward the pompous monster who has stayed quiet until this point. "Would you like to explain?"

"I would." His voice is as deep as the Mariana Trench and equally as dangerous.

My petulant side wants to mock him, to take away some of the power of that tone. But I keep my mouth shut—for now.

Levi leans forward, addressing the table. "Two nights ago, the police had to go to plot 236 to intervene in an unsanctioned fight between two wolf shifters."

My teeth grind together at the reminder. Samantha made me aware of the incident within an hour of her officer breaking up the fight.

"Those were adolescents," Juan points out as the mythic in charge of the offending parties. "They spent the night in the holding cell and have litter pickup duty for the next month. Are you demanding further punishment?" The last comes out with a tinge of a growl, and in that rumble, I hear an ally.

"No. I don't blame them for fighting or doing so there." Levi holds up his hands, placating the wolf. "What I need to point out is, this is the fourth incident requiring police intervention on that land in the past three months."

"I'm perfectly aware of what is happening on *my* land." My defensiveness forces the words out before I can stop myself. "What concern is it of yours?"

The monster still doesn't meet my eyes, staring hard at the

agenda in front of him as he addresses me. "As you know, I own the property beside yours. My business opens in just over a month. A luxury spa doesn't need the piece of land next door steeped in toxic magic, constantly attracting bad elements."

Even as I long to rail against him, I hate admitting that there's legitimate reasoning behind his concern.

The land didn't used to be such a problem. Plot 236 was owned by a mythical family that left Folk Haven decades ago and never bothered to build. In a wild hope, I tried to contact them. The only number I found was for a lawyer who promised to pass on my offer to purchase the plot. A year ago, the lawyer acted as proxy, the original owner letting me have the property for a steal.

Plot 236 sits on a perfect section of Lake Galen in the territory open to any species of buyers. Ripe for a large profit. But I never intended to sell the land. I just need to keep it safe.

However, a few months back, a lightning storm passed through, one bolt striking and setting fire to an unobtrusive shack on the property and burning the structure down. There was no other damage, so I thought everything was fine. But it didn't take long to realize that tiny building had some sort of protective magic tied to it. Without that talisman in place, tendrils of evil magic coaxed trouble to the property.

First, there was the impromptu underage kegger that got half of Folk Haven High's senior class suspended. Next, a human driving their new speedboat for the first time somehow launched the thing over the bank so fast that the boat crashed into a tree. The man broke his collarbone and should be happy that was all. Not even two weeks after the wrecked watercraft was cleared away, a group of phoenixes got wasted on Fireball whiskey, built a massive bonfire, and tried to summon their patron god, The Hot One. Samantha had a hell of a time shutting that down, even with my help in dousing the flames. Then, of course, plot 236 most recently hosted a group of fighting werewolves.

"I'm aware of the problem. I still don't see why this is a council issue." Maybe that's intentionally obtuse, but still, Levi could have talked to me directly about his concerns before going over my head.

"It's a council issue," he says to the table, still avoiding my eyes, "because my proposed solution requires approval from multiple departments."

"And what *solution* is that?" I grit through the words, seething at his arrogance.

Levi addresses the entire gathering, as if giving a lecture. "Lake Galen was created to purge toxic magic from this land. We all know there are spots that still linger, and plot 236 is one of them. Water didn't fulfill the job our ancestors had hoped for. The next step is fire."

"Fire?" I choke on the word. "You want to *burn* everything?"

Levi gives a definitive nod. "Scorched earth. A controlled burn, and then we let the land sit fallow. After it is cleansed and reborn, you can do whatever you want with it."

"No." I almost slam my palms down on the table but stop myself at the final instance, fisting my hands and tucking them into my lap instead. I feel like I'm dealing with the flock of phoenixes all over again. "There are other options. And it's *my* property."

"Sitting on *our* lake. Attracting trouble." Tension vibrates through his low voice, and I mentally clutch at that break in his cool demeanor.

Normally, I am the model of rational argument. Professionalism in all situations. I applaud myself on constantly keeping a cool head.

But this topic, this land, I can't be objective about. The first time I stepped onto plot 236 when I was a young girl, I knew there was something powerful about the place. The towering trees and lush undergrowth. The unbroken view of Lake Galen, best admired from under the sagging branches of a weeping willow, whose leaves dip into the water when the lake is high after a heavy rain. Wildflowers rushing over the grassy portions of the land when winter's brief chill disappears. The stream that flows through rocks and roots to feed the lake we all love.

All of that alone should be enough to save the plot. Still, I have another reason, but Levi doesn't deserve that secret.

Not when he wants to set the whole of it ablaze.

Desperate passion I never bring into these meetings coats the words that I force through my lips. "You *cannot* burn it. Anyone who could set fire to such beauty is monstrous."

As I utter that proclamation, Levi's chin jerks, and the mythic finally meets my eyes.

3

———————

LEVI

THAT WORD. I can never escape it.

Monstrous.

The term *monster* was ascribed to me the day I was born. Likely before that as well.

I've done my best to embrace the label. But it's one thing to be called a monster based on my mixed mythical heritage, and it's another to claim I act like what the world considers a monster to be. But this bigotry isn't new. I shouldn't let it bother me.

There are a lot of things I shouldn't do.

Like meet the soft brown eyes of the beautiful selkie I'm battling with now. Long ago, I discovered the effect of Moira MacNamara's gaze. How the melted-chocolate color of her irises muddles my brain and makes my pulse beat in erratic rhythms. And as my blood races, my eyes always drop to her throat, trying to catch sight of a rapid flutter under her pale skin. To hopefully comfort myself with proof that she's as affected as I am. Overwhelmed by odd bodily responses that serve no purpose other than to distract me from my goal.

Instead, I'm captured by the enticing sight of the smooth column of her neck and have to tear my stare away again.

Ignoring her comment and that word, I get back to the point. "No matter how pretty you think it is, the land's sickness will cause problems for the town. Making plot 236 a council problem."

The selkie scowls fiercely, which gives me the urge to smile at her. So, I do.

Moira's eyes flutter and then heat with an intensity that would do the job I'm asking for, if only I pointed her in the right direction.

"There are other ways to cleanse besides fire." The selkie sits straighter in her chair, her royal-blue dress molding to the shape of her body. "A spell."

I can't stop a dismissive snort. "Of course," I drawl. "Have a problem? Call in a witch." Leaning forward, I recommit to holding her gaze, determined to take control of the scant bit of power she exerts over me. "You know their magic doesn't fix everything. You can't just grab a random witch off the street and have them work a cleansing spell."

"Hear, hear," Selena mutters, even as she watches our back-and-forth with a gleeful smile.

"I'm aware of how witches work," Moira snaps. "When I say a spell, I obviously mean, I will hire a witch who specializes in purifying magic."

"Do you have one in mind?" I keep my tone nonchalant and do a good job at ignoring my prick of guilt at not sharing a key piece of information.

The selkie shifts her attention to Selena, but the council member waves a dismissive hand, a collection of silver rings glittering with the gesture. "Don't ask me, girlie. It's not my place or my right to share a witch's specialty. An individual must choose whether to make their skill known. That is our law."

Victory in reach, I allow satisfaction to tug at the corner of my mouth. But I shouldn't have gotten so cocky.

"Fine." Moira's tone is all business. "Then, I request The Council hold their decision for a time with the understanding that I'll actively pursue a cleansing solution for plot 236."

"Really?" I barely bite back a scoff. "You think it's that easy? You're going to pluck a cleansing witch out of the air because you want to?"

Moira's smirk is all self-assurance, mixed with a strong dose of condescension. "If you choose to doubt my research skills, then that is your deficiency."

Her confidence has my groin tightening. Luckily, I'm sitting down, so no one sees as I subtly adjust myself under the table.

"What does The Council say about me handling an issue on *my* land?" Moira's underlying meaning whispers under the question.

Wrestling control of plot 236 from her could set a bad precedent. If one thing holds true among mythics, it's that we are extremely protective of our territory.

Which I could argue is the exact reason I brought this up.

"I propose a month," Juan rumbles as his meaty fingers fly over his keyboard. "A cleansing act must take place before the next council session. Twisted magic is a danger to the town." He glances up from his screen. "We would intervene on any property to flush it out. Not just yours."

"A vote," Georgiana states, "for a one-month stay on The Council approving a cleansing burning. All those for the stay, raise your hand."

Three hands go up. Moira's, obviously. Juan's, which is no surprise, as he suggested the solution. And Georgiana's.

I held out hope that the prim-and-proper siren would fear the taint of toxic magic enough to want to act fast. However, I am not entirely surprised. I've long known the siren is among the faction in Folk Haven that would like to remove monsters from the town altogether. She's rarely voted in favor of a proposal I presented.

What surprises me is, the witch is on my side.

"All those against the one-month stay," Georgiana says despite the obvious result.

So everything is on the record, I raise my hand, and Selena joins me. She shrugs Moira's way, but the gesture doesn't come off as apologetic.

"Twisted magic sends roots deep and far. Like weeds. The sooner it's gone, the better." Her voice drops into a hard note. "You accept responsibility for any harm your hesitation causes?"

The selkie's face gets just as serious. "I will."

"Please add *cleansing of plot 236* to next month's agenda." Georgiana directs to the wolf, ready to move on to the next bullet point, and I try not to grind my teeth at the not-satisfactory solution.

A month. That'll leave barely any time to perform the burn before my spa opens. There will still be a scent of smoke in the air when guests first arrive. I'll have to find a way to spin that. Maybe applaud the cleansing effects of charcoal.

Based off the vote, some people at this table believe the use of fire might not be necessary. That Moira will find a way to purge the twisted magic from the land.

They have too much faith. The only purifying witch I know is closefisted when it comes to her powers. The only thing that can pry her hold open is an exorbitant fund. Even if Moira finds a witch who is willing, the selkie will no doubt balk at the price.

With years of training at tamping down my frustration, I do so again as Georgiana moves us on to the next agenda item.

"We have two petitioners asking to speak to The Council. A

Morgana and Amethyst Shelly. Both witches, but this item has been added by you, Moira."

Along with the rest of The Council members, I turn to look at the selkie, who seems undaunted by our confusion.

"They came to me in a professional capacity."

Moira runs Folk Haven Realty. If witches are looking to buy property, they shouldn't need to speak directly to The Council. Moira normally provides the necessary identification information, and we unanimously sign off on their acceptance. There's rarely a deviation. Unless—

"They wish to purchase outside of the witch territory."

The room goes quiet. No doubt each one of us has the same thoughts in our head.

Moira knows the rules. She is good at her job, which includes directing mythics and humans away from properties not available to them. She's never brought an issue like this to us before. Why would she do so now?

"I think I should let them explain. I'll go check if they've arrived." The selkie stands from her chair, straightening the stiff material of her dress once she's upright.

Moira MacNamara looms over the table, taller than even her normal impressive height. She must have on a set of heels. With long strides, she crosses the room, and as she's stepping out of view, I spy her quick press of a hand to the hair behind her ear. Probably making sure her riot of curls are staying exactly where they should be—held back by an unforgiving bun.

Severe.

Sexy.

Stop it, I groan in my head. With Moira out of the room, I should focus on eradicating these small bursts of attraction rather than giving in to them.

None of us chat while the selkie is gone. I mentally scroll through the rest of the tasks I need to get done today.

Tour the building to make sure everything is on track.
Phone call with my marketing team.
Approve the changes to the website.

I'm not even halfway through when Moira reappears, two women in tow. Both are white with a paleness that begs to never be let out in the sun, for fear of immediate combustion. Their crimson hair only emphasizes the lack of melanin, although the shorter of the two has a flush of red on her arms that indicates she's not as careful about applying SPF as she should be.

The two witches aren't the only new arrivals. Behind them trots a cat. The animal moves in an odd way—less feline, more doglike somehow. It's also larger than most house cats I've encountered.

"What a curious creature." Selena swivels in her chair, reaching out as if to pick the animal up.

In response to the approaching hands, the cat arches high, letting out a growl rather than a hiss but menacing all the same. Instead of flinching away to avoid a swipe of claws, the witch council member goes still, interest sharpening her gaze.

"Please, don't try to pick him up." The witch with sunburned arms steps forward but makes no move to restrain her pet, who's still rumbling a warning.

"Is he a rescue?" Selena asks.

"Not yet." The redhead tucks her hands into the pockets of the worn overalls she wears. "I'm afraid he's still very much in the middle of his peril."

Selena transfers her curiosity to the young witch, and I wonder if having the attention of Selena Evermore is some-thing anyone wants. "How so?"

The new arrival pulls out an empty chair at the table and gives a subtle wave to the seat, as if offering the place. The cat relaxes enough to claim the higher ground, dark eyes flitting between all the mythics in the room.

"I'm pretty sure he's a man cursed into cat form."

At that proclamation, the other new witch sighs, but she doesn't naysay her companion.

"Pretty sure?" Selena clarifies.

"If I had to apply a number, I would say, ninety percent sure. But I'm still waiting on two ingredients for a spell that can give me a definitive answer. Until then, I'd say it's better practice to treat him as such. Just in case."

I—along with the other council members—stare hard at the feline, as if he'll open his mouth and start up a conversation. But he only sits calmly, if warily, in his seat.

"Fascinating. Do keep me updated." Selena reclines in her chair; her focus never leaves the animal.

But the reddened witch steps between the council member and the cat, using her body as a shield. "I don't think I will. Witch-patient confidentiality and all that."

Juan snorts and then clears his throat, as if all he meant to do was cough. But I find myself hiding my own smile behind my hand. As council members, we hold a position of power among our factions. Power that was granted through a fair election, but still. Other witches defer to Selena. But this newcomer either has no notion of the power, both political and mystical, that Selena wields or she doesn't care. Even her tone of voice—slightly distracted, as if she's thinking of five other subjects while holding this conversation—conveys a sense of ... not disrespect exactly. More like disinterest.

"Very well, girl. I'll find out what I want on my own." Selena's attention at the beginning of this meeting was as sharp as a butter knife. Now, she's a carefully honed butcher's knife, and I feel pity for these two women on the cutting block.

"If we could move on to the matter at hand?" Georgiana's voice regains the attention of the room. "Council Member MacNamara informed us you have interest in property not available to witches, but she has brought you to speak to us, which I assume means there are special circumstances. Please state your case."

"Yes, thank you." The slightly taller witch moves to the end of the oval conference table, pulling documents out of her bag as she goes. "My name is Morgana Shelly. This is my sister, Amethyst." She waves toward the younger witch, who takes a seat next to her cat. "We are here in Folk Haven and in this council meeting because we would like to serve the community by opening a library. Specifically, a library containing mythic-related texts, including spell books and histories of species."

At that proclamation, the room sits in stunned silence. A skill these sisters seem to have mastered. While Morgana allows us to process her statement, she places a packet of paper in front of each of us.

I read the cover of mine—*Folk Haven Public Mythic Library.*

"You mean to house our grimoires in a public library?" Selena chokes on the question, as if the woman told her she was going to perform blood sacrifices in the town square. Actually, the witch council member would probably prefer that.

"All grimoires in the collection would be voluntarily donated, recovered from misplacement landing them in human hands, or collected after the last member of a line is deceased," Morgana explains as if teaching a class.

"Misplacement?" Selena hisses the word like a curse.

Morgana's face remains impassive, as undaunted by the council witch as her sister. I wonder about their level of powers. From my knowledge of witches, there is a scale their abilities fall on. Could it be that these two surpass Selena?

I sit forward, intrigued with this turn of events, more easily pushing aside my annoyance from earlier as the situation plays out.

"Amethyst and I have spent the last five years traveling the country. We've gone to most every major city in the continental US and plenty of smaller towns in between. A pared-down record of our travels is in the packet I handed out." She waves toward the papers in front of us, and I flip open to the first page, impressed to find a well-laid-out table of contents. "Our mission was to scour every used bookstore we came across to find and recover legitimate mythic-related texts that had somehow fallen into human hands. That includes grimoires."

"We have sixty," Amethyst chimes in. "Not including our family's."

Selena's mouth gapes open, for once unable to hide her emotions behind a veneer of disinterest. I take back my earlier unhappiness. This is the best council meeting I've ever attended. Glancing across the table, my eyes clash with Moira's. Shocking myself, I realize we're grinning at each other. She's enjoying this as much as I am.

Realizing who she's sharing her delight with, Moira jerks back and then scowls at me before clearing all emotion from her face and shifting to focus back on the witches.

My guts twist.

So what if she doesn't want to share a laugh with me? Should have known, what with me being so monstrous to her.

"But grimoires would only be a small portion of the collection," Morgana continues. "We have histories. Legends. Many we've already legitimized; others we would request input from Folk Haven residents on their validity. And we are here because the collection we've gathered has grown too large for us to remain mobile. We need a safe place to store the texts. But in addition to that, our purpose has always been to share our findings. Information should be free."

"Information is power, girl. You don't just give it away." Selena struggles to reestablish her veneer of detached interest. Her efforts aren't working.

Morgana meets the older witch's eyes, cool gaze unblinking. "If that is the case, then I would wager I am the most powerful person in this room."

I half-expect her to pull out a mic and drop it. I get the urge to stand up and applaud her.

And I'm even more impressed when Morgana doesn't push for a true display of power, backing away from the posturing. "But that is not the case. I simply have an extremely large collection of books with delicate, coveted information. I want to give that to the town of Folk Haven in the form of a library. I've found a house that would serve my purpose perfectly. If you all would, flip to page ten."

And we all do, finding a picture of a beautiful Victorian house.

"That is the Novac residence," Georgiana snaps.

One more council member's feathers ruffled. Morgana has a battle on her hands.

"It is," the witch agrees. "And my understanding is that Delta Novac wishes to sell."

The siren turns fiery eyes on Moira. For some reason, the glare has my hackles rising. As if I plan on defending the selkie.

Ridiculous.

"So, you're shopping property in winged territory to everyone now? You think sitting on The Council gives you the right?"

Moira keeps a neutral expression. "The Shelly sisters found the property themselves and *then* contacted me."

"We've been renting in town for the last few weeks. Trying to decide if Folk Haven was the right home for this collection. We overheard a conversation about the house. Nothing was shopped to us," Morgana explains.

"There are houses available for purchase in witch territory," Selena points out. "And within the town, which is open to any and all mythics."

That almost has me snorting out loud. Her description sounds like the town is a welcoming place, which it might be to some. However, I'd like to see them try buying property with the *monster* label attached to their name. Sellers suddenly become a lot less interested.

"We want this house because of its winged history." Morgana taps a finger on the picture. "Delta Novac's father kept his hoard in this house. Dragons naturally create magical protections around their hoards, and those forces mingle with the physical space where the collections are kept. Even with the hoard gone now, a level of protection remains." She leans forward, displaying the first sign of emotion since stepping in the door. Determination. "I am aware of the value of my collection. The power that resides in all the knowledge I've gathered." She nods toward Selena. "It is important to maintain safeguards while also providing access. This house is key."

"This house belongs to winged mystics," Georgiana insists.

Amethyst heaves out a tired sigh. "If wings are all that's standing in the way, I should be able to manage a set. Will take me some time though. Can't recall which book had the spell, but I'm sure the brew required a month of steeping. At least."

The whole table stares at the young witch, but she doesn't seem to notice as she fiddles with one of her red braids. I have to dig my teeth into my lower lip to keep from chuckling.

"What my sister is trying to say"—Morgana brings the room's attention back to her—"is that we don't understand your territorial divides. They seem arbitrary and more likely to hinder your society rather than allowing all mythics to thrive."

I do laugh then. A quick bark I don't even try to stifle.

When all eyes turn to me, I decide to say my piece. "Morgana makes good points. I like the idea." My voice rings through the quiet space.

"You would," Georgiana snaps before pressing her lips shut.

I hold her poison-green eyes, undaunted by the disgust in them. "Of course I would. I come from a portion of the mythical population most often excluded. Shoved into the farthest corner of the lake. The idea of redefining borders, paired with the philosophy of shared knowledge, appeals to me."

As does the tracking of histories. Most of the fear of monsters comes from our unknowable powers. But who's to say we're unknowable? Maybe if people kept better records, then our existence wouldn't be cause for alarm and bigotry. There's plenty of lore on dragons, who can take a shape I would argue is potentially more terrifying than my other form.

But of course, dragons were an intentional formation by The Winged One.

While I am merely a mistake.

Glancing across the table surface, I once again meet Moira's judgmental gaze. And even though I want to shrug off her disdain as easily as I do Georgiana's, I can't help the gutting sense of loss, knowing she labels me as *less than* for something I can't control.

Every muscle in my body tenses when she opens her mouth.

"I agree with Council Member Abadi."

4

MOIRA

THE WORDS LEAVE a bad taste in my mouth, even after we conclude The Council meeting, and I walk out to my car.

"I agree with Council Member Abadi."

Damn him for giving me cause to do that so soon after trying to screw me over. For giving me cause to do it at all. I had plenty of reason to dislike the monster without his petition to set my property on fire.

As I stride into the muggy summer morning and down Town Hall's front steps, I spy the Shelly sisters and their cat companion heading toward the center of town. Like the cleansing of plot 236, the issue of selling the house to the witches has been given another month, so The Council can fully vet the request. Morgana claimed she and her sister were fine with waiting, as they've rented the apartment above Clean Feathers Laundromat for the next few months. They might have earned a single point in Georgiana's favor with that announcement, seeing as how the building is owned by

Esmerelda, a harpy. Funneling some rent money into an Of the Wing pocket can't hurt their bid to buy a house in the territory.

A mythical library. The idea has merit. Enough that I thought The Council needed to hear the witches' argument instead of me pushing the women away from the Novac property.

Seems I'm not the only one. Levi's words reflected my thoughts. Well, not the whole being part of a disregarded faction. Of the Fin mythics make up the largest portion of Folk Haven's mythical population. If anything, my kind's unrelenting grip on this town aids in stoking the monster resentment.

That thought doesn't sit well, and I press fingers against my forehead, trying to force away an oncoming headache as I unlock my car.

"Moira."

I don't have to turn around to know who called my name. That deep voice hooks into my brain with backward barbs that keep me from disengaging. There's no escaping him. I school my features to disinterest and face Levi as he jogs toward me.

The man should look ridiculous, running in professional clothes. Instead, I get action-movie vibes, where the hero is a spy in corporate disguise.

"What?" I snap, not meaning to let my emotions bubble to the surface.

A frown tugs at the corners of the monster's mouth as he stops in front of me. Luckily, with my heels on, we are exactly eye-level. Not many people in this town can look down on me, and I plan to keep it that way.

"Can we talk about plot 236? If you're worried about the cost of a fire cleansing, I want to offer to pay for the service—with the understanding that it will take place in the next few weeks."

I gape at him. The dead-fish expression is all I can manage for a good ten seconds. Then, I crack.

"You relentless asshole!" *Keep your cool*, a barely audible and easily ignored part of my brain whispers. "I'm not worried about the *cost*. I'm concerned about the fire!" I want to shove Levi in the chest, but instead, I wrench open my car door and chuck my briefcase into the passenger seat before turning my glare back on him. "I have a month to find a better way, and I will. Don't offer that shit deal like you're doing me a favor. Especially when you didn't even bother talking to me before going over my head to The Council. You think I'd want to enter into any kind of agreement with you after that?"

From the tightening of his jaw, I can bet the monster is grinding his teeth. Good. I hope he wears away every one of those pearly whites, and I pray to The Finned One that his massive dental bill is all my doing.

"I went to The Council because you've made it abundantly clear—on more than one occasion—you'd rather not breathe the same air as me." He drags long fingers through his silky black tresses in an agitated movement, yet the strands settle back into perfect waves the instant he's done.

Damn his well-behaved hair.

And damn him for making a small amount of sense.

When I first met Levi, the day he contacted my real estate agency to buy a house in Folk Haven, I had nothing against him. On the phone, he sounded polite, and when we were face-to-face, I struggled not to melt as I took in his sexy, professional demeanor. The guy knows how to wear business casual. I had no trouble guessing his button-up covered a well-formed body. And despite being in a relationship at the time, I did something I never do at work.

I flirted. Bantering with him came naturally as we toured the two houses for sale in monster territory at the time. After months where I felt like a shadow of myself in a dying relationship, Levi reminded me of the hot excitement of new attraction.

Not that I planned to do anything about it, but silently, I appreciated the coy looks and knowing smiles.

Then, a few weeks later, I went out to dinner with my friend Sonya. I can still remember the conversation.

"You sold a house to that monster Levi, right?" she asked while pouring us each a glass of pinot noir. "The gods were in a good mood the day they made his face."

I laughed and offered to set her up with the new guy in town, ignoring how the idea settled wrong in my stomach.

Sonya waved the offer away. "I'm good. And he's not exactly new. He lived here when he was a teenager, but I guess you must have been off at college by then."

Disappointment stung my chest in an unexpected way. Something to do with missing the chance to get to know the monster earlier. Before I met Hamish.

"Are his parents still here?" I asked between sips of wine. "I might know them."

Sonya leaned forward, ready to offer up prime gossip. "Levi moved here with his mom. She doesn't get out much, I don't think. But his dad. You really don't know who he is?"

When she told me, all good feelings toward the monster evaporated.

From that moment on, I avoided interaction with the town's newest member, conveying cold detachment whenever we had to speak. I hoped to keep my distance.

Then, just a few months after moving to town, Levi petitioned The Council to add a monster seat. And damn if I didn't have to put aside my dislike of him and vote for the movement to pass. The monsters did need representation as much as I despised the man bringing up the issue.

Avoidance became impossible. Instead, I opted for subtle hostility, so Levi would always know that despite the years passing, I hadn't forgotten or forgiven the sins of the past.

"What cause did I have for thinking that you'd listen to me?" Levi's question pulls me back to the hot summer sidewalk and his piercing black eyes, staring at me in accusation. "That you would listen to the reasoning of a *monster*?"

The way he says that last word, as if his mythical designation were the cause of strife between us, boils my anger to the brim of my patience pot.

A scoff forces from my throat. "I couldn't care less that you're a monster," I inform him. "In case you haven't heard, my brother just mated a dragon. If they ever get around to procreating, I'll have a few monsters in *my* family."

Levi rocks back on his heels, sliding his hands deep into his pockets as his face crumples in confusion. The sight has me wanting to shove him back further, but I refuse to give in to the petty urge on a public street. The monster already has me growling like a hungry bear shifter.

"Then, why don't you like me?"

The. Audacity.

"Are you truly so self-involved? You have no idea why I, a *MacNamara*, would have a blue-whale-sized bone to pick with you. A *leviathan*." I spit the grandiose name that history proclaims to be a terrifying beast.

I, meanwhile, know the truth of the mythics descended from that line. They spawned a petty, vindictive thief.

"What does my particular brand of monster have to do with anything?" Levi asks.

For a moment, there is so much righteous anger coursing through my veins that I cannot force any comprehendible words from my throat. After expelling a heated snarl, I bare my teeth at the monster, wishing I could masticate him.

"It has *everything* to do with this. Your father stole a selkie pelt from my great-grandaunt." I funnel all my outrage into the glare I level at the cocky monster before me. "One hundred years later, he *still* has not given it back."

Just as I'm about to slide into my car and peel away in furious triumph, Levi opens his sinfully tempting lips.

"You're wrong."

5

———

LEVI

I AM no stranger to monsters getting blamed for crap they did not do. And if I know one thing for sure, it's that my father does not—and has not—stolen any selkie skins.

The timing of Moira's story is not in question. My father is one of the long-lived mythics. Most magical creatures have life spans similar to humans. But some creatures, like my father, never grow old. Or if they do, the aging happens at a reduced rate.

So, yes, it is entirely possible that my father, a leviathan, crossed paths with Moira's great-grandaunt.

But I refuse to believe he stole her most precious belonging. Not even a belonging. A piece of her soul.

My father is not that kind of man.

But the world only sees him as a monster.

Moira whirls on me, glowing with beautiful, bothersome fury. Of course she's mad. She blindly believes a falsehood told to her by a person with a monster grudge. I've received plenty of angry, undeserved comments over the course of my life.

"I am not wrong. My grandfather—her nephew—told me the story."

"And that's all it is. A story. Made up."

A growl-gasp leaves her throat, and I wonder if the selkie will try to hit me. But, no, Moira MacNamara might have a hidden temper, but she knows where to draw the line.

"Just because you have a skewed view of history"—she steps away from her car and into my space—"doesn't make the story wrong."

There's a fresh scent surrounding her, like the cold ocean waves that crash against rocky cliffs in Maine, coating everything in a chill but leaving behind a glorious, clean beauty.

Stop comparing her to the sea! You're arguing with her!

I grind my teeth before responding. "I'm the one actually acquainted with the man that you're accusing, and I know he'd never steal from a selkie."

Moira's stare takes on a new level of intensity. "You *do* know him. So, why don't you give him a call? Right now. Ask him about my aunt."

Damn it. I neatly stumbled my way into this one. I struggle for a response, something smooth that also shuts down her argument.

All I manage is, "I can't."

Great fucking job with that.

But it is the truth. I literally can't get in touch with my father. Haven't been able to in five years.

"You can't," she scoffs. "Just like you can't identify the creature who tried to steal my brother's pelt."

My annoyance spikes.

Two months ago, Moira arrived at The Council meeting with a warning. The morning after the dark moon, when Calder MacNamara removed his selkie hide, a nightmarish creature attempted to take it. A dragon named Delta—Calder's new mate—dived into Lake Galen to chase after the thief, managing to wrestle the pelt free. The creature fled without its prize.

Naturally, because the description matched no known mythic, everyone assumed it must have been a sticky-fingered monster—and therefore my responsibility.

"I have talked to every one of my constituents, and none know of a being like Delta described. At no point have I condoned attacks or theft between our kind." My fists clench and ease as I try to rein in the urge to grab this selkie and pull her close and ... well, I haven't planned past that point. "I want the creature to be found as badly as you do. So, no, I cannot magically present you with the thief simply because you want it. Nor can I speak to my father."

"More like you *won't*," Moira sneers. "Worried you might break some sparkly perfect image you have of the great and mighty leviathan? Fine. Whatever. Not like I'd expect him to be honest anyway. I know the truth, and that's what matters."

Each one of her comments buffets me like gales in a storm, and I only barely manage to stay afloat. My desperate grab for a lifeline comes in the form of snapping back at her. My version of self-preservation.

"You know *one* version of the truth. Honestly, I'm surprised. I never thought Moira MacNamara would blindly believe everything she was told." Trying a derisive chuckle, I only manage a strange bark. I blame that subtly enticing scent. It's choking me.

"You're wrong," she snarls.

Even though we're in the middle of growling at each other, I experience an odd spark of relief.

Finally, I know what happened to make the selkie turn cold on me.

When I returned to Folk Haven just over a year ago, I didn't know what my reception in town would be. I'd spent my high school years here, making a handful of casual friends, and then went north for college. But when I decided to open a business, this town—a mythical sanctuary—seemed like the perfect spot. So, I returned, bracing for the monster distrust I'd experienced in small bursts when I was younger.

When I met my realtor at the first address she'd sent me, my mind was focused on finding a home. Then, she stepped out of the front door, moved in close to shake my hand, told me to call her Moira, and gifted me with a welcoming smile that should appear on all advertisements for Folk Haven. In that moment, I didn't care if she showed me a mold-covered shack, infested with palmetto bugs and copperheads. I was sold.

Instead, Moira walked me through two modern, comfortable houses, pointing out all the amenities while offering jokes and sassy grins along the way. I think I said words back, ones that made her laugh and her eyes sparkle. The gods must have gifted me with those sentences because I can't recall anything other than wanting to bury my face in her neck to breathe her scent in deeper. Every surface she ran her fingers over had me imagining her touch on my bare skin. When she pointed out the granite countertops, I couldn't stop fantasizing about bending her over the cool surface and tearing the pencil skirt off her shapely thighs before kneeling to taste her.

I'd never felt such a strong, immediate attraction, but I kept that longing to myself when she mentioned a boyfriend.

A short time after, I heard through the relentless Folk Haven gossip mill that the pair had split up. I planned to ask her out. But when I next saw Moira in Coffee & Claws and offered her a warm greeting, the selkie's expression was harder than the countertops in my new kitchen. The shift in personality jarred me, and I struggled to figure out what I might have done wrong. Every interaction after that was the same until I realized what the truth must be.

When I had been a customer, Moira had dialed up her saleswoman persona to get me to buy a house. Once the papers had been signed, she went back to her normal dislike of monsters. Prejudice, just like plenty of other mythics.

I wanted to rage and roar, furious that she hated me without knowing me.

But wouldn't that reaction make me the monster she believed me to be?

Maybe not.

Turns out, I got it wrong. Moira's grudge was born from a lie. All her animosity is unfounded, which would be encouraging if I didn't just piss her off for an entirely new reason.

Fucking great.

In my frustration, I can't help pushing her.

"The moon is made of cheese," I taunt. "Witches are selling winning lottery tickets." I keep going with the preposterous, made-up facts, enjoying how each one has Moira's cheeks flushing a deeper shade of crimson. "Bigfoot grows cannabis in Canada. Merpeople fart fairy dust."

"No, we don't."

Moira and I both whip around to spot Carl, a sergeant on the police force and one of the mermen of Lake Galen, watching us with a bemused expression.

And instead of calming down when faced with my ridiculousness, I lean in. "There you have it!" Great, I'm shouting about sparkly farts in public. "A secondary source! Guess we can cross that off my list of facts that are totally true."

Moira draws a veil of respectability over herself with a deep inhale. The sight only has me wanting to get her riled up again. Some public figure I am.

"Hi, Carl. Council Member Abadi and I are having a debate about research." She presents him a friendly politician smile.

The merman glances between us again before offering a hesitant nod that conveys he doesn't believe a word of what she said. But he heads inside, leaving us to our strange argument.

"Fine." The snap of the one word draws my attention back

to Moira's face, where her fury has reemerged. The switch-flipping might scare me if I wasn't so impressed. "You need another source? I'll get one."

"Really? You're planning to fly to the Mediterranean to track down my father?" At least, I believe that's the ocean he chose to go to with it being the closest to his home. But his letter didn't specify. It also didn't give a return date.

I could tell Moira what the letter said. Tell her that I'm not refusing to speak to my father to be petty.

But I keep the information to myself.

"No." She brushes her hands down the front of her dress, straightening wrinkles that aren't there. "I'll consult the closest thing mythics have to historians." Moira plants her fists on her hips, hitting me with a power pose. "Sirens. A leviathan stealing the pelt of a selkie is a grand tale. They have to have a song about it."

Curse the gods, her snarky smirk does strange things to my chest. I long to wipe that expression off her face. With my mouth.

That's called kissing, and remember, you don't want to do that with her. She's infuriating, not infatuating.

Keep getting those wires crossed.

"And you're what? Going to waltz up to Georgiana and demand she sing it for you? Good luck remembering that."

Spend even a small time around sirens, and people soon learn the reason their songs are so appealing is because no listener can remember the lyrics when the song has finished.

"Doubt any of them would write the words down either. You know as well as I do, sirens are as protective of their songs as witches are of their grimoires."

I expect her triumph to wane. Instead, a wild gleam enters Moira's gaze.

"But they couldn't refuse if they *had* to tell me."

"And I'd be a millionaire if I had a million dollars. You're not making sense." And I *was* a millionaire before I sank all my money into this spa.

In college, my roommate was a computer science major, and together, we designed and launched an app, guiding users through in-home massages. We had a decent amount of success on our own, and then a large health corporation offered to buy our company. Both of us had different career dreams that didn't involve managing an app, and the decision to sell was easy. Which was how I ended up with the startup funds for Haven's Relaxation, the luxury spa Moira's toxic land is threatening.

My teeth grind again at the thought.

The selkie grins wide, and the expression causes a clash of wariness and excitement under my rib cage.

"I'm making perfect sense," she retorts. "You're just not keeping up, little monster."

I almost choke on my tongue at the title. Little monster? What am I, a gremlin? And yet there's a small flame of warmth that starts up in my chest at the title that sounds awfully close to an endearment.

How pathetic of me to cling to it.

Unaware of the chaos she's causing under my surface, Moira keeps talking. "There's one prize that never changes. Win, and you can request a favor or a piece of knowledge from the sirens."

"Win ..."

"Galen's Gauntlet."

Of course. Georgiana just finished telling us that everything is in place for the competition. A biennial tradition that celebrates the siren who freed a group of mystics over ninety years ago from the menagerie built by a sorcerer. He fashioned his twisted prison on the land Folk Haven and Lake Galen now sit on. And it's his evil magic that still lingers in certain areas.

"You don't *decide* to win Galen's Gauntlet. There's always at least fifty other competitors as interested in the siren favor as well as the cash prize and everything else the victor receives."

Moira swats her hand in the air, as if none of those matter. "You can't talk me out of this." Then, her flippant air solidifies into a serious note, and her brown eyes hold me in their thrall. "I can forgive you for not knowing. But I cannot forgive you for standing by and letting your father continue to hold the skin. It is not his to keep. And when I prove to you he has it, then you have to help get it back."

I could repeat that my father does not have it, but she wouldn't believe me. Instead, I choose to use her confidence in a falsehood against her.

"Fine. But if we find out that you're wrong, then we move ahead with the fire cleansing immediately after the Gauntlet."

Moira's eyes widen along with her mouth.

"Unless you think the story is fabricated?" I weasel, digging my claws into her.

She snaps her mouth shut, and suddenly, there's a silver dagger in her hand.

"What in all the gods?!" I stumble back a step. "Where did you get that?" *Does she plan to stab me for the continued insults?* Maybe I was wrong about the line of civility my fellow council member maintains.

"I keep it in my purse." Moira doesn't plunge the knife into my gut. She instead presses the blade to the pad of her thumb, drawing out a scarlet drop. "Blood vow, or it didn't happen." She offers the blade, hilt first, to me.

"Gods, Moira." I grip her wrist, forcing the hand holding the knife down. "Not on the street."

She flicks her gaze around, as if just remembering where we are. Folk Haven might have a larger population of mythics than the rest of the world, but there are still plenty of humans in this town, and only a fraction knows about the magical qualities their neighbors possess.

"In my car," she mutters, sliding behind the steering wheel and slamming the door shut.

I circle around to the other side, glancing at my watch and cursing myself for letting half the morning go by because I can't help getting tangled up with this selkie.

The sedan is an oven, having baked in the sun while we sat in the nice air-conditioning for the last hour. As I set her briefcase on the floor and tuck my long legs into the passenger seat, Moira starts the engine and blasts the cooling system. For a stretch, I get warm air pressed into my face. Sweat gathers under my arms, more so when I turn to find the selkie leaning toward me, her face closer than it's ever been. Her lips right there. Her cold sea scent filling the steamy car.

"Just stab yourself and get this over with." She offers the knife again.

Her bloodthirsty words shoot more heat through my veins.

"I'm competing too," I announce.

Her thick lashes flutter with surprise. "What? Why?"

Because I'm not enough of a bastard to make you go through that mindfuck of a competition on your own.

"Double our chances of winning and getting what we want. I vow to use the prize money to pay for the fire cleansing when we find out the story is false."

Moira scowls, and I snatch the knife before she decides to slice my hand herself. There's only a bothersome sting as I cut my thumb. She offers her small wound to me, and we press our bloodied skin together. A shot of fire scores through my body, and from the selkie's gasp, I guess she feels the same.

"And I vow," she says in a breathy voice, "when we discover what my family told is true, I'll use the prize money to purchase you a first-class round-trip ticket to wherever your father's hideout is."

Good luck with that.

I would feel guilty if I thought I might be wrong. But the

man who raised me could never have done what she's describing. I know it deep in my soul. My father is not a villain.

"Here." Moira pulls her injured hand away from mine and then reaches into the purse in her lap, pulling out a palm-sized first aid kit and an alcohol wipe.

"Run into a lot of mini emergency situations?" I joke.

"Do you want a Band-Aid or not?" She reclaims her dagger, uses the wipe to clean off the few drops of blood, and then tucks the blade into a pocket inside the purse.

Remember for the future, if Moira has her bag, she has a weapon.

Next, she pops the top of the first aid kit and takes out a small tube of Neosporin and two Band-Aids.

"You know we don't get sick, right?" Still, I hold out my thumb to be doctored.

"You know there's no academic research to back that notion up, right?" Her biting comeback sets off that tightening in my groin again. "And you know diseases constantly mutate, right? Do you want to be patient zero in a mythical epidemic?"

Her soft brown eyes meet mine, holding me in place, as if she cupped my face in her hands.

Gods, why do I feel a groan rising in my throat? And not a frustrated one.

"No," I mutter.

"That's what I thought." The selkie is unable to let me have the last word.

I keep perfectly still as Moira holds my palm still and dabs the disinfectant on the cut. The thing will heal as if it never existed by tomorrow, but she treats the nick as though my life were hanging in the balance. I try to ignore how much I like her paying me this caring kind of attention. It's on the tip of my tongue to tell her about the bruises under my shirt, leftover from a morning wrestling match with Sev. They don't need Neosporin to heal.

But maybe a kiss? The brush of selkie lips against the discolored skin?

At the twitch south of my belt, I pull my hand from hers and reach for the door handle.

"I'm late," I mutter, which is true. Only I forget what I must do for the rest of the day.

"Band-Aid," she snaps, tossing one at my retreating form.

I snatch it from the air without a thanks and slam the door shut, power-walking away before Moira notices the bulge behind my fly.

Why does my body have to react this way to a mythic who hates me?

6

____

MOIRA

After the short drive to my office, heat still buzzes through my veins from the blood vow. Having never made one before, I don't know if this lingering effect is normal. It's almost as though I'm still connected to Levi. Like he's tugging a string suspended between us from across town.

That was a rash decision. Why did I let him get under my skin?

Literally and figuratively.

Even my brothers can't piss me off the way Levi Abadi does. And now, I'm bound to him. Temporarily.

Once I unlock the front door to Folk Haven Realty, I step inside and use the privacy to give myself a whole-body shake. The maneuver doesn't help. If only I had time to go home and shower. But oddly, the thought of getting naked while this sensation lingers has my face flushing hot.

What if he can somehow see me?

"Don't be ridiculous," I chide myself as I stroll through the waiting room of my business and into the back office.

I take comfort in the familiar surroundings, settling behind my desk, where I hold full control. Pulling out my laptop, I open my email and send a short message to Zelda Skyborn, the siren heading the Gauntlet planning this year.

Interested in GG.

—Moira

By the time I get back from a quick trip to the bathroom, there's already a response.

Come by my house tomorrow at 7 p.m. Bring what you need.

—Z

Cryptic, but I know exactly what she wants in the same way she picked up my meaning from the single sentence. We don't have any reason to think a government agency will hack into our small-town email accounts, looking for messages about a magical tournament. But as technology advances, so does our paranoia.

Bring what you need. By that, she means the entry fee.

Entering Galen's Gauntlet isn't cheap, but that means the winning pot is big. Still, half the entrants barely care about the money. They want the bragging rights.

But I want information.

A quick search shows me seven p.m. will still give me close to two hours before sunset.

Another reason my nerves are on edge is the moon. Or lack thereof. Tomorrow is the dark moon, and I can't wait to don my selkie pelt and swim in Lake Galen, reconnecting with the other half of my being. We only allow ourselves full freedom on the darkest night of the month, using the pitch-black waters as a form of shielding.

I can't wait.

I'm writing a note to stop by the bank—guess I'll see Council Member Juan twice today, as he's head of security— when the bell of my front door opening jingles. My next appointment is not for an hour, so I lean around my monitor to see who's wandered in.

Fuck. I almost mutter the word aloud but manage to keep the curse in my head.

"Hello, Miss Moira. How are you doing this fine day?" Albert Durrand strolls into my office without invitation and settles himself in the seat across the desk from mine without a by-your-leave. His wide smile and handsome face scream, *People let me do whatever I want, whenever I want because I'm a good-looking white guy.*

Maybe that's true in most situations but not with me. His charm slides right off my bullshit shield.

"Mr. Durrand." My politician smile is fully in place. "I don't remember scheduling an appointment. Did you need to check my availability? On another day?" *How about July never?*

"Oh no. This is just a quick drop-in. I'll be out of your curly hair in only a moment, *mademoiselle*." He says the last word with an authentic roll that has me thinking he might have spent a stretch of time over in Europe. The comment about hair almost has me raising a hand to check if my wild mass is still tucked in my *take no shit* bun. But I stop myself, remembering that I checked a short while ago in my car's rearview mirror.

Perfectly smooth.

Not that I have a problem with my curls. I simply require them to behave in a certain way on certain days.

With the hiccup of thought I lose the chance to control the conversation as the intruder continues to talk. "I'm here to inquire about plot 236, I believe the number is. When exactly will that officially go on the market?"

What game of The Finned One is playing out? What's with all these people butting their noses into my piece of land?

I have to instruct the muscles in my shoulders to relax out of their instinctive angry tense. Unlike The Council, this man has no say or control over plot 236.

"The owner hasn't decided how they wish to move forward." The owner being *me*. "I'm not even sure how you got the idea it would be up for sale." I certainly haven't told anyone about plans to put it on the market. Even if I didn't want to keep it for myself, no way in any of the realms would I sell to Albert.

Not that I have any damning information about him. From what I know, the human is renting a place in town and works for a digital marketing company. The first time we met, he offered his services to increase Folk Haven Realty's online presence.

Thanks, but no, thanks.

Marketing property in a mythic-filled town is a delicate process. Most times, I'm focused solely on selling to members of the magical community. Humans are allowed to buy property in Folk Haven and on one section of the lake, but I put them through an extensive background check beforehand.

From all outside appearances, Albert should be a man I'd happily welcome to the Folk Haven community. Handsome, energetic, young. One of the reasons the original founders of this town decided to sell property to humans was because mythics often find partners in the human population. That's how we've survived so long. My father is human.

An eligible man should be a perfect new resident.

But the guy gives off bad vibes. That's the only explanation I have, but it's enough that I'd steer my clients away from selling to a man like him. And it is the kiss of death for him to buy anything of mine.

Still, I don't need to share that with him.

"You know, people in small towns gossip." He winks at me, and I fight the urge to gag. "Sure you can't give me a hint?"

If he were someone I respected or at the very least wanted to keep happy, I'd put on my own charming smile and avoid his questions by stroking his ego. But I don't care if Albert gets his own bad vibes from me in return.

Realty in Folk Haven is different than probably most anywhere else in the world. Some might say I have a monopoly on the market, and they wouldn't be wrong. I am the only real estate agency in town. But that's because I know the rules. Sellers are welcome to try finding a buyer on their own, but anyone living on the lake must get The Council's approval. That's a bylaw in the town.

When it comes to property in Folk Haven, that's not regulated as closely, but for the most part, mythics want to sell to other mythics or at least know they're not selling to a human who will blow up our carefully cultivated community.

That's why my process involves thorough background checks. Money isn't everything in our town, and I didn't pick this job for the paycheck.

"I can't." I use a blunt tone and wonder what level of rude I need to reach before he'll leave. "Now, if you could—"

"Just a moment." The human holds up a hand to cut me off.

A more toxic version of the anger I felt this morning condenses in my gut. At least I have a small amount of respect for Levi. More so now that I'm almost certain he didn't know about my great-grandaunt's pelt.

But Albert has zero of my respect, and he's dropping into negative numbers. He flashes me another smile that should be attractive, but I was ten times more turned on by a monster's frown.

Wait, no. I was not turned on. Definitely not.

"I would be eternally grateful if you could give the owner of plot 236 my offer."

The man sets a folded piece of paper on my desktop, sliding it across the glass surface toward me like we're in some mob movie where money is discussed in hush whispers, for fear the Feds might overhear. I glance around my otherwise empty office, wondering when I fell into a corner of the universe I'd rather not be in.

Fighting back a sigh of annoyance, I pick the paper up with a tight, disingenuous smile, wanting more than anything for the guy to get out of my face. The idea of getting into a spat with him is much less appealing than it was with the sea monster council member. Sparring with Levi was invigorating. Exchanging a handful of sentences with Albert is draining.

"I'll pass it on," I say.

"Wonderful. You keep me updated. Just think of the percentage of that number that'd be yours." He winks again, which ups his bad-vibes factor by ten because no one in real life actually winks.

When he strolls out of my office, disappearing down the street, I open a window despite the warm, humid day, over-whelmed with the urge to replace the air the human exhaled in my office.

Only then, with the thick Georgia breeze blanketing me, do I unfold his piece of paper.

I read the number once. Then again. Then a third time for good measure.

The digits don't change, and I know why Albert swaggered in here with such confidence.

This amount is more than triple what I paid for plot 236. But instead of changing my mind, the massive offer only spikes my concern. This kind of money is more than an overeager homebuyer.

This is development-company money.

"Shit," I mutter, crumpling up the note and chucking it into my waste bin. Juan isn't the only council member I'm going to be visiting again today. I need to talk to Selena.

A spell to completely shield Folk Haven from the rest of the world would require hundreds of witches, all with a protection focus, casting constantly. I'm not sure that many protection witches even exist in the world, much less in our town.

However, there are smaller protections in place. Wards buried in the earth on the way into town, spelled to discourage people like Albert—someone backed by a larger company—

from taking interest in our off-the-beaten-path home. Lake property is lucrative even if it's tucked away in northern Georgia.

If humans are here, trying to buy up prime real estate, then the wards are failing.

Until Selena and her witches get that fixed, I'll have to keep a wary eye on Albert Durrand.

7

———

LEVI

MOST GUYS DON'T GO to their ex-girlfriend when they're looking to relax. But most people don't end a relationship, only to become best friends after the fact.

"You'd better not be bringing that IPA shit in my house," Satine calls from her perch on the edge of her roof. She balances on the spot easily, unconcerned by the fifteen-foot drop when she has a set of wings ready to hold her aloft. The monster uses them now, launching into the air and gliding down to me in a graceful swoop.

"I brought you sours."

I hold the six-pack up, and she reaches out to accept the offering, cradling the beers in her taloned hands. Satine stares up at me with cloudy-purple eyes I've always found intriguing. No pupils, but she can still see fine. Better even than the average human.

There are a lot of interesting aspects to Satine's appearance. Large patches of scales cover portions of her skin, the diamond-hard protection blending seamlessly in with her skin. Both surfaces are a royal blue, the color more vibrant than the murky greenish waters of Lake Galen. She told me once that her father's scales are an icy blue, which must serve him well, as he lives in a hidden dragon colony in Antarctica.

The difference between Satine and her father is greater than the color of their hides. As a full-blooded dragon, Mr. Drakos has a human form and a beast form. The first allows him to walk unnoticed among the human population, like mine does. The second resembles the myths passed down through the centuries of giant reptilian creatures soaring through the sky and breathing fire.

But Satine is a monster. Father a dragon, mother an undine. There were no rules to her creation, and she came out different.

"You look beat." She flicks a wing at me, knocking the leathery appendage against my shoulder in a gentle shove. "You up for a game or just want to drink?"

The cut on my thumb still stings, and my mind flits around to different topics. If I try my hand at our usual game of chess, she'll have me in checkmate before I make it through a single beer.

"Let's drink. Been a busy day."

"Yeah, mine too."

She saunters into her house, the easy sway of her indigo body lulling me into a relaxed state. Not an aroused one though. I got over those feelings a while back when we realized romance wasn't the connection we felt to each other.

Being around Satine is calming because of her comfort with herself. I'm a selfish ass to feed off the hard work she's done for her own mental state, but I can't help basking in the presence of a woman who found a way to be completely comfortable in her monster-ness.

At least, that's the face she portrays to the world. Not that the world gave her any other choice.

The most common type of mythic falls under the broad

category of shifter. Most of us have two forms: human and other. Witches don't; they remain humanoid unless they cast certain spells. Satine also has two forms. But her forms are other and other. She has no self that easily fits into the human world. So, she lives a hidden life, interacting only with those of us who know and accept her.

Apparently, she also has a vibrant virtual life, and I hope through her online friends, she's able to fulfill her social needs. Every time I think of how the general world would treat Satine if she stepped out from behind the careful shields she'd built, my rage flares to life. Not only on her behalf, but also for every monster.

Satine is the one our kind point to when warning others about inter-mythical relationship.

"Careful," they whisper. "You might have a child like her. A mistake."

Those people don't know anything, and their bigoted views only poison an already-dangerous world.

"You complain to me about your business. Then, I'll complain about mine," I offer.

"Deal." Satine throws a grin over her shoulder, short fangs flashing.

She leads me through her high-ceilinged house, past an impressive computer setup, and out onto her back porch. Screens keep the bugs away, but there's an additional shimmer to the wires. An illusion spell. The same sparkle coats every window in Satine's house. I can't imagine how much she paid to have a witch come out here and work this kind of magic, but I guess it's hard to put a price tag on safety. Satine's home sits on a far-removed part of the lake, but that doesn't mean some nosy human couldn't stumble their way out here and see something they don't understand. I don't blame Satine for using a chunk of her hard-earned paycheck on the spells.

Thoughts of witch magic lead me back to Moira.

Does she know how much the spell she wants will cost her? Will she find the witch she needs? Should I help?

"Okay." Satine folds her wings tight against her back as she settles into an egg-shaped hanging chair. Once she's snug against the plush cushions, she cracks open one of the sour beers and throws a grimace my way. "Me first. My boss is throwing around the idea of an in-person team-building retreat again."

"Seriously?" I roll up the sleeves of my shirt and undo the top few buttons before reclining on a lounge chair. The first sip of my beer has a magical effect, easing tension from my shoulders. "Doesn't he think you have a medical condition?"

"An autoimmune disease. And yes. He asked if I could get a doctor to clear me." She huffs before pressing her can to a set of thin blue lips and taking a deep gulp. I'm glad I brought her a full six-pack. She wipes her mouth and keeps on with her rant. "Like, seriously? He thinks a doctor scribbling on a piece of paper would magically cure a chronic condition? I know I'm not really immunocompromised, but *he* sure as shit doesn't!" Satine drags her claws over the scales that cover the top of her head, the motion reminiscent of a human combing fingers through hair. The dragon-undine hybrid doesn't have any fibrous material to work with, but she makes do.

"Did you tell him to go screw himself?" I ask.

If my friend had pupils, no doubt she'd be rolling her eyes at me right now. "I wish. No, I gave him some long explanation about my medical restrictions and risks and kept going until he conceded the point."

"Well, that's good, right?"

Satine shakes her head before another quick sip. "Now, he's pressing me to join the retreat virtually. In his words, 'Show your lovely face to the rest of the team, so we can connect and become a stronger unit.' Seriously, what the fuck is his problem? I'm his best employee. Why can't he get off my back and let me do my job?"

Hearing about her struggle has me twitchy on her behalf. This is more than an extroverted boss pushing his work views on an antisocial employee. The guy doesn't know how much his demands are torture to her.

Satine *wants* to interact with the rest of the world.

It's the world that doesn't want Satine.

I bet she'd love to go to the team-building retreat. Bond with her coworkers.

But they'd run, screaming, if they saw her appearance. Unable to appreciate the beautiful woman before them simply because of her differences.

"What are you going to do?"

She shrugs. "He hasn't made it mandatory. Yet. If he does, then I might be job-hunting soon."

"Maybe fake camera failure the day of?"

Satine tilts her head from side to side. "That might work. But it still opens me up to him asking for another video meet in the future. And too many camera failures mean more questions and prodding. Humans getting too curious spells danger."

A rule that every mythic learns at a young age. Hopefully not the hard way.

"Okay, I'm done," she sighs. "Your turn."

Satine and I have only ever been honest with each other, so I don't hold back. Not that I reveal everything that occurred in The Council meeting. There's an understanding of confidentiality to our discussions unless we agree to make a public announcement. But I tell her about the growing pain in my ass that is Moira MacNamara.

I still can't believe she pulled a knife on me in the middle of town. *Who has a special knife pocket in their purse? Is she a secret assassin? And why did the sight of the sharp blade have my cock twitching?*

I keep that reaction to myself too.

"You're competing in the Gauntlet? Just to prove a point?"

"And for the cleansing. To move it forward." I draw deep from my beer, letting the hoppy flavor distract me from the stress of the day.

Satine snorts, and I glare over at her.

"What?"

"It's just ... you say that like you think you're going to win." Her thin lips stretch into a rueful grin.

"Of course I'll win." I straighten in the wicker chair, glaring at her. "I'm descended from sea monsters. Born to dominate any water-based competition."

"But you have to keep your human form," she points out. "Yeah, you're in shape. But so is everyone else entering. And don't take this the wrong way, but Moira is more ruthless than you." Satine nibbles on her lower lip with a fang. "I mean, I'll cheer you on. But don't expect me to bet on you to win."

"I'm plenty ruthless!" The deep rumble of my voice should strike fear into the hearts of my competition.

Again, I get the sense that Satine is rolling her amethyst eyes. "Ruthless people don't have to point out they're ruthless. The world just knows."

My chair lets out a creak of protest when I collapse back, a sullen pout pulling at my mouth. "The world treats me like I'm ruthless," I grouse.

Satine makes a hum in the back of her throat that sounds like agreement. On this point, she can't contest my view. Even though I have a face to wear that is acceptable among the human masses, the rest of the mythics know what I am and treat me according to a set of guidelines fashioned out of fear.

I am a product of an unapproved union.

A pair that birthed the unknown.

I am a monster.

Fear me, I guess.

8

MOIRA

HOLDING Galen's Gauntlet in the middle of the day has always seemed odd to me. The ceremony and intensity of the competition beg for a midnight course, lit only by the occasional flaming torch.

But I guess a sunny day means the crowds gathered have a better view of all the competitors and the trials we're about to put ourselves through. The mass of mythics pull up folded chairs to the banks, passing around snacks and pulling beers from coolers. No doubt half of them tailgated before they showed up.

That's the beauty of Galen's Gauntlet; the biennial tradition serves multiple purposes.

For fans of sporting events, this is the ultimate game. Competitors from all different mythical groups are put to the test against a range of challenges. Many of them dangerous, although no one has died in the Gauntlet since the '80s. The sirens and witches now make an effort to keep everyone alive, knowing a death would dampen the celebratory aspect of the competition. This whole event is held in tribute to the mythic Galen, a siren who tore her wings apart to slay an evil sorcerer that was capturing mythics and keeping them in cages like his own twisted zoo. Today, he is only known as The Collector, and this lake covers the land he formerly owned.

Mythics took it back.

For those in Folk Haven who think the Gauntlet is too barbaric of a tradition, they can comfort themselves with the charitable aspect. All competitors pay an entry fee, and all spectators buy tickets to attend. A portion of that money, which is always a huge pot, goes straight back to the town.

Sporting event, traditional celebration, charity fundraiser. Galen's Gauntlet does it all.

Today, this ode to a past mythic will serve one more purpose. Helping me rub the truth into the face of one cocky sea monster.

Speaking of the pain in my ass, Levi saunters up to my spot on the floating platform serving as the starting line.

I'm not proud to admit I've been avoiding him these past two weeks. My goal was to discover a cleansing witch before we saw each other again. The task hasn't been easy. Mythics in general get twitchy when they feel as though someone is hunting them, so I attempted to keep my queries casual. Just a selkie looking for a little magic.

First, I stopped by the post office, where Heather, a witch, works the front desk. She merely shrugged and offered me stamps. Next, I went to Ramla University, where I knew two witches were professors, teaching alongside my brother Seamus. Neither one was willing to share that kind of knowledge. Slowly, when I could take breaks from work, I made my way through the witches I knew in town, getting thoroughly rebuffed by each one. Then, two days ago, I was drinking wine at my friend Sonya's house, lamenting my failure, and the siren reminded me of a mythic I'd overlooked.

The next morning, I drove east, along the branch of Lake Galen housing witches, and sought out Madeline, the former school nurse for Folk Haven High and a known healing witch. Finally, the woman gave me a scrap of information I could work with when I asked after a cleansing witch.

"She doesn't like her specialty, so she won't be thanking me for telling anyone about it. She's the worst kind of enemy to have. Sneaky. I'm sorry, child, but don't ask me again." Madeline shook her head, beaded braids clacking with the movement and tapping against ebony cheeks. She swayed back and forth in her rocking chair as I hovered on the steps of her front porch.

Even though I wanted to push, I held myself back. Her vague statement at least told me there was a cleansing witch in town, she was a she, and she wasn't a woman to cross.

"Moira," Levi says in greeting, dipping his chin. The movement causes his dark hair to swish forward, brushing against his strong jaw.

The fact that I notice the small detail frustrates me. Then, there's his lack of a shirt.

Dear Finned One, why can't the monster compete in his normal business-casual wardrobe?

When Levi wears a button-up, I can almost convince myself he doesn't have a sculpted body underneath. Even the swimsuit he sports mocks me with a tight fit. Everything is on display.

Everything.

I tear my eyes away, finding the monster watching me with a curious tilt to his head. While I have the urge to glare so hard that I burn his skin off, I'm aware many of the competitors surrounding us are constituents. Voters who chose me as their political representative because they trust me to be responsible on their behalf. Determined to behave myself—to a point—I paste on my *I'm a professional and I can handle anything* smile and face the water, keeping him in the corner of my eye.

"Council Member Abadi. You showed up."

His lips tighten and then smooth into his own insincere expression of bland politeness. "Of course. I know this is a challenging competition. You can use all the help you can get."

My fingers curl into fists, but I keep my face cool. "Please don't limit yourself on my part. I'd hate to have your resentment when I reach the finish line first."

"Oh, don't worry about that. I would never be so immature as to resent a fellow council member." His lips twitch in a second-long smirk.

Smug bastard.

"Ready yourselves!" The call comes from a siren swooping over our heads.

She's not the only one winging above the inlet we're gathered in. Some sirens ride the warm breeze of the day while others sit, perched in the highest branches of trees overlooking the water. Every single one wears a coating of red paint on the tips of their wings in tribute to Galen and the sacrifice she made.

My great-grandmother was one captured by The Collector. If it wasn't for Galen, I might not exist.

The heaviness of that realization settles on my shoulders as I cross the floating dock to the starting line. Glancing to my left and right, I see an unending stretch of competitors of all different mythical types. Many are descendants of the original captives, like I am. Some are simply mythics who heard of a town in Georgia that was a safe place for their kind.

We all mix now, rivals for however long this competition lasts but allies against the human world.

Just then, I spot a surprisingly familiar face.

Is that Seamus?

My brother stares straight ahead, crouched low and ready to dive into the water.

What the hell is he doing here? He should be among the spectators!

But before I can yell out to him—or at him—a horn blasts, and the race starts.

The water cradles and encourages me as I plunge beneath the surface. I would be much faster if the rules allowed for me to wear my selkie skin, but all competitors must stay in their human forms. Keeping the competition as fair as possible when there are mythics of varying abilities taking part.

When I come up for a breath, the water churns around me with others swimming as fast as they can get their limbs to move. A lot of them shoot ahead.

Maybe I should have trained for this, I consider for the first time.

A blast of heat presses against the left side of my face, and I duck underwater in time to avoid a rolling fireball.

And so the obstacles begin.

Being stuck underwater doesn't bother me; I can hold my breath for hours. If there are any dragons in the competition, I bet they didn't have to dive, immune as they are to fire. Some of us have natural advantages. At least based on what the obstacle is.

An image of Levi pops into my head. What powers does he have? I have no answers. I haven't even seen his secondary form. All I know is, his father is a sea monster, and I've heard a rumor that his mother is a witch. Still, even if I knew the exact abilities his parents have, that would give no clear answer about their son.

Monsters are wild cards, which is why many mythics fear them.

And that fear turns into alienation.

A small spark of sympathy tugs at my chest, but I shove it and thoughts of my nemesis aside as I power forward. My pulse rate picks up as I paddle harder, discovering an exhilarating high from this race I didn't expect. This was supposed to be a means to an end, but I think I might be enjoying myself.

For now.

A cluster of bodies forms ahead as the fire continues to push everyone under the surface. When I reach the mass of squirming bodies, I realize a chain-link fence spans the width of the inlet we're in. Spotting competitors swimming on the other side, I know there must be a way through. In the murky water, five feet below me, I watch a merman slip his body through what must be a gap in the fence. I curl my fingers around the cool metal and pull myself down hand over hand, not wanting to miss the opening. I find the hole and slip to the other side.

Easy enough.

Above me, I don't spy any dancing flame colors, so I take a risk and resurface.

All clear.

Another head appears beside me, and the woman pushes blonde strands out of her face. I recognize her as Penelope, a harpy who works as the town's dentist. She meets my eyes and gives a toothy grin that drops away when a puff of green powder hits her straight on the forehead. Her eyes roll up into her head, and her full body floats to the surface like a dead fish. A cackle above me is all the warning I get before dodging to the side and missing my own neon knockout.

Sirens soar overhead, wearing thick gloves and lobbing the green balls at competitors. I spot Seamus as one hits his arm. From the way the limb relaxes and he stares at the immobile piece of himself, I'm guessing the witches rigged up some type of paralyzing agent.

I dive under the water, hopefully escaping their notice and aim. However, to the side, I see a glimmering cloud of the emerald powder. A werewolf swims into the stuff and then loses consciousness too fast to realize his mistake. His body relaxes and floats to the surface.

Avoid green powder at all costs, I warn myself as I push through the water.

As I dodge around another shimmering cloud of the stuff, I wonder how long the effects last. Would be great if those mythics were down for the count, but my bet is, the effect is temporary. No room for me to slow down. After not seeing green for a stretch, I decide to resurface to get my bearings.

Glancing to the sides, even as I paddle forward, I'm energized to realize the herd has thinned a great deal. And with open water ahead of me, I might have a chance—

A groan. A clang. Metal bars cut off my forward progress.

"No!" I gasp, wrapping my hands around the heavy iron that snapped me up like a bear trap. I'm in a cage, and this won't be as easy as the chain-link to get around.

I recognize this obstacle. The sirens change the Gauntlet every time, rearranging old tricks and implementing new ones. Having attended the event as a spectator since before I can remember, I know all the classics. This trap was last used four years ago, and I don't need the gleeful chanting above me to remember the name.

Love cage.

The crowd roars in approval, and I curse my luck.

There's only one way to get out, and it has nothing to do with physical strength. Like many of the aspects of the Gauntlet, this challenge hearkens back to the namesake. Galen found some of her strength to rebel in the love she had for a fellow prisoner, a selkie male who always found a way to sneak into her cage.

Their love is legend, and to earn my way out of the love-cage obstacle, I have to kiss the hell out of whoever got caught up in here with me.

Might as well get this lip-lock over with.

"You ready to get out of here?" a deep voice asks.

A familiar voice that tenses every muscle in my body.

Please, Finned One. Anyone but him.

But the gods have always found amusement in the strangest of places, including this cage. Which is why when I turn, I find the lowest mythic on my list, waiting for a kiss.

Levi.

9

———

LEVI

"Damn it!" Moira screeches the curse before throwing her body back at the bars, her fingers scrambling for a seam in their mechanism.

I try not to be offended by her obvious horror at having to kiss me.

She hates my father. It's not about being a monster, I remind myself.

Ignoring the false ring in that thought, I let my body drift closer as I continue to tread water. The cage gives us about a foot of airspace, the rest dipping below the surface like an iceberg.

"Moira—"

A body slamming into our cage from the outside cuts off my statement. The selkie pauses her escape attempts while we watch in fascination as Seamus MacNamara wrestles with a bewitched rope. From the way he tears at the writhing thing, our place in this cage almost appears cozy.

Finally, with a deep grunt, he's able to wrench the snakelike object off. Then, he ties the spasming rope to the bars of our cage, offers Moira a quick, "Hey, sis," and swims ahead, leaving us behind.

The rope twitches in a furious rhythm, as eager to get free as my selkie cellmate.

"You know there's only one way to get out of this cage," I reason. "We might as well get it over with."

"Go for it, Moira!" The encouragement sounds from the shore, where Owen—one of the MacNamara siblings—stands in front of a crowd of selkies, grinning as he mercilessly teases his sister. "No one is watching! I swear!"

I can't see her expression, but my guess is, she's plotting multiple murders.

Moira whips around, eyes a fierce fire. "Fine," she hisses.

I expect a reluctant, quick peck. What I get is a furious woman lunging at me, grabbing my face, and smashing her lips into mine. The act has no affection in it, but I groan low in my gut anyway. The angry coupling is a firm stroke against all my nerve endings.

And the selkie doesn't break away. She commits fully to the demonstration, plastering her wet, swimsuit-clad body against mine. Without thought, I wrap an arm around her waist and use my free hand to grip the upper bars of the cage, so not a single brain cell has to be wasted on keeping us afloat. I can revel in the hot seduction of her furious lips sliding against mine.

As Moira sucks on my lower lip, something inside me shifts. A twisting in my chest. A filling of a space I didn't realize was empty. Everything in this moment, in the world, adopts a sense of rightness.

I am whole. The beast presses at the boundaries of my skin, desperate to roar with triumph and shake the sky so that the world might know that—

My mind cuts away from the conclusion when Moira bites me.

I love it.

My cock grows hard and heavy between us. Just as I'm about to press my hips against hers, there's the loud groan, this time not from me.

The cage parts around us, and a siren's musical voice speaks to us from overhead. "You lovebirds had better get a move on." She winks and then wings away.

Before I can remember why I'd want to move anywhere, my selkie tears herself free of my hold. Wide brown eyes give me a wild glance before she plunges under the surface of the water.

No! The thought growls through my head, almost breaching my throat before I keep the desperate shout at bay.

Every cell in my being wants to lunge forward, recapture Moira, and drag her to the rocky bottom of the lake. Take her hard as the water presses on us from all sides. Watch bubbles spill from her mouth as she cries out in ecstasy.

I shake my head, trying to rid my mind of the erotic thoughts that I have no right to act on.

The need might drive me to do something I'd regret. Something monstrous. Just so I might have her.

Moira is not my mate, I scold myself. *I need to focus on the competition.*

Finally, I press forward, cutting a fast path through the water as I follow a bend in the inlet. Ahead of me, more sirens hover in the air, lingering over turbulent water. Last I checked, Lake Galen didn't have any whirlpools. Looks like I've reached the next obstacle.

Moira is ahead of me shouting something as she treads water at the edge of one of the dangerous rapids. A spike of anxiety spears my chest, but then a siren swoops down to the tempestuous surface and the waters suddenly calm, allowing the selkie to paddle through. I move to follow, but as I approach, the churning of the waves starts up again.

My throat aches to let out a fierce sound, something inside me furious at the barrier between me and the selkie.

"You must solve my riddle to cross," the siren floating above me calls out. Massive white wings sprout from her back, beating softly to keep herself in the air. "What stretches to the ends but never stops?"

I open my mouth and then shake a sudden fuzziness from my brain. *She sang something to me.*

Her song had better not have been part of the riddle. No one can remember a siren's song other than one of their kind.

My mind tries to work through the words I did hear, but all I can think is, *Moira is getting farther from me.*

"An ocean," I say, guessing randomly.

"Wrong, monster."

There's something about how she says my species that briefly snares my attention away from Moira's retreating form. I glance up to find the siren smirking at me. I don't know this woman by name, but I've seen her around Folk Haven. She spends time with Georgiana and Pamela, one of the more vocal mythics when it comes to monster distrust.

She thinks to lord her power over me?

Every day of my life, I work to make myself calm. Reasonable. Manageable for those around me so as not to cause discomfort or fear. But I will not allow this bigot to separate me from what I want and taunt me with her hatred while she does it.

My father rules an ocean, and I am his son. No pitiful waves in a lake will frighten me.

I dive into the whirlpool.

The current tears at my flesh, dragging and tugging. Doing everything it can to fling me back the direction I came. I will not allow it. With a snarl and a series of powerful strokes, I traverse the roiling mass, bursting out the other side.

I can hear the siren shouting curses at my back, furious I did not follow her rules. If she'd wanted me to respect the dictates of her game, then she should have shown the same respect to me.

Far ahead, I spy the dark, curling hair of my selkie, and I aim my body toward her. The water suddenly drags heavy against my limbs, as if the liquid were solidifying into gelatin. The slow pace has me even more frantic to reach my selkie.

Not mine. Not my goal. Forget about Moira, the logical part of my brain scolds. *This is about winning. She is not the prize.*

Trying to listen to that logic, I reluctantly take my focus off her as the water around me eases to a normal mass, and I scan the way ahead.

We've come to the next obstacle.

A forest of bubbles drifts on the surface of the lake. The shimmering orbs very in size and color, and they carry an ominous air. The noise of the spectators is somehow muffled here, leaving only the sounds of sobbing and hysterical laughter drifting from ahead.

"What the fuck?" I mutter to myself as I swim toward the edge of the collection.

A quick dive below the surface reveals the way isn't clear of obstacles. The water is shallow, and the bubbles dip low. Worried what will happen if I touch one, I return to the surface and navigate carefully.

The world stays utterly quiet around me as I progress and lose sight of the shore, as if I entered a maze with hedges that muffle all noise. A dread clutches at my chest, and I fight off a descending fear that I'm alone, stranded. There's no sign of other competitors. Just me dodging these randomly moving globes.

A purple bubble the size of a golf cart bobs on a small wave off to my right. When it drifts another few feet, I suddenly have a clear sight of Moira. I almost convince myself to dismiss her when another mythic appears at her side. The mountain lion shifter shoulders Moira out of his way, sending her straight into a white bubble. The thing pops with a high-pitched squeak.

I expect Moira to retaliate against the manhandling, maybe shove the shifter back or shout an insult his way. Instead, she opens her mouth and lets out a shriek.

The noise is pure fear.

Even twenty feet away, I can see the whites of her eyes. Moira flounders in the water, movements frantic, as if attacks were coming at her from all directions.

"Moira!" I bellow her name, abandoning my forward movement as I dodge the deceptively innocent bubbles to reach her side. Once close enough, I wrap my arms around her. "I'm here, Moira. It's okay. I've got you."

But she continues to scream in utter terror, her normally soft brown eyes seeing something mine can't. An instinct arises, filling my limbs with the tingling fire I associate with my magic. Knowing how people view me, I tend to keep all signs of my mythical self hidden. My form and my abilities.

But with Moira writhing in this unidentifiable terror, I call up my magic without second thought. A pressure seeps out of my skin, invisible to the eye and containing no more sensation than a light brush of wind. When the magic pressure touches Moira, she gasps in a deep breath, cutting off her scream. Now, she pants, each exhale ragged with continued fear, but the overwhelming terror visibly eases as she blinks, and her hands relax from their claw shape.

"I won't let anything hurt you," I murmur against her hair as I keep us afloat and away from more bubbles with continuous kicks of my legs.

She is lush against me. All strength and softness. Holding

her elicits an easy joy that could only be surpassed if she wrapped herself around me like she did in the cage.

I know the instant Moira fully comes back to herself. She stiffens, and then a set of hands shoves my chest, and I allow her to move away.

"I'm fine," she snaps, brown eyes glaring over my shoulder, not meeting my gaze.

I'm sure she'd like to believe the side effects of touching the bubble went away on their own, and I'm happy to let her go on thinking that. I don't like the idea of Moira feeling indebted to me for comforting her while she was afraid.

Still, the cold dismissal doesn't exactly boost my confidence.

"I heard laughing and someone crying. I'm betting that each color is a different emotion," I offer the knowledge while dodging a blue bubble the size of a Jet Ski.

"Yeah, I got that." There's a bite to her words that has me staring even harder at the selkie. She still avoids my gaze as she paddles past me, into a gap that'll let her move forward.

As I let out a shaky breath, I realize I might not have touched the white bubble, but the situation affected me too. I've never seen Moira scared. She is always the epitome of professionalism—until I throw her off-balance. Then, I'll earn a peek at her temper or sarcastic humor. I've seen her around Folk Haven with her family, laughing and joyful. Beautiful moments I tucked into the back of my mind.

But I've never seen her fear, and the glimpse of it shocked me. Caused my own fear response to switch on.

This strong woman revealed a crack in her armor, and she didn't do it deliberately. And I saw the crack. Probably the last mythic in this town she'd want to be vulnerable around.

So, as much as I want to ask if she's okay, I keep my mouth shut. As much as I want to catch up to her, press a comforting palm to her back, I keep my hands to myself.

"Gods-damn it!" Her curse whips me back to the present,

and I'm already moving toward her when I realize her eyes are on the cliff face rising above the bubble forest.

The lip of the ledge is the finish line, and a single mythic is currently rolling himself over the edge, securing a victory.

"Fucking Seamus," Moira mutters as the man disappears. "How'd he manage that?"

As we lose sight of him, all the bubbles dissolve, and the roar of the watching crowd erupts, as if someone cranked up the volume. I forgot we were being watched this whole time. The witches must've done something to spell this part of the course, making the spectators less obvious. Or maybe I was too focused on Moira to think about the hundreds of eyes watching my every move.

What did the townspeople think of the monster council member comforting the finned council member as she screamed in fear?

Hopefully, they were all too fixated on the competitors approaching the finish line to see the break in both of our composures.

"Neither of us won." Moira heads to the nearby bank, her torso rising from the water as her feet find ground.

I watch as droplets slide over her skin, unable to help myself from noticing how the wet black bathing suit forms to her body. Two hard nipples press against the shiny fabric. Tearing my eyes away, I meet her disgruntled glare.

"Guess this didn't make any difference." With that, she turns toward the cliff, trudging forward, no doubt to watch her brother collect his victory.

As I watch her go, I hold my thoughts to myself.

We might not have won, but everything has changed.

10

———

MOIRA

A BUILDING less ornate than Town Hall but still imposing in its own right stands at the opposite end of Main Street—Wolf Trust Bank. The name always reminds me of the *Little Red Riding Hood* story.

Ignore the large teeth, little girl, and trust me.

Despite the odd thoughts the name inspires, I do in fact trust the wolves that run this bank. The pack is an integral part of Folk Haven, and there's not a place safer in town limits than a vault guarded by werewolves.

Which is exactly why I keep my most sensitive documents in a large safety deposit box available for council member usage. I'm already mentally flipping through the papers when the front door of the bank swings open, almost bludgeoning me in the face.

"Oh gods! I'm sorry. I ... Moira?" The deep, accented voice plays over my name like rolling ocean waves.

Dangerous if I let my guard down. But the moment I see his

face, my defenses slam into place. I will never let this mythic drag my head underwater again.

"Hamish." I'm proud of myself for not spitting my ex's name. "How are you?" *Also, I don't care.*

The only reason I'm not shoving by him is, we're approaching noon, which means the sidewalks are steadily filling with townsfolk seeking lunch. I refuse to look anything other than composed when speaking to Hamish Barclay.

Expecting a quick response of *good*, I step back and give him plenty of space to continue on his way.

But Hamish moves with me, keeping close.

"I'm doing well. Really well in fact. I'm expecting tenure soon. The admin at RU loves me." A charismatic grin creases the dark stubble on his white cheeks, and each syllable he speaks rings with Scottish roots. A selkie who grew up in our ancestral home. That accent used to melt the panties right off me.

Now, I want to set his pants on fire just to see him suffer.

"Good for you." There. Small talk complete.

I make as if to step around him, but Hamish holds out an arm to stop me.

"I watched you in the Gauntlet."

That, more than his arm, has me pausing.

"I thought you said the Gauntlet was barbaric." At least, that's what he claimed two years ago when I asked him to attend with me as a spectator.

One broad shoulder rises as his gaze traces over my face. "I've been known to judge things too quickly."

Understatement of the year. Our relationship, after the glow of the honeymoon phase started to wear off, was all judgment. And I let myself be measured by him. I internalized every time he found me wanting.

Is he changing?

The thought feels like a betrayal. How many times did I tell myself that Hamish would be different? That he would be more accepting? That he would stop judging me as long as I didn't give him anything else to judge?

"I'm glad you gave it a chance," I say, keeping my politician's face in place. Surface-level pleasant, even as I prowl like a caged animal inside.

"I wasn't surprised to see you competing." He leans toward me, bringing the scent of seaweed with him. A touch too salty.

"You weren't?" I step back once more, telling myself there's a difference between retreating and keeping the peace.

If I hold my ground against Hamish, no doubt the fury I found after ending our relationship will crawl up my throat and spew onto him all the words I should have defended myself with when we were together.

Another fact registers: Hamish saw my passionate make-out session with Levi.

For the first time, I'm happy that lip-lock took place. I hope every second of it felt like a paper cut to his pride.

"Not at all. You've always been ... aggressive." He offers a half-smile I used to find charming, as if we were sharing an inside joke.

Instead, the word goes off like a silent grenade tossed between us, flinging shrapnel of our past.

Aggressive. Desperate. Overbearing. Needy. Stubborn.

So many labels he applied to me in every different way until I thought I was no better than a blood-starved leech.

This time though, instead of denying the identifier, I nod. "I am aggressive. It's served me well." Though not in the Gauntlet, seeing as how I still lost and am not closer to Great-Grandaunt Blair's pelt.

Hamish blinks, surprise flicking through his blue eyes. Then, the grin is back, and I have to breathe in deep to stay steady. To brace myself not to flinch at whatever he says next. A compliment? An underhanded praise? An outright insult?

With Hamish, I never know.

A warm pressure settles on my shoulders, and I do jerk at the sensation. I'm about to tug myself free when I glance to the side and realize the new arrival is my brother Owen.

"Hey." Owen beams while pulling me in for a one-armed hug.

My throat is suddenly thick with some choking emotion. His affection in this moment could be the support I need.

Or Owen could turn to my ex and start talking about the good ole days when I was dating a selkie that the whole family loved. If he takes that route, I'll need to truly retreat because it won't be long before traitorous tears escape.

Please don't pick Hamish over me, I silently beg even though I know that's not fair. I never told my family how Hamish treated me. They don't know there's a choice to be made.

Owen loosens his arm but keeps ahold of me. Then, he turns to the Scottish selkie, and I press my lips together, holding my breath so hard that it's possible my blood stops flowing as well.

"Hey, fuckface."

Silence falls between the three of us as the greeting settles. Hamish's confident expression slackens into shock. I'm battered with a wave of relief so massive that I lock my knees to keep from wobbling. Somehow, I maintain my professionally detached demeanor. All the while, my brother keeps on a cheerful expression.

"That's ..." Hamish clears his throat, pulling himself together. "That's uncalled for." Now, he's all sincerity, his voice roughening with emotion. "I know Moira and I aren't together anymore, but I always counted you as a friend."

"Did you?" Owen could be discussing discounted solar panels with how cheery his voice stays. "Because I always counted you as the guy who screwed with my sister's head because you were intimidated by how awesome she is. She's too decent of a person to rub in your face that leaving you was the best decision she ever made, but I'm not. I popped a bottle of champagne when she told us you all were through. After I chugged that bubbly, I did a celebratory naked cannonball in Galen and praised The Finned One."

Thank the gods Owen has a grip on me because I'm having trouble with keeping balanced as my mind recalibrates.

My family didn't like Hamish. Or at least, Owen didn't?

I'm going to need time to fully accept that fact. For now though, I can do what comes easy—banter with my brother.

"I know you think your body is a gift to all dimensions"—my tone is dry, helping to keep the grateful tears from my eyes—"but I don't think The Finned One is looking for an eyeful of your bare ass."

"Let's agree to disagree." Owen's stare stays on Hamish, and I watch in real time as the false sunny expression hardens into a level of intimidation I wasn't aware my brother could achieve. "You don't deserve to talk to her."

"I did nothing wrong," Hamish hisses.

"You made Moira unhappy." Owen releases me to step forward, into the other selkie's space. "That means, you did *everything* wrong."

My heart clenches, and I'm almost willing to let my brother brawl in my honor. Even though Hamish has a few inches on Owen, my ex has maybe half the muscle mass.

But I can fight my own battles. And I also choose when I'm above certain conflict.

"It was so nice to run into you, Mr. Barclay." I pour sugar into my voice until he might choke on the sweetness. "Remember to come to me whenever you have a town concern. That's my job as your council representative."

The tightness of his lips shows I hit my mark. He never liked the idea I might have more power than him. That was the eye-opening point of our relationship, sad as I am to say it because I should have realized sooner.

A year ago, when Hamish and I were still together—living together—I told him I was running for the soon-opening Of the Fin council seat, a dream I'd had since I was seventeen. He tried to talk me out of it, saying I was already busy enough with barely any time for our relationship. There was even a moment he brought up me leaving the real estate business to work on starting a family with him.

I balked and had an epiphany that he was not the man for me, much less my mate. I got out as fast as I could and put my name in the running for the council seat the next week.

This past year has been the happiest I've had in a long time, and through the separation, I finally started to see Hamish's love for what it really was—manipulation.

I hook my arm through Owen's and drag him with me, around the man I'm no longer letting control any part of my life, only to come face-to-face with another mythic threatening my mental stability.

"Levi!" my brother crows, stepping forward to slap the monster on the shoulder. "Been a while."

Levi obviously just came out of the bank but decided not to continue on his way. Instead, he stands still on the sidewalk, dark eyes tracing my body before flicking over my shoulder, no doubt to alight on Hamish.

How much did he hear?

"Hello, Owen." The monster's voice sounds a note lower than usual, and I can't suppress a traitorous shiver.

"When was the last time I saw you?" My brother affects a thoughtful expression as he taps his chin and then snaps his fingers in triumph. "I know! You were making out with my sister in a cage!" Owen turns a gleeful grin on me. "Remember, Moira?"

How is it that one second, I want to hug my brother, and the very next, I want to strangle him until his eyeballs pop out of their sockets?

"It was three days ago. Of course I remember." Underneath my words, I hope Owen picks up on my secret message.

If you don't shut your mouth, I will sew it closed with unbreakable, enchanted thread.

"What about you, Levi? Remember that?" Owen ignores the unspoken warning.

The sound of shifting feet behind me alerts me that Hamish still lingers.

The monster's stare locks with mine. "Couldn't forget if I tried."

Heat suffuses every inch of me until I'm sure the humidity of the summer day will turn into steam when it touches my skin.

"I hate you," I mutter, stalking away from the group toward the bank, regretting the decision to come here in the first place.

"Which one of us?" Owen yells after me, but I don't respond.

Because, other than Hamish, I'm not exactly sure of my answer.

11

MOIRA

WHEN THE KNOCK comes at my office door that afternoon, I'm an island among an ocean of papers. Without any appointments today, I thought it would be the perfect time to continue my search for a cleansing witch among the Folk Haven population, and since I don't keep any electronic records related to mythical status, sorting through hard copies is the only way to look.

"Who is it?"

My real estate office consists of three rooms. The large waiting room with broad windows looking out on Main Street, a small bathroom, and then my back office. In case of walk-ins, I left the front door unlocked, but after Albert Durrand's unannounced visit, I made sure to lock my office door. First off, because this is sensitive information I'm handling. Secondly, I don't need anyone seeing me in the disheveled state I sink into when researching.

"Levi." The deep rumble cuts through the walls and straight to my chest, setting off a whole flurry of unwanted emotions.

Damn The Finned One's games. He's found me. Not like I'm hard to find, here in my workspace. Only this morning, after the bank run-in, I decided to avoid him for as long as mythically possible.

"Just a minute," I shout.

I kissed Levi Abadi. The idea still sends me reeling, mainly because the kiss was so monumental. I'd thought I'd lunge in, practically bite his face off, and then escape from that cage to win the tournament. Instead, I plastered myself to him, experiencing the rough press of his mouth against mine as if he were simultaneously kissing every sensitive spot on my body.

If only that were the worst moment of the day.

Levi Abadi held me while I screamed.

The strange part is, I don't even remember the fear. There and gone. What lingers is the memory of his arms wrapped tight around me, comforting in their unrelenting hold. And those words he whispered. Kind, soft, caring. Enough to make any person melt.

Later, I discovered Morgana was the witch to contribute the bubbles, and I briefly considered slashing the new arrival's tires out of spite. But I immediately talked myself down. She was only trying to do her part as a new witch in Folk Haven, helping with a local tradition. And I had known what I was getting into when I signed up for the Gauntlet.

At least, I thought I did.

"Can't avoid him forever," I mutter to myself, rising from my seat on the floor. My desk is large but nowhere near big enough for my explosion of documents.

Carefully, I walk on my toes, stepping in gaps between the papers as I make my way to my door. Grabbing my phone off a filing cabinet, I swipe open my security-camera app, double-checking that I am about to come face-to-face with the monster who made me feel things. His trademark luscious, dark locks show up on the camera as well as the defined point of his nose.

I scan my office, searching for my heels but they hide from me. I must've tossed them into a corner at some point.

Whatever. At least I know my carpet is clean.

Careful not to disturb my morning's work, I crack my office door and slide out, shutting it behind me. Immediately, I regret not spending the extra moment to find my heels. They would give me the few inches I need to be eye-level with this man.

Now, he gets to look down on me.

As our gazes clash, the healed cut on my thumb tingles, as if the blood vow were still in effect.

It's not, I remind myself.

And even if I find a way to save my land from getting burned, Great-Grandaunt Blair's pelt is still in the possession of a man who never deserved to touch it. The thought sends a spike of hot anger through me, forming my face into a scathing glare.

"Yes?" The word snaps out, and I do nothing to soften the impact.

Levi doesn't flinch, but he also doesn't appear too happy with my greeting. The mythic stares at me with an intense focus, as if enough eye contact could dig out an important answer to a question that plagues him. I don't know what the question is, but I do know I must look a mess with my hair falling out of my normal bun, sleeves pushed up past my elbows, and pants wrinkled from crawling around on the floor.

"I came to talk about the Gauntlet," he finally admits.

With a slice of my hand through the air, I cut off any trip down memory lane. "I did what I had to do to win. Nothing more."

His lips twist, but then he gives a curt nod, and I try not to let my surprise show. For some reason, I thought he was about to push for more.

"Fine. But we need to acknowledge that everything we did was on full display for a good portion of this town's population.

And more than that, as council members, we're under constant scrutiny. It's important we take that into account when interacting with each other."

"You're telling me, no more public make-out sessions?" I try to keep my voice mocking and light, but the question comes out breathy. "Not a problem."

Levi's nostrils flare, and I cross my arms and stare around my waiting room, as if the decor held more of my interest than he does.

"What I'm trying to say," he continues, tone careful, "is that when we argue in public, we set an example. Any animosity we hold for each other could be seen as contention between the monsters and the Of the Fin mythics. But if we instead display cooperation, our constituents might follow suit, resulting in a more harmonized town. Which is what The Council hopes for, correct?"

My eyes continue to avoid his, landing on the wood-carved coffee table I had commissioned when I took over this business. The surface shows Lake Galen. All the coves and inlets jutting off the larger waterways. None of the divides are present on the map, but I know where each line is drawn by heart.

Morgana's words whisper through my mind. *"We don't understand your territorial divides."*

I'm beginning to agree. Maybe the separation was important at the conception of Lake Galen. Ensuring all mythics felt there was space for them here. But after decades of intermingling, why can't the lines start blurring? Are we merely holding on to them for tradition's sake?

As I mull over the thought, Levi speaks again. "I also want you to know, I haven't talked to my father in years."

My focus flies back to the monster's face then, and I try to read the tightness around his eyes.

Did they have a falling-out? Could the legendary monster have betrayed his son too?

"I don't think the silence will last forever," Levi continues. "When we next speak, I promise I will ask him about your great-grandaunt. And I hope in swearing this, you can accept that whatever sins my father might have committed, they are not mine. That I would never steal from a selkie or any other mythic. That I only want what is best for Folk Haven, which is why I joined The Council."

A pleasant buzz hums in my rib cage at the sincerity of his words, and I let myself hope. A decades-long wound in our family's history could heal with the fulfillment of Levi's promise. Tracing my gaze over the curves of his face, I let my long-smoldering animosity dampen, appreciating his ability to put aside his pride to help right a wrong.

"Thank you." Letting my arms fall to my sides, I relax enough to offer the start of a smile. "Knowing you don't condone the theft goes a long way. I'll stop holding it against you. And, yes, I think working together rather than butting heads all the time is what Folk Haven needs."

Levi's strong features soften into a smile, the curve of his lips strangely distracting. They're still pillowy, even when stretched wide, and I recall the exact pressure of them against my mouth. My hand twitches at my side, fingers wanting to press to my own lips at the memory, but Levi distracts me by holding out a folder I didn't realize he had clutched in his hand.

"I also wanted to apologize for how I approached the topic of plot 236 at The Council meeting. I should have done more research. I don't blame you for being annoyed."

Research? My thoughts flick back to the papers strewn across the floor in my office, and hope balloons under my ribcage as I accept the folder from him. *Is this the contact information for a purifying witch?* The possibility fills my chest with warm relief, as I know that we can solve this problem together.

Unfortunately, Levi keeps talking. "I met with Xavier yesterday. Of course, you know he's the head of the fire department, but you might not be aware that as a dragon, he has experience with performing cleansing burns. This would be even better than a controlled burn because a dragon burn is much like a volcano eruption. The soil is even richer after the incineration. Here." The monster reaches out, flipping open the folder and pointing to the first piece of paper inside. "These are properties he's worked on for reference. There are also before and after photos."

As Levi rattles on about the pros of a dragon cleansing burn, I keep a pleasant smile on my face. Under the surface of my calm expression, I am howling, animosity roaring as hot as Xavier's hands would if I agreed to this arrangement.

Which I won't. Pretending to read through the information my fellow council member gathered, I meander toward my business's front door. Levi follows beside me, all the while talking animatedly about timetable and soil composition. Opening the door, I angle my body to naturally guide him out to the sidewalk, which I'm glad to see is currently empty of pedestrians.

"Thank you for showing me this," I cut Levi off mid-sentence.

"Of course."

When he gazes down at me, there's a softening around his eyes that only increases the inferno in my belly. For some reason, the sharp emotion burns deeper and hotter than ever before, and when he blinks in surprise, face losing the excited animation from a second ago, I know my smile has transformed into something sharp.

"Only I wish you hadn't troubled yourself." My voice drips with sweet poison. "I still have until the next council meeting to find a witch. And I will." Gripping the door to my office with white-knuckled rage, I grin wide, showing all my teeth in a threat a monster will surely understand. "In the meantime, you can go fuck yourself."

The door shuts with a definitive snap, and I drive the dismissal home with a snick of the lock and a flip of the front sign to *Closed*.

The monster calls my name, but I ignore him, strutting back to my office, dumping his folder in a small trash bin on the way. A gesture he no doubt sees through the front window.

Good. I want him to experience this same mysterious gut-stabbing that I am. When I shut my office door, I finally identify the emotion.

Betrayal.

He doesn't owe you anything, I remind myself. *Stop being ridiculous.*

Instead, I vow to be productive.

An hour later, I have a short list of names and a mission.

I will find my witch.

12

LEVI

THE SIGHT of my childhood home brings on an uncomfortable mixture of nostalgia and trepidation. That's not the house's fault though, but more the woman who lives inside.

As I pull my car into the gravel drive, I wonder if I'll ever be able to show up here and experience simple joy at visiting my mother.

I doubt it. I love my mother, and she loves me. But the woman lacks tact and has never realized how sharp some of her barbs are. I've got scars under the surface from many of them. At least they're healed, and I'd like to think of myself as stronger for them.

The humid evening air sits heavy on my skin as I step out of my car. In between the trees, fireflies blink on and off, bringing color to the dense green mass of the forest that surrounds my mother's home. The structure seems out of place in the woods of Georgia. The house sits high on stilted legs, as if the owner's chief concern were flooding. The clear sky blue of the siding and steeped roof give off a beach-bungalow vibe rather than a lake house.

But what do you expect from a sea witch?

My mother had this home built when I was thirteen and she moved us to Folk Haven. I now live on an entirely different branch of the lake, far enough that I could easily convince her a weekly visit would suffice for our quality time. The buffer helps maintain a good relationship.

But the idea always sours when I consider why there is so much space between us.

My mother lives in the territory of Lake Galen set aside for witches. I was only allowed to purchase a plot in the space left for monsters. Even though I am half-witch, I will never be able to claim that title.

Some might try to soften the blow, stating that no mythic other than witches can buy here either. But don't they understand how monsters are created? That denying us space near full-blooded mythics most often means cutting us off from family?

A fate I would also have to ask a future mate to accept if they are not a monster as well.

A hazy image of Moira threatens to overtake my mind, but I shake my head to wipe it away. Her harsh glare should have burned any thoughts of her away at the root. But another face blares in my mind. The conventionally attractive selkie with a European accent. The one my fellow council member used to date. I heard only a handful of the words exchanged between him and Moira's brother, and that was all I needed to decide Hamish was a certified piece of shit.

I'd make a better mate than him.

Stop it! You are not her mate!

I'm convinced the intense connection I felt toward her was some effect of the love cage. An extra spell we didn't notice. One that only worked on me.

I'm not even sure monsters are allowed fated mates. The thought scrapes a ragged wound in my gut that I do my best to ignore. My father is hundreds of years old, and he's never found his gods-gifted partner as far as I know. It certainly wasn't my mother.

The damp wood creaks under the soles of my shoes as I climb the flight that leads to the front door. I don't bother knocking. She's expecting me.

Only the voice I hear when I walk farther into the house isn't the one I anticipated. Familiar but not belonging to my mother. Momentarily, I wonder if my pondering manifested the sound. But then I round the corner and find Moira MacNamara sipping a glass of wine at my mother's kitchen island.

Gods, why do you torment me?

The thrum of wanting radiates in my chest still. So, not a spell from the Gauntlet after all, since the longing is still here. But maybe an aftereffect of the blood vow?

Just admit you're attracted to her and move on. The problem is, this intense magnetic pull feels deeper than fleeting lust.

"Ah! My baby bird has returned to the nest. Come, let me kiss your beak." My mother strides toward me, arms wide, and I feel my cheeks heat at the childish greeting I hoped no one else in the world would ever hear. Especially the beautiful selkie currently smirking at me.

"Hello, Mama." Despite the embarrassment, I hug her as hard as she does me and lean down to let her place a smacking kiss on the end of my prominent nose.

I get my height from my father. And my eyes, and my skin, and my hair. My mother is a short, pale brunette with blue eyes that sharpen to sapphire blades every time she casually reminds me that I look nothing like her.

"Come in!" She hooks her fingers around my wrist, dragging me into the kitchen, and then pauses to stare at my hand.

"When did you cut yourself?" Her attention lands on the small scar on the pad of my thumb.

All my muscles strain to turn toward Moira, but I keep my focus on my mother. She gets odd about magic not controlled or administered by witches.

"I was wrestling with Sev. His claws came out." Not a complete lie.

Sev is a monster I grapple with on occasion to help him disperse some pent-up aggression. He's not always careful with the sharper parts of himself. Better my mother think he left a mark on me than know I'm making blood vows with selkies. More accurately, one selkie.

The witch smirks. "Monsters." The word isn't sentimental, and I try not to flinch at the dismissal. "I was just chatting with your fellow council member. Why didn't you tell me how charming she was?"

My mother turns to Moira, lowering her voice, as if imparting a secret, even though we can all hear. "He only ever complains about you."

"Mama, how's your garden?" I throw out the desperate question in hopes of changing the subject.

Normally, Violetta Radeva is happy to talk for hours about the wide range of poisonous plants she cultivates in her yard. But today is different.

"Oh, really?" Moira keeps her seductive brown eyes on me as she sips deeply from her glass. After swallowing, she licks a stray red drop off her lower lip, and I don't know whether to groan in need or run in fear. "And what exactly do I do that offends him?"

My mother finally releases me, strolling to her stovetop to stir a bubbling concoction.

I don't need a supernatural nose to figure out what it is.

Soup, like always. My mother can only manage to cook food if the item is boiling in some sort of broth. She likes to say that witches know how to brew things and no one should demand anything more from her. Even when the weather is so hot and oppressive that one might as well be swimming through the air, you can bet Violetta Radeva will have soup on the stove.

I never went hungry.

"Oh, you know"—she waves a dismissive hand before picking up her own glass of wine—"he throws around those words men always do when they are intimidated by a woman. Bossy, hardheaded, frigid—"

"Frigid?" Moira bites through the word with teeth as sharp as daggers and a lethal glare.

"That is *not* what I said. I never called you frigid." With my hands up, I step toward the back door, thinking I might need to escape if I want to avoid a rabid selkie attack. She has her purse, which means she's armed.

"You might be right." Violetta hums as she sips her pinot noir and then gives a distracted nod. "That must have been something Selena said. You often share the same sentiment. One might think you two gossip about your fellow council members after each one of your meetings." My mother offers a playful smile over her shoulder, endlessly amused by the trouble she's making.

But that's Violetta Radeva, lover of chaos. When the world burns, she puts marshmallows on a stick and makes herself a s'more.

I abandon my escape, unable to leave Moira alone here. Running my gaze over the selkie's face, I watch as she affixes a polite, remote smile. No indication that my mother's comments bothered her in the slightest. But with one of her hands under the counter, she could easily be palming that silver dagger of hers.

"What I find interesting is that just this past council meeting, I expressed a desire to purchase the services of a purifying witch, and neither of the council members you mentioned felt the need to inform me one lived in Folk Haven. Much less that they were friends or"—a spark flares in Moira's eyes as she looks at me—"related to one."

As hard as I try to remain stoic, my head drops in chagrin.

But I had good reason to keep silent, I remind myself.

My mother doesn't make a habit of shopping her services around. Despite her natural specialization in purification spells, she's never had much interest in them. And then there's her minuscule fuse. Violetta is the easiest person to switch on a temper, meaning people are more likely to leave this house cursed than in possession of what they asked for. And she doesn't have to be angry either. Curses amuse her to no end, and my mother loves to laugh.

Best to keep a buffer between her and most everyone else. I didn't want to endanger Moira. Especially now, while I'm dealing with this intense connection that flared to life during the Gauntlet. The longer I'm around her, the more I refuse to believe I imagined the rightness of us entwined together.

But as I heat under the low simmer of Moira's anger, I watch the flimsy chance of us setting aside past grievances burning away.

This is not going well.

"Oh now, don't hold it against them." Violetta abandons her soup to settle on the stool beside Moira, placing a hand on the selkie's bare arm as her voice smooths into a motherly tone. "Why don't you tell me what you need a purifying witch for?"

Moira's entire focus settles on the witch, and it's as if they were the only two in the room. The hairs on the back of my neck rise, and I step forward, wanting to force my body between them.

"There's a plot of land retaining evil magic. I want to remove all trace without physical damage to the area."

"Hmm. And this land means a good deal to you, doesn't it? Why is that?" My mother's voice has gone cotton soft.

A growl rumbles in the back of my throat, and her blue eyes flick to me in surprise before immediately returning to Moira.

"You're strong," the selkie says.

And with those two words, a pressure I didn't realize was forming suddenly breaks, and I suck in a deep breath.

Violetta leans back on her stool, removing her hand from Moira's wrist. "Strong?" Her voice is pure innocence. "Well, I would hope so, but I don't see why you thought to bring it up."

Moira sips her drink, watching the witch beside her. When she speaks again, the words are playful. "I must be special to earn a magical effort from you without payment."

My mother scoffs, even as the edge of her lip curls. "Who says I'm not getting paid?"

This is like watching a duel. Normally, I would always put money on my mother to win. Today though, I think she's met her match.

Moira places her glass on the countertop. "And what price would you ask for the cleansing spell I need? For three acres of tainted land?"

The witch swirls the red liquid in her glass, watching the miniscule waves she creates. I can smell the dry berries and alcohol from across the room but no bitter scent of one of her garden plants added to the mixture.

An image pops into my mind—of Moira clutching her stomach in pain as my mother watches with mocking triumph. No matter that the woman raised me, if she slipped poison in my selkie's drink, I'd have my hand around her throat, demanding the cure. Knowing I could reach that height of violence has my mind spinning faster than the wine.

"A finger."

Moira and I both stare at my mother's hard face. Then, we share a look between ourselves.

That's when the shout of laughter comes. Violetta leans

over in her chair, giggling hard. "Oh, you two! So gullible. No, no. That was a joke. I'm not a monster."

The barb comes small and stinging, like a splinter appearing in a sanded piece of wood. I feel the pressure of Moira's eyes on me and meet them, registering her shock.

Meanwhile, my mother continues to chuckle. "I'll leave the dismemberment to the experts. Like my ex." Another bark of laughter.

This time, I don't let the comment affect me. I've had decades of her digging at my father that the sentiments rarely register anymore.

The selkie clears her throat. "And the price you want is?"

My mother sobers, stare fixating on Moira, the swift change disconcerting even though I've seen her make the shift hundreds of times before.

"I want you to give those Shelly girls what they want. The house. Let them build their library." Her lips form into a matronly smile. "Doesn't that sound lovely?"

Moira is already shaking her head. "My stance on the Shelly issue is not available for purchase. To be clear, no form of payment will relate in any way to my seat on The Council. This is entirely a personal pursuit."

Maybe her rigid stance can be attributed to my presence, but I get the sense Moira would have said the same even if I wasn't here. Unfortunately, that display of integrity only has me more enamored with the woman.

Violetta pouts for a count of five and then sighs away her disappointment with a dramatic gust. "How ... noble of you." The second word seems to choke her, and I find myself fighting a smile. My mother is a self-centered woman, but there are times I find her reactions amusing.

"Maybe this will suffice." Moira brings her hand out, where I can see she's holding a pen and a notebook. She scribbles a quick note, then rips out the paper, and slides it across the counter to my mother.

The witch picks it up with a smirk that quickly drops away as her brows climb high. "Truly?"

Now, my curiosity is piqued. I lean forward, trying to get a glimpse of what I'm certain is some astronomical number figure. But Violetta crumples the sheet in her hand, and when she spreads her fingers again, all that's left are ashes.

Thoroughly out of the loop, I rest back against the fridge, my arms crossed.

"If you can cleanse the land, then yes. Truly."

I watch my mother's face go thoughtful. Then conniving.

"Agreed. However, I'll need thirteen gallons of seawater."

Moira nods. "I can collect that for you." A trip to the coast and back is a full day's drive. Long but doable.

Violetta smiles that honeyed, harmless expression that hints at manipulation. "If only it were that easy. You see, the spell calls for the water to be gathered by my hands. Unfortunately, I can't fathom leaving my home for such a long stretch."

A frown pulls down the corners of Moira's mouth as she works through the problem.

But my mother has a convenient solution, of course. "Hands that hold my blood should suffice. Why not ask my sweet boy, Levi, to accompany you?"

The tension in the room spikes yet again as every muscle in Moira's body tightens. As she slowly turns to me, I wonder if she might shatter; she's strung herself so tight.

"Will you?" she presses the words through clenched teeth.

And maybe it's my mother's blood that elicits my response. "Will I what?"

If I look down to see a silver dagger protruding from my chest the next second, I might not even blame her. The smart-ass comment was unnecessary, especially because the moment my mother presented the solution, I knew I'd say yes.

A trip, the two of us together—alone—could help forge a bond my beast has been demanding ever since we got a taste of her in that cage. I need more time with Moira to figure these feelings out.

"Will you come with me to the ocean?" Moira's question rides an exhale as she paints an icy calm over her face.

"All right." I do my best to maintain a stoic countenance.

Moira offers a stiff nod as she stands from her stool, smartly making her escape before any permanent damage is done.

"Thank you for the wine." She turns her brown eyes to me. "I'll be in touch."

As she passes by me, I lower my voice even though I know my mother will still hear. "And you'll owe me one."

Moira whips her head toward me, gaze narrowed. "Owe you what?"

I shrug. "Haven't decided yet."

My mother cackles as the selkie storms out of the bungalow.

13

MOIRA

I SOLD Levi this plot of land.

Over a year ago, I'd stepped through those doors to watch him climb out of a luxury car, looking like the embodiment of good sex. In that brief instance, I truly hated Hamish. Up until that day, I'd been growing resentful of the way my boyfriend at the time was treating me, but when I saw Levi Abadi, I envisioned Hamish as a barrier between me and the monster I wanted to lick from head to toe.

Then, I experienced a small brush of shame but not enough to keep me from flirting with Levi for the rest of the day. I didn't think of it as flirting at the time. To me, it'd just felt like talking with a thrum of delicious tension.

Later, when I was in my shower, using my waterproof vibrator and imagining the monster stroking my clit and pounding into me from behind, I admitted the truth to myself.

The true shame came later. When I found out what Levi was short for.

Erotic fantasies about a leviathan are strictly prohibited.

Then, a traitorous voice whispers in the back of my head, *But Levi wasn't the one to steal the pelt. He would never. He's only helped the mythics in this town.*

"Well, he's not helping me by trying to set my land on fire," I snarl at myself.

Selfish. The word twists through my brain. But is it because I'm worried putting off a cleansing burn is selfish? Or is it a command to *be* selfish and enjoy time with the man my body has never stopped wanting?

Guilt scratches along my nerves. Only halfway through my morning coffee, I allow my crankiness to drive my actions. With a quick punch, I blare my car horn, letting the monster know he needs to get his ass in gear.

"Bad Moira," I mutter to myself before swallowing a large gulp of my latte.

I need Levi's cooperation on this little adventure, which means the best move is to remain cordial for the day. I also need Violetta's help, which is why I held myself back from asking her about my great-grandaunt's pelt. Even though the woman was with the leviathan decades after the theft and she clearly dislikes the monster now, I doubt she would have warmed to me if I'd brought up another woman Levi's father craved so much that he stole part of her soul.

I'm sorry, Blair. I swear I haven't forgotten you.

Levi steps onto his front porch, shading his eyes before waving. My hand rises on its own, returning the gesture before I decide if I want to or not.

The problem is, my brain malfunctions whenever I'm near him.

A single thought plays on repeat. *I know how his body feels.*

If Levi weren't in view, I'd bang my head on the steering wheel a few times to try eradicating the reminder.

As he strolls toward my car in a pair of navy-blue shorts and a white T-shirt that sets off the golden undertones of his skin, my mind bombards me with the memories of how I wrapped myself—legs, arms, lips—around him.

Curse The Finned One's games, Levi felt good.

Hot yet soothing in a strange way I've never associated with kissing a man before.

"It was for the race," I remind myself, hoping saying the words out loud are enough to push the intrusive thoughts away. Returning my coffee to the cupholder, I grip the steering wheel tight as Levi slides into the passenger seat.

"Morning," he murmurs in a deep rumble that affects my nipples in a way a voice shouldn't.

"That's yours," I say by way of greeting, pointing to the other coffee cup between our seats.

As I shift into reverse, I notice Levi doesn't accept my best attempt at an olive branch, so I throw him a glance before backing out of his driveway. The monster stares at me, confusion in his dark eyes.

"I didn't poison it," I snap.

"Of course not." He drops his gaze and picks up the cup, taking a quick sip. Then a deeper one. His focus flicks back to my face. "This is a flavored coffee with oat milk and cocoa powder."

"Bingo." I brace my hand on his headrest as I turn in my seat to stare out the back window. My car is new enough to have one of those rearview cameras, but after almost flattening Seamus in our parents' driveway, I don't trust the thing anymore.

"This is my order," Levi says.

"I'm aware." Reaching the road, I shift into drive, starting this hours-long journey.

"How do you know my order?"

Gods, this monster and his questions. I stifle an eye roll. "I asked Neri to make what you normally get." I name the barista currently dating my brother, the one I managed not to back into with my Subaru.

"Thank you, Moira." He says my name in a strange tone that has a shiver threatening to overtake my body.

I shy away from the unwanted sensation.

"Guess this makes us even, right?"

Levi barks a laugh at my poor attempt at getting out of an open-ended favor. "Not quite."

When we reach a Stop sign, I bring up the navigation on my phone. The GPS swirls around on the map, confused as it tries to locate my car.

"Does that ever work here for you?" the monster asks between sips of his drink.

I sigh. Technology functions fine for the most part in Folk Haven. Everything, except for navigation. Neither The Council nor Mayor Nightson has contracted a witch to cast a spell with this result, so either one is doing it on their own or there's some other magical force at play.

"Not until we get through town, but I hoped I could get the destination ready, and it would sync up."

"I can type it in when we get clear." Levi holds out his long-fingered hand.

Giving him massive side-eye, I reluctantly hand over my phone. "Don't snoop."

He crosses his heart. "Promise."

Oddly, the gesture sets me at ease. "There's an audiobook app. You see it?" I direct him as I follow the only road that traverses Lake Galen, passing out of the monster territory into the Of the Claw territory. "I downloaded a book for the drive."

A mystery has mass appeal, right?

Neri recommended the latest romance she'd read, but no way was I going to sit through a detailed sex scene with Levi at my side.

"Got it." He swipes his finger across the glass screen, and a moment later, a pleasant feminine voice drifts from my speakers.

Twenty minutes pass before we finally make it to Main Street, passing straight through town. We could've shaved off time if Levi had picked me up instead of the other way around. I live less than a ten-minute drive from town, but I couldn't give up the element of control that being behind the wheel provides for me. Plus, I get carsick.

And even if my sensitive stomach wasn't an issue, it seems wrong to make him drive simply because he lives farther. That's not his fault.

Once again, Morgana's words play through my thoughts, and I must admit that whether the monsters like the land they are allotted, it's not fair that their portion is the farthest from civilization. Clearly, our ancestors were trying to back them into a forgotten corner. Maybe hoping they would leave altogether.

"*He* did it," Levi announces as we're about to cross into South Carolina.

I flick him a mocking glance. "Really? Not even halfway into the book and you think you know who the murderer is?"

The small-town sleuth just discovered the body a chapter ago and has barely started sorting through suspects herself.

"Isn't it obvious?" Levi lounges in his seat as he sips his coffee, every inch of him confident. And strong. And handsome. And—

Stop it!

He keeps talking, and I focus on his words rather than his body. "That ex-boyfriend is a creep. He got jealous, snuck into the house in the middle of the night, and murdered the groom. Boom, mystery solved."

"Boom, mystery solved?" I scoff. "Is that your tagline? You plan to move out to Hollywood and star in the next big cop drama?"

Levi shoots me a grin. "That would be an interesting premise. The straitlaced selkie cop and her wild-card monster sidekick. You know, I think I like the sound of that."

I snort. "Don't get your hopes up. You only think the ex did it because the author *wants* you to think that. They never write the most obvious suspect as the killer. Work on your sleuthing, Sherlock."

"You'll see," he grumbles.

Two chapters later, the ex-boyfriend's body is found, stuffed in the freezer with the bouquets.

"Ha!" I crow, waggling my finger Levi's way. "Told you." He grimaces, and I poke him a few times in the shoulder because I can't seem to help myself. "What was that again? Who did you think the murderer was? Please, Council Member Abadi, share your glorious cozy-mystery wisdom with me."

"Fine," he huffs. "But it's definitely the best man."

"The best man!" I squeak with the absurdity of his statement and can't hold back my derisive laughter as he attempts to prove his theory true.

Before I know it, we're halfway across South Carolina and deep into a debate about which clues to believe and which are red herrings, and if the author intended to misdirect us, and if mystery writers enjoy torturing their readers. Never would I have thought I could have such an easy conversation with the monster next to me.

As Levi argues his point, he waves his hands in the limited space he has. When we stop for gas and a bathroom break, the debate continues, even outside the car, and Levi gestures with his full arm length, limbs practically flapping like siren wings. The imagery has his mother's nickname coming to mind again.

Baby bird.

The man does have a very beak-ish nose, but his face is strong enough that the feature adds to his handsomeness.

Not that I want to think about his attractiveness.

"Sure you don't want me to drive?" he offers during a brief break in our lighthearted bickering when I start the engine.

"I get carsick if I'm not behind the wheel." My teeth snap shut at the end of the sentence, as I'm surprised the statement made its way out of my mouth. I don't like admitting weakness in front of anyone. Much less this mythic.

"What about boats? Are you always the DD?"

When I glance to the side, I see his sparkling grin, and I roll my eyes in response.

"Yes, in fact. That's the only reason Owen invites me anywhere. He always wants me to drive the pontoon back and forth from Marlin's Marina every Margarita Monday."

Levi chuckles, the sound rising from deep in his chest and warming the entirety of the car. The heat amplifies his scent, though I struggle to place it. Salt spray maybe? Cool sand? Burning ozone after a lightning strike? His cologne is like someone bottled an ocean thunderstorm.

Brake lights flare in front of me, all the cars ahead slowing dramatically. Used to keeping a safe following distance, I decrease my speed in plenty of time, even as I try to crane my head to see over the traffic.

"You think this is construction or an accident?" Levi murmurs the question as he plucks my phone off the car dashboard. He pauses the book and zooms in on our route. From the corner of my eye, I see a long red line on the screen. "Looks like we're backed up for a mile or so at least."

"Damn it," I groan, dropping my head to the steering wheel for a few annoyed bangs.

The drive to the coast is six hours, which means twelve total if we want to be there and back in a day. This sudden stop is going to add to that.

"It's going to be fine," Levi says, returning my phone to its spot. "We'll get through this in no time."

He's as right about that as the ex-boyfriend being the murderer. Half an hour later, we've gone maybe half a mile.

"Sorry, but I have to turn off the AC." I reach for the central controls. "I don't want the engine to overheat."

Levi nods, and we roll down the windows as the refreshing air from the vents shuts off. The smell of exhaust and hot asphalt smothers his pleasant thunderstorm scent, and I reach for my water bottle as I feel myself begin to roast.

I'm regretting the short-sleeved romper I pulled on this morning. I wish I had on a tank top.

"You can take your shirt off." The words escape my mouth before I realize the oddity of them. I'm used to being around my brothers, and while Seamus tends to be the button-up type, Owen and Calder lean toward clothing optional. I don't think they put a shirt on from May to September unless they're working—and sometimes not even then.

"Do you want me to take my shirt off?" The question rumbles out of Levi's throat, increasing my body heat another few uncomfortable degrees.

"I just meant, if you're hot. Temperature-wise." *Why did I tack on that last part?* "I mean, I'd like to take my shirt off." *Hello, hole. Let me dig myself deeper into you, please.*

Levi lets out a strangled chuckle before clearing his throat. "Do whatever you're comfortable with. And I think I will. Take my shirt off."

"Good." Now, I want to bang my head on the steering wheel for an entirely different reason.

"I think so." I can hear the smirk in his voice, and listening for it is the only means I have because I refuse to look over as my fellow council member strips off that thin cotton barrier.

Another minute of oppressive heat passes, and we roll forward a grand total of two feet. Sweat gathers in my armpits and beneath my thighs. If this goes on much longer, I'm going to look like I peed myself.

"You've seen me in a bathing suit," I announce, as if Levi needs reminding.

"Correct."

Only the bathing suit I wore during the Gauntlet covered a lot more than the one I have on under my clothes. I threw on the bikini at the last minute, in hopes I'd have a moment to swim while gathering the spell water. Glancing over, I find him watching me with a curiously curved-up brow. I focus on that expression, so I don't drop my eyes to the light dusting of hair on his sculpted chest.

"I'm taking off my romper. And it's not weird that I'm going to be driving in a bikini. Got it?"

He nods, lips pressed tight together. Thank the gods he doesn't give me a hard time or else I wouldn't be able to throw the sedan in park, unbuckle my seat belt, and shimmy out of the all-in-one clothing item. The relief isn't overwhelming, but my discomfort moves down a notch, and I reassure myself that I'll be able to put the outfit on later without sweat stains.

"Better?" Levi asks once I strap back in.

"Marginally." I accelerate into the yard of open space that's appeared before my bumper. "Wish there were a breeze."

Levi makes a noise of agreement in the back of his throat and then starts rifling through a backpack he brought with him. He comes out with a stiff manila folder.

Then, the magnificent monster proceeds to fan me with it.

"Oh my gods," I groan as the minuscule air movement teases over the damp curls sticking to the back of my neck. "Thank you."

"You're welcome. And I must be a saint for doing this for you after you so cruelly shot down all my murder theories."

I can't help it; I grin over at the monster, reveling in the pleasant buzz in my chest as I watch a shirtless Levi fan me while bantering at the same time. That's when I realize, despite the uncomfortable conditions, I'm enjoying myself. With my rival. I never imagined this as a possibility.

"You can't expect me to go easy on you. How will you ever learn?"

His smirk is playful sin. So distracting that I almost miss the cars in front of us accelerating at a steady pace.

"Maybe I should be the teacher," Levi offers. "If you'd listened to me about the cleansing, we could be on a dock right now, sipping cool drinks and taking a refreshing dive."

Despite the imagery he tries to sketch with his words, every muscle in my body tenses, and the heat returns with a vengeance. Almost as if I were standing in the middle of plot 236 as dragon fire engulfed it.

I can't let that happen.

As I refocus on the road, my teasing tone is gone when I respond, "I realize this trip and my land are inconvenient for you, but I have no control over the traffic." Each syllable snaps out of me, and in the corner of my eye, I catch Levi flinching.

"Moira—"

"Let's listen to the book." I slide my finger across the phone screen and then turn up the volume, cutting off further conversation.

The monster takes the hint, settling back in his seat. Still, he continues to fan me.

One of the biggest tensions in this small war we have waging is that I know, in many ways, Levi is right. The land, steeped in evil magic, is dangerous. Fire would purify everything completely and quickly. My insistence on finding another way is a risk.

But I can't help knowing, deep in my gut, that the land needs to be preserved. The urge is hard to explain to anyone who hasn't felt it, and the illogical way I cling to the purity of plot 236 constantly has me fighting my own self-doubt.

Which is strange for me. In most every other area of my life, I am a confident, badass bitch.

With this land, every time someone challenges me on it, I feel like I'm faking that confidence. That I'm clutching on to my control with fingernails because I can't give a list of the reasons I am right.

As we roll past a collection of emergency vehicles and crumbled cars, I sigh in relief. Both because we can pick up speed, but also because the horrendous accident didn't involve us.

Gods, protect their souls. I silently send the prayer to the entities in a far-off dimension. I have no idea if they heard or if they did, whether they involve themselves in the lives of humans. But I doubt it hurts to ask.

As we return to highway speed, I roll up the windows and turn on the AC. If only I could get dressed again. I'll have to ride in my bathing suit until our next rest stop. That and the heavy silence make the hours left to go loom with discomfort.

"The mother of the bride did it," Levi says.

My lips twitch, but I can't find it in me to respond.

14

———

LEVI

WARM SALT WATER and sand swirl around my feet as I dip the final gallon jug under the surface. As the container fills, I mutter a string of words and sounds that mean nothing to me. Still, my mother made sure I memorized them exactly.

This isn't the first time I've helped her with a spell. Over the years, she's asked me to chop herbs or arrange a set of crystals in a certain pattern. But all those tasks were treated as cavalierly as requesting I put away dishes or assist with a dinner. At no point did I receive an actual lesson in witchcraft.

Because like the rest of the mythical world, my mother assigned me a label at birth.

Monster.

And as much as she loves me, monsters can't be witches. We can only be strange amalgamations of our differing parents and therefore a subtle or overt threat to the magical community. A community that doesn't want to provide any more power to us than we already have.

The squawk of seagulls sounds overhead, a chorus backed

106

by the rhythmic crashing of waves on the shore. I glance up at the birds as I screw the cap on the final bottle. They pay little attention to me, more interested in a family farther down the beach with young children that can't seem to hold on to their food.

A grumble sounds in my own stomach as I step out of the water and set my load next to the twelve other jugs. Moira and I will have to make a few trips over the heated sand to carry these all to her car.

As I search for my selkie, I spy her out in the water, past the breakers, head and shoulders bobbing in the place between ocean and sky. Even this far away, she's gorgeous, her curls loose and damp, floating in the water like the seaweed around her. She keeps her eyes closed, face up to the sky, a relaxed smile on her lips.

I've never seen her so peaceful before. I'm torn between letting her continue in this meditative state and getting closer to soak in as much of her joy as I can.

Selfishly, I choose the latter.

The scent of salt fills my nose as I dive under a wave, and the taste lingers on my lips as I surface. Every inch of my body sighs with contentment, surrounded as I am by the sea. I might be a strange combination of mythics, but both my parents are tied to the ocean. Sea monster and sea witch. Salt water is in my blood.

As I draw beside Moira, I notice the shimmer of moisture on her cheeks. At first, I'm sure it's the ocean spray, but then a fat tear spills from the corner of her eye, and my gut drops with its descent.

"Moira?" I keep my voice soft so as not to startle her. "Are you all right?"

She blinks, and I can hardly see the normal soft brown of her eyes, her pupils so dilated.

"I miss the ocean," she admits in a ragged whisper. Then,

possibly realizing how raw her confession was, she shakes her head and loses some of the dazed fog in her gaze. "I haven't been here in a while. And I've never—" Her voice catches, and she turns to stare out at the glorious blue expanse. "I've never swum in the salt water in my other skin. It's too dangerous."

My heart aches for her, even as I understand her fear. A selkie's connection to their mythical half exists outside themselves. A pelt that can be removed and kept apart from them. That leaves their kind more vulnerable than creatures like me. I can never be separated from my other form, though there are times I wish I could be.

No wonder she holds so much anger on her great-grandaunt's behalf.

I still don't believe my father stole the skin, but if he knew Moira's ancestor, then he might know what happened. Whenever he gets in touch with me, I plan to keep the promise I made and question him about it.

"The lake is a fine substitute," Moira says when I don't respond. A hollowness echoes in her voice. Her attention flicks to the shore, where I've piled the collected seawater. "Are you ready to go?"

I find myself infused with the sudden urge to gather her in my arms, hold her close, and promise to drive her to the sea every day. Or better yet, swear to collect this ocean and bring it back to Folk Haven with us.

Neither of those is an option, so I offer the best alternative.

"There's a bed-and-breakfast that also acts as a spa not too far from here." I gesture south. "I hoped we would have time to swing by it. You know, so I could look around. Get inspiration for my business." Haven's Relaxation is already in the final stages before opening, but I've always figured the spa would grow and improve over time with new ideas. "Since the drive out here took longer than we'd expected, how would you feel about booking a couple of rooms and staying the night? That way, you can swim a bit longer, I can do my research, and there's no risk of you passing out behind the wheel on the drive back."

Moira blinks at me once. Twice. Then, a radiant smile crashes across her face and straight into my chest, pulverizing my heart and reforming the organ into something new. Something that beats only for her.

"Deal." And before the word is done leaving her mouth, the selkie splashes me with a playful flick of her hand and then dives into an oncoming wave.

A growl rumbles out of my chest, the noise a blend of happy, aching need. She will ruin me, but I will enjoy every moment of my descent into destruction.

I give chase.

15

———

MOIRA

"I'm sorry, the honeymoon suite is all we have available." The woman at the front desk leans forward and drops her voice. "Apparently, the bride ran off with the maid of honor. It's all a big scandal." She straightens, a delighted smile on her face, as if gossip gives the woman life. "Since they made the cancelation last minute, there was only a partial refund, which means I can give you both a discount. How's that sound?"

Sounds like she's asking me to pay to spend time in the love cage all over again. Only this iteration includes a bed.

"What's the sleeping arrangement in there?" Levi asks, staying practical, as we both know it is now officially too late to drive back to Folk Haven. Not unless I want to be on the road at two a.m.

"You would have the entire upper floor. King-size bed, full bathroom, plus a Jacuzzi tub. And a beautiful view of the ocean from your balcony."

Simply the mention of that lovely, unending expanse of salt

water stirs up the longing in my heart. I had no idea how much immersing myself in the sea would affect me.

"Any couches?" Levi asks.

The woman nods enthusiastically. "A cozy love seat facing toward that unbeatable view I mentioned."

Doesn't sound big enough for my five-foot-ten height, much less Levi's over six-foot body. My travel companion glances down at me, a question in his dark eyes.

A king bed is plenty large enough for two and some distance between. I'll build a pillow wall between us.

"Okay. We'll take it." Reaching into my purse, I shield the glint of my dagger as I search for my wallet.

Levi beats me to it, sliding his credit card across the counter.

As I open my mouth to protest, he leans in, lips close to my ear, breath cool against the damp hair still clinging to my neck. "This was my side excursion. It's on me. How about you get dinner?"

"Sounds like someone plans to order Kobe beef tonight." I let my half-lidded gaze match the snark of my words.

Levi straightens, a wide grin showing off his sharp canines. I pull my gaze away in time to mask how his happiness affects me.

Too much.

"And you said you were interested in a tour of our spa? I'm happy to accommodate." The woman flutters her lashes at Levi, as if she didn't just book him the honeymoon suite with another person.

Most likely, she picked up on my reluctance and decided to shoot her shot with the devilishly handsome monster. I might give her kudos for the initiative if there wasn't a burning twist in my gut at the thought of my monster sneaking off with this tan-skinned beauty.

Wait, did I think of him as my monster? Bad Moira. Do not get possessive of your rival.

Then, Levi offers the woman a grateful smile, and my palm is suddenly itchy for my dagger.

"That would be fantastic." His attention returns to me. "Do you want to come along or head to the room?"

"Spa," I announce, not willing to examine my sudden urge to stay by his side. My fingers twitch, as if they want to reach out and slip between his.

Maybe I spent too much time in the sun today, and it's short-circuiting the connection between my neurons. Wires are crossed. I can't be responsible for my behavior.

Levi raises a brow but doesn't say anything, and the three of us head out. The spa is in a different building than the overnight rooms, and the briny, humid wind caresses my skin as we traverse the brick walkway to get to the neighboring building.

While the B & B employee shows us the different serene spaces, I find my attention drifting away from her words and to the man she's aiming them at. By now, I must admit, Levi Abadi is a surprisingly good travel companion. Even with the traffic, the drive felt about half the time, and I've already downloaded the next book in the cozy mystery series for us to listen to on the way back. My mouth twitches with a smile as I imagine him calling out wrong murder suspect after wrong murder suspect.

His gullibility was almost ... cute.

Wait, what?

I give a firm head shake to clear the thought.

"You don't like lavender?" The pointed question takes me a moment to process, and I glance at the desk attendant, who's holding up essential oils.

What were they talking about?

"Uh, no." My brain flops around like a fish on a dock for an answer that isn't, *I prefer the smell of thunderstorms on a monster's skin.* "Eucalyptus is nice."

The woman—Sandy, as I see on her name tag now—says, "Ah, yes. That's an invigorating one. Excites the senses."

Glancing over at Levi, I find him staring at me, eyes searching.

"What?" I prod, not a fan of being caught unaware. "Something wrong with eucalyptus?"

"No," he murmurs.

And without revealing the thoughts playing behind those dark eyes, he goes back to listening to Sandy's tour. By the time she's done, my stomach is demanding attention, not satisfied with the sandwich I packed for the car trip and ate more than five hours ago.

"Food?" Levi asks, a twitch at the corner of his mouth when my stomach growls a response.

"Gods, yes."

We don't bother with the car as Sandy points down the road, claiming there are multiple restaurants within walking distance. We find one, open and airy, smelling of salt, the way a good seafood restaurant should. Levi pulls a stool out for me at the bar, and I tamp down on the strange swishing reaction that elicits in my stomach.

"Will you make fun of me if I get a strawberry daiquiri?" the monster asks, watching the bartender whip up a red slushy drink in a blender.

"Only because you seem to be under the incorrect notion that a daiquiri is tastier than a margarita." I smirk over the top of my menu and earn a grin in return.

"What looks good?" Levi reaches for a menu after placing an order for both our cocktails.

"Seafood tower." Oysters. Clams. Crab. Lobster. Scallops. Shrimp. What more could a selkie want?

"Mmm. Want to share?" He leans close, bringing the scent of lightning with him. "Menu says it serves six. So, that's, like, two of our kind. Right?" Tapping my menu with a long finger, Levi misses the way my attention adheres to his face.

This is odd. This banter and casual hanging out is not something I ever expected to take part in with a leviathan. But here I am. And the strangest part is how I relax more every moment I'm around him.

My memory skips backward, scanning over the last few months of my relationship with Hamish. There came a point when I worried about starting a conversation, for fear he'd insult the topic I chose or chide me for discussing work. I would just sit quietly and wait until he said something.

Shame flushes my cheeks—a common emotion when I recall the ghost of myself I turned into with Hamish. Flicking my eyes to Levi's face and then away, I realize that I have no urge to shrink around the monster. The fact that we argue invigorates me rather than deflates me.

It almost feels like ... foreplay.

Nope. Wrong. This is just a business dinner, and you need to pretend the love cage never happened.

"Fine." I snap my menu closed. "But if you try to take more than your fair share of scallops, remember, I've got my dagger on me, and I've stabbed a man for less."

Meeting his eyes in that moment, I expect to see laughter. Instead, there's something like heat.

When my drink arrives, I take a long, cold sip, needing to cool myself down fast.

Too bad I forgot about the alcohol content. Two hours later and three margaritas deep, I'm warm with an inner glow, grinning goofily across an empty platter at an equally buzzed monster. Levi loudly slurps the dregs of his drink—a piña colada this time—and then lets out an impressive burp.

His gaze shoots to me, and I get to watch a delicious red wave wash over his face. "You didn't hear that, did you?"

His question holds the tiniest hint of a slur, and suddenly, I'm giggling so hard that I slip to the side and out of my stool.

Before I face-plant on the floor, a strong arm hooks around my waist, and I'm pulled flush against a hard body.

"Council Member MacNamara, are you drunk?" Levi asks with his best attempt at a serious tone as he stares into my eyes.

And I only laugh harder.

Somehow, I manage to pay the bill, and the two of us meander back to the B & B, arm in arm, under the bright glow of moonlight cast by the almost-full orb in the sky. We butcher a few classic German drinking songs that tipsy gnomes regularly spout off in bars in Folk Haven.

As we climb the steep staircases to our honeymoon suite, both of us make too much noise shushing each other as we repeatedly trip on steps that I'm sure are not a regulated height. Then, Levi slips a key into the door, and I'm hit with the first wash of partial soberness since finishing my drinks.

We're alone in this room together. All night.

Part of me bubbles in excitement at the thought. But another more logical part crawls out from under the hazy blanket of booze long enough to remind me that I don't know what I'm feeling and I definitely don't know what Levi's feeling.

We step inside a cozy space. The ceiling slopes upward in the middle, and there's plenty of headroom for both of us tall people.

"Do you think we'll find the fiancé's dead body in the bathtub?" Levi asks as he meanders around.

"You just want to try out your horrendous detective skills in real life, don't you?" I snort an unattractive chuckle while taking in the sliding glass doors—outside of which, it's too dark to see the ocean—single gargantuan bed, and the massive Jacuzzi tub Sandy did not specify was *in* the bedroom. Luckily, the bathroom has a door, so I don't have to pee in front of my fellow council member.

I think hard on that title, trying to ingrain the importance of it on my slippery, drunk brain.

We work together. Work.

Gods, Levi's body could really work mine out.

Bad drunk brain!

"They gave us robes." Levi comes out of the bathroom, holding up some fluffy white terry cloth. "Guess we don't have to sleep in our bathing suits."

Sleep. Together.

Launching forward, I snatch my robe and escape into the bathroom, mumbling about a shower. The evasive maneuver was necessary because I was equally as close to shoving Levi Abadi onto the bed and mounting him.

What in all the gods' names has taken hold of me? Did I piss off a lust witch?

I don't think we have any of those in town, but who knows?

Trying to remember what being a responsible adult entails, I strip off my clothes, rinse them in the sink to get out the day's salt, sand, and sweat before hanging them up to dry. The shower is a glass stall.

Big enough for two.

The traitorous thought taunts me as I step under the spray. As I try to only think of scrubbing the salt from my skin and hair, my focus strays toward the door I didn't lock.

Waiting to see if the knob turns.

16

MOIRA

Levi doesn't come into the bathroom. After drying myself off and shrugging into my thick robe, I self-diagnose as close to fully sober. A slight unbalance and a hazy edge to my thoughts, but nothing to show I'm terribly inebriated. I expect I'll find Levi already passed out in the bed, sent to sleep from too much rum. He should've binged on tequila, like me. Then, maybe his nerves would have this needy thrum too.

I hang up my towel next to my clothes and leave the bathroom.

"Thank gods, I need to piss!" Levi grabs me by the shoulders, gently moves me out of the doorway, and then slams the thing shut.

A second later, I hear a heavy stream and have to cover my mouth to muffle the laughter.

For some reason, his frantic dive into the bathroom brings back a tinge of my warm glow. The move was so honest. An exchange a couple would have.

Maybe you aren't as sober as you thought. Stop making more of this trip than it is.

Searching for something else to focus on, I wander over to a little desk, spying a piece of paper with notes scrawled across the page. The words detail everything Sandy showed us today, albeit in an unsteady, drunken hand. I'm impressed his memory is functioning this well after our happy hour. I'm trying to decipher one of the messier sentences when Levi exits the bathroom, drying his hands on a towel and wearing his robe and a relieved expression.

"That was a close one."

"Sorry. Didn't realize I was endangering your bladder."

He shrugs. "I was considering the balcony. Glad it didn't come to that."

I snort and then tap the paper. "Very studious for a drunk man."

"Excuse me." He affects an affronted voice. "I am tipsy at most. But everyone knows *selkies* are lightweights."

I roll my eyes as a goofy grin steals over my lips. "Please. Look at this." I hold up the paper. "Did a toddler write this? Did you use a crayon?" I toss it back on the desk. "And why are you scribbling all these notes anyway?"

Levi spreads his arms wide, and I struggle not to trace the lean muscles shifting under his golden skin. "Look at this place. They've been around fifty years. Still a massive success. This is what I want Haven's Relaxation to be."

"This?" Disbelief colors my voice. "You can't make a place like this."

Levi's face, which was alight with optimism a second ago, drops into devastation so fast that my heart breaks with the fall.

"Why?" His voice is a pained whisper. "Because a monster could never make something so peaceful?"

Shock at his vulnerability crashes into me.

"Oh gods, Levi. No. Is that what you think I said?" Suddenly, I'm in front of him, my palms pressed against his chest, as if he needs my touch to know I tell the truth. "I meant, this place has a homey feel to it. Like the cover of that cozy mystery we listened to. They're all overstuffed furniture and woven rugs and plants hanging in macrame! All of that is cute and great. For this. But you need to make a place like *you*. Sleek, modern." My voice takes on a touch of dreaminess. "Minimalist with a touch of warmth. Glass. Metal. Some plants but not many. Wood. A dark wood. Almost black." I blink myself back to the moment to find him staring down at me with wide eyes.

"Have you been by the spa?" Levi's tone is hushed.

"No. You haven't opened it yet. And I'm not *that* much of a pushy bitch." I grin up at him, and the monster's hard face softens with a half-smile.

"You should come by. It's eerie how accurately you described it."

I preen under the success of my guess. "That's my point. When starting a business, you should be passionate not only about the product you're selling, but also how you present it to your customers." The lessons from my long-ago-earned marketing degree come back full force now that I have an audience. "That way, you don't get tired of the work. Obviously, you gravitated to a simple, elegant style because that's what you like and how you present yourself to the world."

"Funny." The twist to his mouth shows the next thing he is about to say is anything but. "I doubt anyone other than you would use those words to describe me."

That makes no sense. I rifle through all the memories I've saved of Levi, not dwelling on the massive number I've tucked away. Other than this trip and the time in the Gauntlet, he's always professionally dressed in clean, unwrinkled clothes of neutral colors, hair styled but not too much, and driving an expensive, understated car that purrs gently when he starts the engine.

"If that's not how people see you, then they need to visit Dr. Forrester." I name Folk Haven's optometrist. "Because I'm right. Like always. I don't know why that's so hard to believe."

Crossing my arms over my chest to stop from fondling his, I glare up at Levi, not liking his self-deprecating tone. I can insult him. But he can't.

"Come on, Moira." He reaches out, plucking one of my damp curls off my shoulder and twining the strand around his long finger. "Who is going to call a monster elegant?"

The idea buzzes in the air between us, so annoying that I wave my hand to dispel it. "And what do you think selkies look like when we change? Let me tell you, we're not sexy, like merpeople. My other form isn't in any line to win any beauty pageants. Think seal. But massive!" I hunch my shoulders and wave my arms like I'm swimming, doing a poor job of explaining my other form. "We're a bunch of oddballs. But I love that half of myself. Just because you're a mash-up doesn't mean there's anything wrong with that." Stepping forward into his space so the man can't look anywhere but at me, I hold his dark gaze. "What do you feel when you change? What do you look like?"

I blame the tequila for my invasive questions, but I'm suddenly rabid to know. A witch and a leviathan got it on and produced him. Our world calls Levi a monster. *I* call him a monster. But what does that mean?

"Beastly," he mutters, releasing his hold on my hair and dropping his lids to escape my bitchy pushiness.

Pressing my wrist against my mouth, I blow a very mature raspberry. The noise causes him to jerk his head back, jaw dropping in shock. Yeah, not a move I normally make at council meetings. But this is Moira mixed with margaritas, so the guy is getting a shiny, new version of me. More fun, even less willing to put up with bullshit.

"Vague." I poke his chest. "How big do you get?"

I think I remember hearing that the first leviathan—the monster so famous it earned a legendary name—was the offspring of a dragon and some other mythic. Dragons are huge. Plus, once they transform into their enormous, scaly state, they can't change back for a few decades. Bummer.

Levi sighs an exasperated gust, and his breath smells like coconut.

I wonder if his skin tastes like coconut.

"My bottom half might fit in the tub." He waves to the massive porcelain bowl suggestively sitting in the middle of our room.

Staring at the Jacuzzi for a moment, I try to remember what I asked. The basin could easily fit three of me.

"So, not dragon-sized, but still a hefty boy." I pat his chest and then give him a push backward. "Show me."

"What?" He chokes on the word, eyes wide and tinged with panic.

"Go sit in that tub and change. Come on. Let's see what you've got."

"I don't think that's a good idea." Levi dodges my insistent hands but not very well. Still unsteady on his feet.

"Do you get stuck that way for a long stretch?"

"No, but—"

"If I had my pelt here, I'd show you. Remember"—I point to my chest and do the weird floppy dance again—"blubbery seal creature over here."

He snorts but still avoids the tub.

"When's the last time you changed in front of someone?"

Wrapping my arms around his trim waist, I try dragging him toward the tub. Levi stands in place, and my feet slide on the hardwood floor.

"A few months ago. With a friend. She's a monster too." He says the last bit like it's a special club I'm not allowed into. Like I don't understand.

And he's right. But that doesn't stop the strange spike of painful heat under my ribs when I realize he easily changed in front of some other woman. My liquor-soaked brain conveniently forgets we were only on the most precarious of cordial terms this morning.

"And you trust this friend more than me?" I demand as I circle behind him to plant a shoulder into his lower back and try for a mighty shove.

Levi simply turns and catches me when I stumble past him.

"In a lot of ways, yes." No matter how gentle of a tone he uses, the words still stoke a fiery emotion that is definitely not jealousy.

"Fine!" I back away from him, hands up. Then, I smirk my most *I'm fucking smarter than you* smirk. "Don't change for me now. Whatever. I'll have to wait to see you do it in a few weeks, I guess."

Levi's brows dip. "Huh?"

"Oh, you didn't hear?" I pretend to examine my nails, all nonchalance. "I'm going to ask my mother to invite you to our dark moon swim. Have you met my mother? Let me tell you, Sorcha MacNamara doesn't take no for an answer. She will reel you in as easy as a minnow on a fishing line. You have no chance. And you'll change in front of my entire family." I don't know why I won't let this drop, but some instinct tells me I need to get him to show me his other form. That I need to see all parts of him.

"Moira," Levi rumbles the warning low in his throat.

"Or you could just get the whole thing over with now. No need to bring my pushy mother into this. Up to you."

I watch a delicious muscle tic in his jaw.

"Fine." He stalks on only slightly unsteady feet over to the tub, perching on the rim with his legs inside. "Though I don't know how she could be pushier than you."

I might feel a little guilty for the threat, if we weren't both aware that he *could* put off my mother if he really wanted to. That he's acquiescing means Levi wanted an excuse to change. Even in my tipsy state, it's obvious to me he's longing to show the other side of himself and not be met with disgust or fear.

Silently, I swear to treat him with the utmost care, no matter what he changes into. If Levi is a Frankenstein monster–looking creature, I won't flinch. If he resembles one of those terrifying anglerfish with their long, needlelike teeth, I'll keep my cool. Even if he turns into something like that bony selkie-pelt-thieving white monster Delta described, I'll let him know that every side of him is normal and deserving of respect.

Levi loosens the tie on his robe but doesn't give me a full frontal. Not that I expected he would. But I wouldn't have minded ...

Sparks race over his skin, the rapid flashes blotting out my retinas momentarily, like someone took a picture with the flash on directly in front of my face. After I blink away the spots, it takes me a moment to acknowledge what I'm seeing.

And I appreciate the view.

Levi's other form maintains a handful of his human features. Waist up, he's formed like a man. But down from his hips extends a massive scaled tail. The long limb curls in a powerful mass, looping around itself multiple times before the finned end drapes outside of the tub onto the floor.

Guess the Jacuzzi doesn't fit him after all.

The two parts of the monster blend seamlessly, aided by the continuous color of solid black. Skin and scales and pupils are dark with a tint of blue, where the light reflects. Muscles flex and shift as he settles his massive onyx body deeper into the tub. The most hypnotizing detail of his appearance is the sparks. Small flickers randomly scattered throughout the black, hovering under the surface, giving his skin the deep, endless appearance of the night sky filled with stars.

He's glorious.

"You bastard," I murmur, barely noticing his flinch. "You're sexy, like a merperson."

Then, I stumble, my head swirling.

17

LEVI

Sexy.

The word ricochets through my head, leaving me more off-balance than the fruity drinks I downed earlier.

Is she joking?

I'm distracted from the doubt when Moira loses her balance while standing still. My arm flings out, hand reaching toward her. She grabs hold, using my limb to steady herself, smiling all the while.

"Amazing," my selkie murmurs, her fingers tracing the length of my forearm. She connects the sparks under my skin like she's drawing a picture or solving a puzzle. All the while leaving me confused and heated.

I can't remember the last time someone touched me in this form. With Satine, I only ever changed a handful of times when we took a swim on the night of the dark moon. But we didn't touch then, and the few times we were intimate, I maintained my human form.

Now, Moira is here, stroking me as if she weren't in contact with a monster.

"Are you doing something to me?" She keeps her focus on her curious fingers while asking the question.

"Huh?" The sound croaks from my throat as I try to focus on her words rather than her caresses.

The selkie leaves off her touches to wave near her head. "Feels like I drank a few more margaritas. But with top-shelf tequila."

Ah. "That's"—I clear my throat—"a power I have."

Her brown eyes catch on mine, slightly unfocused but still present. "Seduction?"

"No!" I lean closer to her, reaching to place my hand on her waist but stopping an inch away. "I'm not enchanting you. This is more like"—I search for the best description—"a relaxing effect. I've always thought of it as cleansing related to emotions and worries. An inherent power from my mother's bloodline. She uses spells, but I use my will. Of course, her power is more potent and far-reaching than mine."

Moira tilts her head and then nods. "That's an interesting evolution." She spreads her palm over my forearm, and I smother a groan at the touch. "Are you doing it on purpose right now?" Her voice comes on an airy breath.

"In human form, I have to. Give it a push and some direction." I stare down at my dark form. "I've never examined how it manifests when I'm like this. But I'm not trying to use it."

The intoxicating pressure of her skin against mine disappears, and I whip my head up, seeking her out.

Moira steps back and then turns, striding away from me, swaying slightly with each step. I brace for her condemnation while I fight the urge to transform and chase after her. I'll need to change back soon anyway. She's clearly had enough.

Then, Moira turns, wearing a curious smile. "The effect isn't as strong over here. I'm normal tipsy."

She chuckles, the noise lightening the air in the room, and I can breathe.

The selkie strolls back to me, her movements relatively steady until she reaches my side. Her knees wobble.

"Whoa. Here." Reaching for her again, I brace a hand on her waist this time, guiding her down to the lip of the tub, where she can settle at my side. Somehow, I convince myself the move was all for her benefit and nothing to do with getting the unpredictable woman as close as possible.

"You cleansed my fear, didn't you?" Her mocha eyes claim my gaze. "At the Gauntlet."

Please don't be mad. "Yes."

"Why didn't you leave me? Keep going? You might have won."

Because you kissed the hell out of me and I convinced myself you must be my mate. "You were in pain," is all I say aloud.

Moira sways toward me, a curious tilt to her lips and a hint of searching in her stare. "You rescued me."

Would that make you want me? "I doubt you were in real danger."

"No. You did. From fear." The selkie straightens, teetering on her seat as she stares toward the dark window. "Does that count?" The question seems more for herself than me. Moira shrugs. "I don't think I have to be in mortal peril. But I also said I didn't believe in all that."

The selkie faces me as I struggle to keep up with a conversation I feel like I'm missing half of.

"Don't believe in what?"

Her eyes crinkle at the corners. "Fate." All her attention weighs on me in a comforting press. "Can I touch you more?" There's no hesitation in her question.

Her normal Moira bluntness sets off a teasing clench in my stomach and has me forgetting the odd statement before the question.

"Anywhere," I breathe out, leaving myself open for her to destroy me.

She doesn't hold back. Moira leans forward to place her hands on my tail, gliding over the diamond-hard scales, mapping the length of each coil. When she reaches the end, the inquisitive woman goes so far as to finger the membrane between the spikes of my fins. I've never examined myself so thoroughly.

With every inch she covers, a brick of lust stacks on my chest. A long time ago, I swore to suppress all sexual urges while in this form. But in this moment, I forget why because all I want is to fuck her senseless.

Moira's palms land on my chest, seeking out the flickering sparks once more. I can't stifle a small groan, but my selkie doesn't back off.

She doubles down.

Shifting to the side, Moira swings her leg up and around, so she can slide herself into my lap, straddling me. I meet a set of soft brown eyes with heavy lids. The neck of her robe gapes enough for me to spy the inner curves of her breasts.

Fuck.

Her bare pussy is under this robe. Pressed against the slit that hides my cock. The member I never use in this monster form. The fact that I have one when I'm like this shames me, and I try to clear away my arousal, so Moira never finds out how twisted I am.

"Praise The Finned One," my selkie sighs. "You're like a living, breathing spa." She leans forward, draping her torso over mine, burying her face in my neck. "Touching you is like getting a full-body massage," Moira moans, shifting against me, trying to get closer. "At least, I imagine this is what it feels like. I've never actually gotten a massage."

I dig my fingers into the cold porcelain of the tub to keep myself from gripping the warm body draped over mine. To keep from cupping her ass and pressing her hips tight against the uppermost point of my tail.

"You—" The word is a gasp in my throat. "You sound like you're about to orgasm."

Why in all the gods' names did I say that?

Rum. I blame the rum.

"What would that be like?" Her breath teases hot over the skin of my neck. "To come, already feeling this good?"

Does she want my brain to melt and leak out of my ears, a puddle at her feet? There's so much heat in my skull that the risk is real.

"We could try," I rasp. "If you want, I mean. Only if you want."

No! Don't do this to yourself! the scared part of my brain roars at me. *She'll find out! She'll be disgusted!*

Moira sits up, and I steel myself for the loss of her.

"Okay."

18

———

MOIRA

MY CLIT IS ALREADY PULSING, a steady beat that demands my focus. That begs for touch.

From him.

Levi gazes at me. At least, I think he does. Without pupils, his eyes are fathomless in their solid blackness. While he's in this form, I have trouble reading his face, but I could hear the emotion in his voice. The monster sounded needy, just like me.

"You want me to?" he asks, voice deeper than normal, with a delicious rasp at the end of the question.

I nod as eagerly as I can manage while still in this blissed-out state of relaxation. My muscles have never been looser, and I want them to tighten with pleasure, only to snap and stretch further.

"Gods, I want it." There's a pleading in my voice that Levi responds to, his lids fluttering.

One of his dark, sparking hands presses past the edge of my robe, curving around my breast and finding a nipple, flicking until the tip hardens. Then, he pulls the terry cloth aside and leans in to suck. I gasp, digging my hands into inky hair that soothes my skin with a silky caress, as if each strand is coated with warm oil.

The monster licks and kisses and gently bites my breasts until they're tingling, all the while whispering my name like a prayer. Then, he massages the two globes, soothing my flesh with every pass.

"No," I moan, loving and hating the relaxing waves pouring off him. "I need more." Wrapping my arms around his back, I grind down on his lower abdomen, seeking pressure for my clit.

Levi grunts, digging fingers with claws into my ass.

Guess those won't be going inside me.

There's a pressure at my back, and I glance over my shoulder to find his massive tail writhing.

Is he uncomfortable? Should I get off him?

Before I can move, he stills. "Lean back." His deep voice reverberates through me.

A seat. Levi's fashioned a seat for me with his tail by arranging the length just right. Following his instructions, I loosen my grip and recline on the scaled mass. The monster tugs at the tie to my robe, pulling the halves apart to bare me completely. There's a shift of his tail, and my body rises a few feet.

Putting my vulva on level with his face.

"Yes," he growls, guiding my legs over his shoulders. "Mine."

At the first swipe of his tongue, I pray to the gods. By the third, I pray to Levi. Then, I lose count and simply try to remember to breathe.

The monster licks my folds as if my wetness were ambrosia. I wonder if his tongue lengthens like his body because when he plunges the warm muscle into me, I could swear I'm full to the brim. With only the slightest tensing of his muscles, the monster rocks me forward and back, guiding my ride on his face.

"Levi! Oh, yes. Don't—oh gods—don't ever stop!" I sob the plea, my begging eyes meeting his dark ones over the stretch of my body.

The cruel monster lifts his head then, night-sky lips dripping with my arousal.

"You taste like the ocean." His slurred words press against my pussy, and I gasp at the highest compliment I've ever received during sex.

Then, holding my gaze, he leans forward and sucks on my clit.

Hard.

I bite on my wrist to muffle my scream as a hurricane amount of pleasurable waves crash through me.

The best orgasm I've ever had. All muscles in my body tensing tight and then releasing, discovering the peak of relaxation. The pleasure imprints on my nerves, as if I need only to remember this moment—his eyes, the cool cradle of his tail against my back, the warm pressure of his lips on my clit—and I will find this place within myself again.

After a stretch, I realize I'm lying mostly naked on a bed made of Levi's lower half. No longer at the height of his mouth, I'm reclined in the deep tub. He stares down at me, starlight face unreadable, his large hands settled in his lap. Right where his member should be.

"Have you ever tried shifting with your dick?" The question bursts out of me, born of a need for him to understand the level of pleasure he just brought me to.

Levi jerks his head back, mouth open, as if to respond. Then, he snaps his teeth shut, his entire face crumpling in confusion.

I stay reclined, still enjoying the occasional pulse of ecstasy that has my pussy clenching. For an expanse covered in hard scales, his tail is surprisingly cozy. I have always preferred a firm mattress. Whatever Levi's relaxation power is, the aura, combined with alcohol, has erased all signs of my professional filter.

"Sorry. That was selfish. I'm horny, and I figured since you retain intelligence in this shape, you might be able to keep your ..." I wave where his hands rest. Discussion of sex in our other forms is more taboo than inter-mythical couples, but here goes my tipsy mouth. "*I* can't. I'm like a Barbie doll seal. All smooth down there. I figure the gods tried to draw the line at bestiality, and my mind definitely is more animal than human when I'm in my selkie form. But I've heard rumors that merpeople and dragons and a few others have their equipment, no matter what form they're in." I sigh when I realize I'm starting to ramble. "Ignore me."

Stop thinking about what his dick would look like.

Flashing with sparks.

Would he taste like a thunderstorm?

"Are you ... are you saying if I had a cock, that wouldn't disgust you?"

Confused by his question, I finally sit up, enjoying the way Levi easily adjusts his tail to accommodate my new position.

"Of course not."

The monster's starry-night face slackens into a vulnerable expression. "But ... you wouldn't ... the gods ..." He clears his throat, and I notice his hands flexing in his lap. "The gods only intended intimate relations to happen in our human forms."

The way he says that last line sounds almost like someone else's voice. As if the declaration was preached to him. Burned into his young brain as an undeniable fact. His phrasing is enough to drive away a decent portion of my post-orgasm haze.

"The gods didn't leave a set of instructions on how we should live." Following an instinct, I rock myself forward, crawling up his long body, only pausing when my face reaches his shielding hands. Where his groin would be.

He's hiding something.

Bracing my palms on his hips, I lean forward and press a kiss to the cool midnight skin below Levi's belly button. Then, I ease my tongue out for a long, teasing lick and enjoy the play of his muscles tensing under my attention.

"Show me," I command.

19

LEVI

MOIRA'S decadent words fill the room, lingering in the air like an intoxicating fog.

Does she mean them? Could it be that the selkie is not repulsed by this form? That she truly wants to see my cock?

"You're sure?" My voice is hoarse—and not from drunkenly belting out songs earlier.

Pushing aside her curtain of damp curls, Moira offers me a teasing tilt of her lips. Her cheeks still hold the flush of her orgasm, and the sight is so tantalizing that I'm ready to beg to service her again. Just to hear my name in that needy, gasping tone.

"I want a taste of you." Her tongue sneaks out, another lick on my lower stomach that's all fire.

Lunging forward, I scoop her up in my arms, enjoying her yelp of surprise, before placing her butt on the edge of the tub. I still haven't gotten a full view of what promises to be a delicious ass, what with the damn robe still hanging off her shoulders and covering her backside as it gapes wide in the front.

135

"I knew it!" Moira's delighted gasp pairs with wide eyes that stare down at my lap. Her eagerness helps with my nerves.

Ever since I hit puberty, I've been able to change into this form at will. And unlike Moira's description of herself, I'm not a Ken doll, no matter what I might first appear to be. In my monster form, my cock retracts inside my body, only extending from a slit between my scales when I'm aroused. My member and balls are now fully on display, resting on my stomach, the same electric-black color as the rest of my body.

As a teenager, I wasn't shy about touching myself, like any other guy my age. But one day, to both of our mortification, my mother walked into the bathroom when I forgot to lock the door. She saw entirely too much. For weeks after, she lectured and made sharp comments about not giving in to those urges when in my other form. She said that the gods never intended for mythics to mate in their beast forms and that I only had my equipment because of a weird monster DNA mishap.

But here's Moira—a leader among our kind and one who's never shy about cutting me down when I get too cocky—telling me that I'm normal. Or at least, not *too* odd.

More than that, the selkie traces her soft brown gaze over me with lust washing over her face and tightening her nipples.

"I'm guessing you haven't used your monster dick much?"

She gifts me with a cheeky grin, and my whole body clenches with need. Need to encircle her with my arms and tail. Hold her hard and close until the pattern of my scales imprints on her skin. Tattoo the marks there to make her mine.

She is fierce, and prickly, and sexy, and perfect.

"No." I keep my response short or else I might end up begging her for every scrap of affection she's willing to dole out.

"Not even with another monster?"

At her question, I try not to wince as guilt squeezes my chest. Satine's face is clear in my mind, glittering blue scales she lives with every day. My friend can only have sex in her monster form, and we did sleep together a handful of times. She was passionate and beautiful during those encounters. But I never transformed during our intimate moments. I never shared this part of myself.

Satine deserved better. I still believe we weren't meant to be more than friends, but I have no doubt she would have appreciated vulnerability instead of me always hiding behind my human-approved face.

"No," I rasp out the response and then grunt when Moira scoops up my hand, which I only now realize I've curled into a fist.

My selkie kisses the knuckles, then licks them, and then bites them, earning a strangled noise from my throat and a thrust of my hips.

Moira shifts on the tub lip and traces her heavy gaze over every straining inch of me. "Well, I think it's fucking perfect."

Letting go of my hand, she slides into the Jacuzzi, her legs straddling a lower section of my tail. The warm press of her pussy against my scales sends a raging pulse of need through me, and I harden further.

As my selkie leans forward, I hold my breath. Mere inches away, she stops.

"Is something wrong?" I gasp out.

Moira meets my eyes, sitting up straight. "You should be the first to touch it."

A half-laugh, half-groan bursts out of my mouth. I'm tempted to tell her I've stroked my dick plenty, lately to thoughts of her. Fantasizing about us trapped in that love cage again, only we need to do a lot more to earn our freedom.

But that was in my human form. This is different.

The earnest way my selkie stares at me has me giving in. Reaching down, I'm careful of my claws as I grip my erection. This time, I groan for a different reason.

Fuck, this is too good.

When I stroke myself, a streak of fiery pleasure races down the entire length of my tail. As if having a larger form means I get to have a bigger orgasm. As my hand moves, Moira's eyes follow, which only increases my arousal.

I pause. "Will you?" The question drips with desperation. *Will you touch me? Will you take me as I am? Will you find a way to be with a monster?*

In answer, my selkie leans in, dragging her pink tongue over the sensitive head. I grunt, barely keeping my full-body spasm in check. I don't want to dislodge Moira—or worse, hurt her. My tail is a powerful weapon if I need it to be.

Pushing my hand away, Moira takes up the job of gripping me. Stroking me. Sucking as much as she can take past her slick lips. Shimmering black slipping against flushed pink.

So hungry for me. As if I'm a delicacy. As if I'm worth consuming.

I mutter curses and thanks to the gods in turn as the pleasure rises ever higher. Before was a mere puddle of sensations while, now, I ride into a tsunami's worth of ecstasy. My tail wants to thrash, my hips want to thrust, but my claws scratch porcelain as I grip the sides of the tub, holding myself still as my selkie's head rises and falls in my lap.

"Moira," I moan her name, wanting her to hear in the single word how she has all of me. No barters. No exchanges. I am hers.

In response, the devious selkie begins to hum the gnome drinking song again, and the vibration is too much for my over-stimulated cock to handle.

"I—I'm about to—"

She pops me out of her mouth, licking the moisture off her lips as her hands work me hard, their tight hold slipping and turning in alternating directions.

Moira's unyielding gaze meets mine, and it's as if we were back in that conference room, two council members battling with words and glares over the stretch of the oak table, oblivious to everyone else around us.

"Give it to me, Levi," she commands.

My body jerks, and I shout a harsh curse as I spill all over her fingers, spurting onto her bare breasts. Her hold remains until I can't take her perfect touch anymore, and she releases me, sitting tall. Towering above the monster she's conquered.

Please decimate me every day for the rest of our lives. The plea plays silently across my brain as I suck in ragged breaths.

When I rake my eyes over her body and find she's tracing a finger through my cum on her skin, I almost pass out from the erotic scene.

"You know"—her voice comes out conversational—"I half-expected this to be stardust." The selkie shoots me a teasing smile.

Somehow, I manage a chuckle and then groan in protest when Moira climbs off me and out of the tub. Still too spent to move, I allow myself to recline and watch my selkie stroll into the bathroom. She leaves the door open, and I watch as she washes her chest. A quiet growl, too low for her to hear, rumbles out of me. I don't like the idea of her wiping the traces of me away. I want to pin her to the ground and slide inside her, press our bodies together with the remnants of my orgasm between us until my scent couldn't be removed from her skin. So, every day, I could smell her icy-ocean scent mixed with mine.

Moira, unaware of my alpha-male urges, finds a complimentary toothbrush and scrubs her teeth, pausing halfway through to retie her robe. Another crime in my opinion. After she rinses her mouth, my selkie wets a cloth and brings the offering to me, fighting a yawn as she hands the damp material over.

"I'm ready for bed," she murmurs, lids already drooping. She teases her fingers through my hair in a gesture that has me wanting to purr. Then, she steps away, blinking slowly, and I start to realize how drunk—on both tequila and my magic—she's been during this encounter. "Don't forget to change back. You don't want to scare the cleaning staff if they come too early."

With that simple statement, all the previous bliss drains from my body.

I know the suggestion is practical. I *know* that.

But all my insecurities about my monstrous form barge to the front of my brain as Moira sidles to the bed and slides under the covers without a second look my way.

What did we do?

Panic-laced bands tighten around my chest, reminding me of that sentient rope from the Gauntlet. Twining and choking until my breath comes faster. Too fast.

I don't regret a moment of what happened, but maybe she does.

With rough strokes, I wipe off my "monster dick," as she called it.

Was that a compliment? Fuck if I know.

My mind scrabbles for the safe sensation of my human form, and with a scattering of sparks, I'm a bipedal figure again. All man, no sign of monster.

But the uncomfortable doubt lingers, mixing with the dregs of my earlier buzz, creating a toxic cocktail.

Was this just a drunken hook-up?

Yeah, we were both tipsy, but I thought we checked in plenty of times. Neither of us forced ourselves on the other. As I heave myself out of the tub, my stare seeks out her lightly snoring form.

She got drunk on my powers.

A logical part of my brain reminds me that my abilities aren't strong enough to trick a woman into sleeping with me. But with the combination of alcohol and the way Moira relaxed further when I changed, she was missing her normal prickly walls. And I don't know if that was a good thing.

When I sat in front of her in my other form and she didn't look away, I didn't want to question her acceptance.

But I also didn't take the time to ask what any of this meant to her. And now, she's fast asleep, clutching a pillow to her chest, curls spread in a twisting mass over the white sheets.

Gods, how I want to slip into the bed beside her, pull her body against my chest, and hold my wild selkie until morning.

But if I wake up and have to watch her cringe away from me, I know something inside me will break. All my life, I've dealt with the fear and distrust that come from sharing my lineage. Until this moment, I thought my hide had scarred to a thick enough barrier that no one's disdain could pierce through.

But Moira MacNamara could gut me with a single word.

I can't risk that pain. Better I give her space. Tomorrow, when neither of us is steeped in the haze of liquor and mythical relaxing powers, the truth of our encounter will be easier to discern.

Reluctantly, I step away from my selkie and find a spare blanket and pillow in a linen closet. Fashioning a crude bed on the floor, I try to find the peace I had in the tub with Moira sprawled on top of me. I can't manage it, but after a time, the sound of her soft breathing lulls me into an unrestful sleep.

20

———

MOIRA

A RAY OF SUNSHINE, warm against my bare shoulder, wakes me.

Sunrise. The peaceful word flits through my head, pairing perfectly with the briny scent of the ocean. Memories of the previous day surface slowly, and I keep my lids closed as I drift through them.

Each one elicits a spark of heat and joy.

Swimming in the sea. Delicious, salty food on my tongue, paired with sweet and tart drinks. Insistent, coaxing pressure at my core. Rolling, bone-melting pleasure. A different salty taste. Teasing thunderbolts with my lips. Levi's deep groan caressing my eardrums and the back of my throat.

A new image forms in my mind. A fantasy of me rising to kneel on this plush bed to face toward the glass doors.

I soak in the breathtaking view of shimmering water disappearing over the curve of the horizon. As I revel in the majesty, a warm, hard body presses against my back. Strong fingers gripping my hips. Hot mouth on my neck. Rigid length sliding along my folds and then past them. Him inside me.

Thrusting.

Taking.

My pussy is already wet as I stretch my arm out, searching for the monster who can make my daydream a reality. But my palm only finds cool sheets.

Finally, I blink my eyes open. The bed beside me is empty. The void seeming as vast as the stretch of water outside this bed-and-breakfast. Propping myself up on my elbows, I scan the room.

Maybe he's an early riser. Maybe he went to find us breakfast.

But those hopes crash like a wave on the sand when I spy a lean, long body stretched out on the floor with only a blanket and a pillow for bedding.

He slept on the hardwood floor instead of sharing this mammoth mattress with me.

There's a jab in my gut, so sharp and surprising that I flip onto my other side and curl into the fetal position, protecting my insides. But the attack isn't physical.

Levi's cleansing powers might have let my guard down, but the part of me I revealed was real.

He didn't like what he saw.

The distancing act is familiar and hurts more because of it. I cannot count the times Hamish slept in our guest bedroom because he needed space from me. How many mornings did I wake up alone when all I wanted was to roll over and find the warm body of the person I loved beside me?

Moving carefully, I slide from the bed and step on the balls of my feet as I sneak to the bathroom, closing the door with a soft click behind me. Then, I press my shoulder blades to the wood and allow a collection of silent tears to track down my cheeks.

Hamish wasn't right. I fight back against the anxiety.

But then why is this happening again?

The only correlation: me.

Being with Levi last night was selfish. A choice I made for no other reason than to please myself. Because in that moment, I wanted him more than the ocean. There was a sense of rightness when I touched his thunderstorm skin. Like a sudden understanding had dawned on me.

This is the man, I thought. *I choose this man.*

And I thought he'd chosen me too.

But Levi was tipsy from mixed drinks and rich food.

Did he want to be with me at all? Or did he just give in because I was practically rubbing myself all over him?

Gods, I was so aggressive. Demanding everything from him. That he change, and touch me, and let me touch him.

I press knuckles against my mouth to stifle a moan.

No, I try to remind myself. *I asked. He said yes. There was consent.*

Through a tangled bird's nest of curls, wide eyes stare back at me from the mirror.

But we were drinking. And now, he's sleeping on the floor.

"You're a lot sometimes." Hamish's accented voice slips in between my own self-recriminations. *"It's a big turn-off for you to climb all over me like that. I need you to back off. Give me space."*

Whatever I felt about last night, Levi has made his stance clear. He put space between us. I need to respect that. The connection was one-sided, and pushing him is likely to result in a more thorough put-down.

Because my nerves are still raw and my heart beats with a painful ache, I give myself the duration of a shower to pity myself, doing all I can to wash the scent of him off my skin. But when I step out from under the spray, I tuck away all those vulnerable emotions. As I dress in yesterday's outfit, the clothes mostly dry from hanging up overnight, I pull on my professional shield.

This started as a business trip—kind of—and I will end it that way.

When I come out of the bathroom, Levi is still asleep. Glancing at the clock, I realize I truly did rise with the sun. It's not even seven yet.

I should wake him up, I reason, my eyes tracing over his strong jaw up to his prominent nose and then along his dark lashes.

Instead, I duck out of the room and find a delicious spread in the dining area on the first floor. When some people are sad, they claim they can't eat a bite. I'm the opposite, piling my plate high with bacon and pancakes and letting the syrup try its best to soothe my soul. Unfortunately, I also eat fast, finishing my massive breakfast in a matter of minutes.

As much as I want to wander off, I can't just disappear. Slowly climbing up to the top level again, I listen at the door. No movement. Unlocking it, I find Levi still slumbering away, looking adorably mussed and vulnerable with his inky hair tangling around his golden cheeks.

"For gods' sake." Frustration blots out my hurt.

I've had a sex fantasy, mental breakdown, self-pep talk, and depression binge-eat this morning, and he hasn't even woken up yet. Stalking over to him, I nudge the monster in the ribs with my toe.

Levi mutters an incoherent string of words and rolls onto his side. Away from me.

My teeth threaten to shatter; I clench them so hard. This quaint B & B is about to become the perfect setting for another cozy mystery. Murder victim: one sleepy monster.

"Levi." I crouch beside him, grabbing his shoulder and giving it a shake.

Finally, he jerks awake, head whipping toward me, midnight eyes widening as shock slackens his jaw. No doubt worried to find me hovering above him. I cross my arms over my chest.

Look, I'm keeping my hands to myself. No need to worry that I'm about to straddle your trim waist.

"Moira ..."

Levi doesn't come up with any more words, and I stare past his shoulder, letting the glint of the ocean draw my gaze.

"I already showered and ate. I'm going to go down to the water again while I can." *Maybe find some peace before the return trip.* Standing, I stroll over to the bed I slept in alone and snatch my phone off the side table. "Text me when you're ready to leave. I'll meet you at the car."

If I were fine, I'd wait for an answer. Maybe share my thoughts on the breakfast currently curdling in my stomach. But I can't be in this room with him leaning away from me, looking anywhere but me, regretting every touch we shared. Not when I'll have to suffer through the agony for six hours on the drive back.

If I wasn't so bent on him not knowing the pain I'm in, I'd consider renting a car.

But I'm stronger than this. All I need is a little boost from a lot of salt water. So, I stride past him and out the door.

I give him as much space as I can, and he doesn't try to stop me.

21

LEVI

"Then, that baby witch tried to claim this cleansing spell is straightforward. Which, in a way, it is. There aren't many ingredients. But the power expenditure!" My mother lets out a scoff from the passenger seat of my Mercedes. "No witch on the East Coast would be able to pull off this spell on their own, is all I'm going to say."

As my mother continues to run through the gossip and power plays exchanged during her weekly coven meetings, I try to pay attention. When I was younger, I would have been glued to her words because Violetta Radeva always waved away her monster son, claiming he had no need to know the teaching of witches. It's not as though I could use them.

That's all my mother thought was important about her knowledge. The usability. Meanwhile, I just wanted her to include me in the largest part of her life. To not be turned away for a part of myself I couldn't change. To have my mother accept me.

Her sharing now should enchant me. Instead, my mind

continues to track back to the other woman I'd pay any price to keep from turning me away.

Moira MacNamara has claimed permanent residency in my brain. And my heart.

And she'll barely talk to me.

Yesterday morning, when she met me, smelling like the ocean, I wanted to press her against the car and steal a hot, long kiss from her frowning mouth. But the selkie immediately slid into the driver's seat. Her avoidance and discomfort were a dark storm swirling around her tense form, proving all my worries were well-founded.

The curiosity she'd had for my body only came from booze and magic.

Disgust cut against my rib cage at the idea that my relaxation abilities had manipulated her. Made her open to sexual acts she would normally never agree to.

The entire car ride, I struggled to find a way to bridge the void between us. But words refused to present themselves, and the boring drone of the audiobook about personal finance instead of the fun cozy mystery somehow made my ability to concentrate worse.

When she parked in front of my house, I blurted out the only two words I found in the six-hour drive.

"I'm sorry."

Moira flinched—actually flinched—from me then, and I wanted to howl in despair at her fear, feeling like the scum of the earth.

"A lot of people do things they regret," she said. "We're adults. We can move on from it."

The pain of her words was so sharp that I glanced down to see if she'd slipped her dagger between my ribs. But there was no wound, and when I climbed from her car, she sped off the moment I shut the door.

. . .

"Oh good. Moira is already here." My mom's statement wrenches me back to the present moment, and I follow her gaze out my windshield.

There she is. My selkie.

Or at least, the selkie I wish were mine.

Moira leans against the trunk of her car, sunglasses shielding her beautiful eyes. But with her curls pulled high in a bun, I have an unobscured view of the way her lips dip in a frown.

There must be a way to fix this. How can I show her I'm not some villainous creature? That I can care for her better than any other mythic?

"Good morning, Violetta," Moira greets my mother when we get out of my car. "I thought you said this only required two people."

The witch grins wide, showing all her teeth in a borderline menacing display. But that's just how my mother smiles. "I did say that. Of course, I meant, two people in addition to myself. Which is why I brought my helpful son along." She pats my shoulder and then strolls over to the jugs of water Moira has set up in a neat line along the gravel drive-up to plot 236.

This close, I can tell something is off about the place. July in Georgia is already hot and humid, but here, there's an extra presence sticking to my skin. Like spiderwebs.

"You two back up a step or ten. I need to spell these before we get to work." My mother waves her hands at us.

Moira moves first, and I follow to where she stands. When she realizes I'm beside her, her body stiffens. Pointedly ignoring me, the selkie slips her fingers in her pocket and pulls out her cell phone.

"No technology!" my mother snaps, her back facing us, which makes the comment eerie.

With tight lips, Moira slides the device into her pocket.

"Don't take it personally," I murmur. "She claims the signal messes with her spells. I'm still not allowed to use my phone in her house despite having walked in on her playing Candy Crush plenty of times."

Moira offers me her polite politician smile, which has me wanting to rip her sunglasses off just to find some emotion on her face. Instead, I search for another topic. Something that might get her to talk to me.

"You mentioned Seamus finally convinced Neri to give him a chance?" Maybe her brother's love life is a safer subject.

This time, there's a genuine tilt to her mouth, and I breathe easier.

"Yeah. He's convinced winning the Gauntlet is what did it."

"You don't think so?"

Moira shrugs. "I don't think she cared. Not about the title anyway. She looked ready to strangle him at the end. You didn't notice?"

I remember standing by while the Gauntlet organizers debated the validity of Seamus's win. All I could do was stare at Moira. My tall, wet, exasperated selkie, whose mouth I'd just gotten to taste for the first time.

And she's asking if I noticed another?

"Can't say I did."

"Well, they've worked things out. He's even moved in with her over the bookstore she's opening. That'll be a good new business for Folk Haven. Maybe you all should start a support group."

I smile at her words, keeping to myself that I'm already in communication with Neri about setting up a space in my spa for books to be sold. The siren easily convinced me many people find reading relaxing. I want to serve every customer the best I can.

A cluster of clouds drifts across the sky, easing the morning sun. I want to praise those fluffy white cumulous creations because Moira pushes her sunglasses off her nose to perch on the top of her head.

"Neri says she'll focus on providing a good selection in each genre, which means plenty of cozy mysteries." She keeps talking to me as her focus trains on the tall trees around us. "I like to pretend that's for me, but Seamus is a fan too. The bookworm found his perfect mate."

The selkie flicks her eyes my way, her gaze widening when she finds me staring at her. But I can't help my fascination with each movement she makes and the words she speaks.

"Do you want a mate?" I ask, unable to stop the question.

Instead of her brushing me off or giving me a hard no, I watch with unease as Moira's face flushes a dark red. The color deepens past embarrassment, and I could swear anger and shame war in her glare.

"If you're going to advise me to behave better than I did on our trip, don't bother. I'm fully aware that taking advantage of an inebriated person is not how to go about finding a mate." Her voice catches on the last word and hits me like a blow to the gut. She shakes her head, as if the intense emotions leaking from her expression could be dislodged with a violent enough movement. All that comes loose is one of her curls. "I made a mistake. I apologize. Let us just move on, knowing I won't ever do it again."

"You can't say that." The words are a growl, an immediate denial of her never allowing herself to accept me the way she did that night.

Her brows dip at a fierce angle. "Yes, I can. In fact"—she shifts, and with horror, I realize Moira's pulled her dagger out while I've been reeling from her words—"I swear."

A flick of her wrist, and the blade arcs toward the pad of her thumb.

I catch my selkie's wrist, stopping her just in time.

"Please," I rasp, terrified she'll continue the movement if I relax even a molecule of my being. That she'll finish a blood vow to never repeat the events of the most erotic night of my life. "Do not make a promise that would keep you from me."

Moira's expression twists with confusion, and just as I am about to interrogate her to get to the heart of this misunderstanding, my mother's voice whips between us.

"Stop playing with knives and come grab a jug!" The witch gestures to the collection. Each one gives off a subtle blue glow. Good thing we're far enough back from the main road, where no random driver will see the obvious display of magic. "Time to get this spell going."

"We need a minute." I keep hold of Moira's wrist.

"What's more important?" She glares with offense and warning. "Your small talk or the cleansing?"

The answer on my tongue is not the same in my chest. This land means a great deal to Moira for a reason I don't understand. Yet. It is one of the many answers I want to earn from her intoxicating lips. The best way to gain her trust is to support her in this.

Meeting Moira's gaze, I carefully let her go. With the same slow movement, she returns the dagger to its home in her purse. The gesture is an answer of sorts. Enough to have me stepping toward my mother.

"Fine. Yes. We're coming."

22

MOIRA

"Do not make a promise that would keep you from me."

As I follow behind Levi and his mother while they walk the perimeter of my land, I can't help playing his words over in my mind. They sound like the plea of a man who wants me. If that's the case, then something must have happened that I missed during our beach getaway. My body aches to demand an answer from him right now.

But I must wait.

Violetta strikes me as the type of woman to leave a situation if she believes she is being disrespected. Normally, I'd be all for badass power moves, but not if it means abandoning this cleansing before it's completed. So, I'll bite back my words and try not to get too itchy as I wait for a moment alone with Levi.

"Is that one empty? Then, go grab another." The witch waves her son away, all haughty arrogance and no please or thank you. Not that he reacts.

Instead, as Levi turns to jog back to the cars, he catches my eye. His gaze is pure heat, which tightens all the nerves in my body.

There are words waiting to be said.

"Here," Violetta barks out. She points a silver-polished finger to a random spot on the ground that must hold a meaning she can detect.

Knowing the drill by now, I step up to her side and pour out about half a cup of the enchanted seawater onto the earth. Violetta moves forward at a swaying pace with her eyes closed, muttering words under her breath, and points to another spot a minute later.

I feel the weight of Levi's gaze on my back before I hear the crunch of his footsteps on the leafy debris of the forest floor. His presence threatens to overwhelm me, so I force my mind to find another sensation to focus on.

The magic tied to plot 236.

There's a gross, sticky presence lingering, like oil on top of water. Clinging to where it doesn't belong. This toxic magic wasn't always here. It appeared when the shack no one knew was a protective talisman burned down.

Now, my land is the town's concern, and no one but me can seem to sense the other pure power that hovers just under the invisible mess. Like embers of a fire, the force lingers in a perpetual state of opportunity. Waiting.

For what? I don't know.

And I don't expect Violetta's spell will affect it. The mystical force is solid—unlike the stretching, clinging evil magic. My guess is, the cleansing fire also would have passed over the stronger force. But so much more would have disappeared in its wake. The hungry flames would have stolen all that stands here, still surviving after all these years.

My jug runs out, and I go to retrieve another. Levi repeats the fetching process once more, not having to walk far as we finish the circuit.

"Lead me to the remains of the first spell," Violetta demands.

When the structure burned down, I had a crew come in and haul away the charred debris, so no one would harm themselves in the space. But stones were used as the foundation, and those remain. Levi's mother crouches by the remnants of the structure, running her hands over the rocks.

"Will you need to construct another building? Something that should be preserved?" I ask as I prop my seawater jug on my hip to ease the dragging weight off my fingers.

"No." Violetta stands, brushing her hands on her jeans. I'm not sure how she's wearing pants in this day's heat. I opted for a sleeveless dress, and I'm still sweating. "This spell was cast by a binding witch. She captured all the twisted magic and tied it to the shack. A temporary solution at best. Mine will purge every trace from the land. Here." She waves at her feet. "Place the jugs here. Caps off."

Levi and I follow her orders, placing the two remaining containers at her feet. Then, we move back, allowing her plenty of space to work. The woman tucks longs strands of brunette hair behind her ears and closes her eyes again. She stretches her arms out, fingers spread wide, each one glinting with silver and gold rings.

The air stills, all breeze and movement pausing like a held breath. Slowly, the luminescent water rises from the mouths of the jugs, splitting into thousands of droplets that spread out wide, some moving past where I can see. After a moment, the liquid pauses, hovering like frozen rain.

When I glance at Levi, I find him gazing around us, his face sharing the same wonder I feel. I would have expected Violetta's son to know the gist of what was coming, but maybe she rarely works magic around him.

Or maybe this is a larger spell than she's ever performed before.

The deep growl of a voice snaps my attention back to Violetta, and I barely stifle a gasp of shock. The witch's skin shows a map of her veins, the lines a dark blue network. She glares into the air as her lips move around words I can't hear.

A pulsing whine starts up in the air, the pitch increasing with the speed of the witch's jaw movements. Suddenly, Violetta's mouth opens wide, as if in a silent scream, her eyes wild.

"Mom!" Levi shouts, stepping forward, concern radiating off him.

But then the witch drops to a crouch, slapping her hands hard against the dirt. The shimmering droplets hanging in the air follow her lead and crash to the ground, plunging into the earth.

As if in protest, the dirt beneath my feet emits a screech that echoes through the trees.

A cleansing force rolls out from Violetta, passing through me on its way. Where her son's abilities spread around me like a soothing caress, hers hits like a power wash, leaving my skin raw.

Good thing I told the mayor and police chief we were doing this today or else the noise alone would have raised an alarm. Still might.

As the effects dissipate, the witch sits down heavily, her body drooping in on itself.

"Mom!" Levi calls again, rushing forward and scooping Violetta into his arms. "Are you okay? Do we need to go to emergency care?"

"No, no. Calm down." She pats his chest. "I'm just worn out. Nothing a good meal and long night of sleep won't cure." The powerful woman turns a toothy grin my way. "Pretty impressive, wouldn't you agree?"

"Yes." I search for the sticky, sick sensation and find nothing where it used to linger. The forceful glow of potential energy remains, prompting me to smile back at the witch. "Amazing."

"I'm taking you home," Levi announces, as if he thinks his mother might try another spell for shits and giggles.

"You come along with us." Violetta points a demanding finger over her son's shoulder. "I want payment immediately."

"Mom," Levi sighs in exasperation.

"It's fine," I assure him, gathering up the empty jugs before following.

Not too long later, I'm perched on a stool in the witch's kitchen, carefully writing out instructions on a set of heavy card stock.

"A recipe?" Levi stares between the two of us after placing a teapot on the stovetop. "You did all of that for a recipe?"

"This is the MacNamara clam chowder." I gesture at the half-finished instructions I learned by heart before I was a teenager. "Show some respect."

"I've wanted this for decades." Violetta scoops a spoonful of loose tea leaves into a strainer.

The monster shakes his head but leaves off his questions. Between penning each step, I watch as Levi's concerned gaze returns to his mother time and time again. The sight has my heart squeezing.

When the tea and recipe are done, Violetta shoos us toward the door. "I don't need you hovering. Moira, you call me when you want to divulge more family secrets." The witch gives me a wicked smirk before shutting her front door in our faces.

Levi stares at the wood, a lost expression in his eyes.

"Hey." I poke his shoulder, and he jerks, eyes landing on me. "Do you want to go grab a beer at Local Brew?" Then, I wince in memory. "Not that I'm looking to get you drunk again. I just thought it might be a good place to decompress."

Suddenly, Levi's entire sharp focus homes in on me, and the monster steps forward, looming because I wore flats today instead of heels.

"Also, it's a good place to talk."

23

—————

MOIRA

"I'VE DECIDED how you can pay me back the favor you owe me," Levi announces as I slip into a back corner booth beside him.

We each hold a beer, just poured by the werewolf bartender. If I'd won Galen's Gauntlet, I wouldn't have had to pay for the drink. Instead, Seamus is the one who gets to enjoy a year of free booze from Local Brew—one of the many Gauntlet prizes. Not that I'm sitting on an empty bank account, but still.

While waiting at the bar, I considered the possible ways of easing into a serious conversation with Levi. But I guess he wants to start us off.

"Oh, really? And what's that? Firstborn child? Commit a murder on your behalf?"

The monster tries to glare at me, but there are too many sparks going off in his dark eyes for me to feel intimidated.

"No." He smooths his features out. "I want you to come to my spa. This Friday."

I swallow my sip of beer hard, surprised by the request. "A

spa day? That's the hardship I have to go through to repay you?" Okay, maybe it *is* a little hard. I've never been to a spa in my life. Never even gotten a manicure. I take care of all my self-care myself. Still, just stating the offer out loud shows how ridiculous the notion is.

"Ah, I'm not done." Levi leans closer to me, bringing his stormy scent with him. "If you like the services, you have to tell everyone. Give Haven's Relaxation the official Moira MacNamara stamp of approval."

I quirk an eyebrow at the monster, trying to ignore the way his proximity affects my pulse rate. "I think you think my approval carries more weight than it does."

He holds my gaze. "And I think you think you aren't a force that will shift the entire direction of this town." Levi clinks the lip of his glass against mine. "You will change Folk Haven, and I want to be on your good side." As he takes a deep swallow of the amber liquid, the man holds my eyes with his dark ones, daring me to contradict him.

As I avoid the enticing bob of his Adam's apple, I mull the idea over.

Change Folk Haven.

I love this small, mythic-filled lake town. But I would be lying if I claimed to be happy with every dictate laid down by our town's founders. Once again, Morgana and her baldly honest words play through my head, and in my distraction, the monster moves closer.

"What do you say, Council Member MacNamara? Will you agree to a preview of my spa before the doors officially open?"

I narrow my eyes and press my lips tight together, trying to fight a smile. "Are you luring me to the spa to get me alone?"

Am I flirting? Is it too much? Am I being too aggressive?

In that moment, I realize I only ever ask myself that last question in a romantic situation. Anywhere else in my life, I'm proud of my forceful nature.

Levi grins wickedly but then shakes his head, and I fight off a prick of disappointment. "The spa will be fully staffed. I have a few other influencers coming to get a preview. A press day, you might say."

I pretend to mull the idea over but then roll my eyes to try and cover up the kindling of excitement. "Fine. I will come honestly review your spa. But I'm a hard customer. You'd better provide five-star treatment."

As I go to sip my drink, I think better of consuming alcohol when near this enticing monster and place my glass to the side for now. I haven't gotten drunk off a single beer since I was sixteen, but I want a clear head for the next part of this conversation, and Levi's proximity is already fogging my thoughts.

Memories rise to the surface of the tub, his long body, his clever tongue—

"Do you want me?" I blurt and then glance around to make sure we don't have an audience.

But things are slow this Monday. A few sirens by the jukebox, a werewolf tossing back whiskey, a gnome guzzling beer, and a group of humans at the pool table. None of them paying us any mind.

No one to hear a council member lowering her defenses.

When I return my gaze to Levi, I find a hungry stare roaming over my face.

"Do I want you?"

Under the table, a hot hand lands on my knee, and I bite back a gasp. Without thought, my legs spread wide. At the invitation, his nostrils flare, pupils dilating until his eyes are almost entirely black. The monster's fingers drag upward, under my skirt, finding the elastic of my underwear.

"You tell me, Moira. Do you think I want you?"

I'm not sure. I'm never sure.

Slowly, he traces the thin strip of lace that presses into my leg. The only barrier between his finger and my pleasure.

At the clear signal, I try to hold on to the confidence that comes easily in every other aspect of my life. To remember that it's okay to ask for what I want. To demand what I want.

"Yes." I inhale the word, taking the sound into me. But he already heard.

Levi delves past my panties, teasing a finger through my folds. Slowly, he strokes, encouraging a growing dampness until I'm slick against his touch. I want to moan, but instead, I take a deep gulp of my drink and try not to choke on the liquid.

"You're soaking," he purrs into my ear.

I nod, as if he needs a second opinion. Covering his hand with mine, I direct his fingers deeper. Inside. When Levi slips two in, I grip his muscular thigh to keep from thrusting.

"Gods," he breathes against my neck, voice hoarse. "Is this for me?"

My pussy clenches. That's certainly one way to answer.

"The question isn't if I want you, Moira." Levi leisurely thrusts his fingers in and out of my core with each word. The cheap plastic of the booth squeaks as I shift in subtle rocks. "The question is, do *you* want *me*."

His thumb presses down on my clit, and I let out an undignified whimper.

"Do you?" the monster asks, his lips brushing the skin of my neck before he gives a gentle pinch with his teeth. "Do you want me?"

My mouth opens, but a louder voice overrides whatever answer I might have given.

"Hey!"

I jump, which sets off a whole smattering of delicious sensations with Levi's fingers still inside me. But I can't enjoy any of them when there's some hulking brute just feet away. For a moment, I panic, thinking he was shouting at the two of us. That he knows what's going on below the table.

But the man isn't looking our way. He's facing the small hall that leads to the restrooms. And he's not alone.

"Please, can you just let me get past?" The delicate voice quivers, and my arousal dies with the fear I hear.

Unceremoniously, I shove Levi's hand out from under my skirt and slide from the booth.

"Moira!"

I don't look back at his call, striding straight toward the situation developing in front of me.

"Not until you tell me what you were singing," the guy—a human—slurs through his words as he grabs the arm of what I now see is a terrified siren.

She's a young girl, probably barely past the drinking age, and I can bet what happened. She sang to herself or with some friends, this asshole overheard, and like everyone who's not a siren, he immediately forgot what she sang. But he remembered it was beautiful. And for some reason, he thinks that gives him the right to demand she perform for him.

Not on my watch.

"Please," she whispers again. "I can't."

"I want—"

"I don't give a fuck what you want." My declaration has the man turning. "Let the girl go."

The white guy's cheeks flush with mottled drunkenness as he sneers at me, dragging the terrified siren closer before reaching out, as if to shove me away. But I merely turn, grabbing his wrist, and utilize his questionable balance to sweep his leg out from under him. The human goes down hard, releasing the siren as he tries to cushion his introduction to the floor. He stays down with my knee in his back and his arm twisted up to his shoulder blades.

I jerk my head at the siren, and she scurries back to her friends. Levi appears at my side, phone to his ear, and I hear Samantha's voice from the speaker. While he gives the police chief a rundown, he reaches into the assaulter's back pocket, pulling out a wallet.

"I'll kill you, bitch! You have no fucking clue who I am!" the piece of scum yells, struggling against my hold.

But I have leverage, sobriety, and a small mythical strength boost in my favor. He's not going anywhere until I want him to. For a moment, the human's friends concern me, but they back up real fast when the bartender pulls out his shotgun. Little do they know, Rodney is plenty deadly without the firearm. They clear out before the cops show up.

Cowards.

Soon, red and blue lights flash in the windows of the bar, and Samantha appears.

"Heya, Moira," the police chief says without her usual cheer. "Whatcha got here?"

"Another bitch? Is this town fucking pussy-whipped?" The guy seems determined to dig his hole deeper.

I give her the play-by-play of what happened, and Levi offers the guy's ID, which he must've found in his wallet.

"Out-of-towner."

I could've guessed. Samantha cuffs the human and hauls him to his feet, unperturbed by his unimaginative insults.

"I'll take it from here. Hopefully, this rotten peach didn't ruin your night." The mermaid nods a good-bye and maneuvers the menace out of the bar.

As the adrenaline wanes, I stagger under the reality of this mess.

A strange human tried to hurt someone in my town.

What if the toxic draw of plot 236 coaxed these men to come to Folk Haven? If I had burned the place weeks ago, would all of this have been avoided?

And tonight, I had Levi—a fellow council member—pleasure me in a public place.

What if one of my constituents, people who trust me to represent them, had seen me? What if I'd been too busy, getting my rocks off in public, to notice the siren's distress?

When is my selfishness going to get someone else hurt?

I meet Levi's eyes. The dark eyes of a monster. A man who already deals with enough shit, being who he is. An inter-mythical relationship would only pile more on top of that, and I think he knows it. Maybe my intense sex drive didn't scare him off, but something drove him to sleep on the floor that night.

That was the right move. Putting space between us is the smart choice.

"You should stay away from me."

I turn but not before seeing the hurt in his starry eyes.

24

LEVI

Moira's words dig into my brain as I try to reason through them.

"You should stay away from me."

Not *I* want *you to stay away from me*, and that small arrangement gives me hope. For now though, I'll do what my selkie suggested. But only because I have business to attend to.

Unfortunately, an arrest in Folk Haven is not always a cut-and-dry procedure. The wards on the road into town are supposed to dissuade humans prone to causing problems from visiting. The witches can't shield fully against humans with chaotic tendencies, but I've heard the effect of the wards is a strong bad vibe, mixed with some stomach cramps. Enough to send most people home a day or so after arrival, if not right away. All an attempt to provide mythics a relatively safe area while still allowing connection with the human world. Michael Dryer, as the guy's ID proclaims him to be, should've gotten the runs before Folk Haven even came into view.

But it seems the wards are failing.

Instead, he ended up at the bar, harassing a woman who'd probably accidentally sung in public, prompting Moira to step in because the selkie is incapable of letting a mythic—not even one of her constituents—suffer.

Gods, the way she took the human down with barely any effort was one of the hottest things I'd ever seen. If I hadn't already been on the verge of coming from the sensation of her pussy clenching my fingers, that would've gotten me there.

One more reason to be pissed at the ignorant asshole causing mayhem in our town.

I slide into my car, slamming the door shut and revving the engine. For a moment, I let my anger claim control and punch the steering wheel. Just once. Then, I suck in a breath through my nose.

She was mine, and then she wasn't. She was pushing my fingers inside her, and then she was pushing me away.

I'm not mad at Moira. I'm pissed at the circumstance. The events that sparked discomfort in her. A doubt.

I have enough of my own trying to tell me Moira isn't for me.

But, gods, how can we not be right?

"Tomorrow," I chide myself, forcing my foot to carefully lighten up on the gas so I don't speed through the small-town roads on my way to Town Hall. "Moira tomorrow. Asshole tonight."

The lights are always on at Town Hall, mainly because it's the police department. Usually, the doors are locked after hours, but I push through them now and reason Samantha didn't have time to lock up while juggling a perp. I find the police chief typing on the computer at her desk. In the back corner of the office sits Folk Haven's single jail cell. At least, the only official one. The guy paces in the eight-by-eight space, spitting curses at the mermaid.

"You just fucking wait until my father hears about this!"

Samantha meets my eyes and rolls hers. But I can tell from the tension in her shoulders that no matter how annoyingly pompous the jerk is, he's also dangerous.

"What do you have?" I lean over her shoulder to peer at the screen, keeping my voice low so we can converse without the drunk man overhearing.

The Folk Haven Police don't always consult with The Council, but in a situation like this, decisions will need to be made that could affect us all.

"You're right about him being an out-of-towner. He's from Atlanta. Social posts say he came here to fish." She flips through multiple browser windows. "Looks like his dad is CEO of a pharmaceuticals company. Big money. Could be a problem." Samantha drags fingers through her short blonde hair in an agitated gesture.

Fuck, she's right.

The most crime Folk Haven normally sees is speeding tickets. Maybe the occasional shoplifting. Problems between mythics are usually handled by the creatures themselves or their council representative, or The Council sometimes steps in, acting as a unit.

Issues with out-of-towners are rare because of the wards.

"My dad will buy this piece-of-shit town. Then, he'll demolish everything and build a sweet-ass resort. Just you fucking watch." The guy burps at the end of his threat, and I clench my jaw until I hear bones creak.

Entitled prick.

"And the second I get out of here, I'm gonna find that bitch—"

I'm across the room in a breath, lunging at the bars. The guy stumbles back.

"Who the fuck are you?" His watery blue eyes widen at the first hint of discomfort.

"Someone whose woman you shouldn't have threatened," I hiss, letting all the menace of my beast flow into my voice as I make unblinking eye contact with the human through the bars.

He flinches and ducks his head, instinctively aware that he's dealing with a predator. No gentle, relaxing aura of power for him.

But no matter how cowed he is in the moment, it won't last.

I stalk back to Samantha's desk, where she watches me, trying to school the shock off her face, and I belatedly realize what the mermaid just heard. Me claiming Moira MacNamara as mine.

I jerk my chin toward the other side of the room, and Samantha rises from her desk and joins me, where we can have a conversation out of earshot.

"If you could forget—"

"Already forgotten. I'm not a gossip." She crosses her heart, and I give a tight smile in thanks.

"Obviously, regulation 34 applies in this case." I redirect the topic of conversation, bringing up the rule stating any non-resident human threatening a mythic is forever barred from entering Folk Haven. Of course, that can't be stated out loud to the man without explaining he was harassing a mythical creature.

That's not information he has any right to.

"We could try using one of the *Footloose* rules, but I get the feeling he's the type to hold a grudge." Samantha rests her hands on her hips, glaring at the ground as she labors to find another solution to this mess.

The occasional problem maker Folk Haven gets every few years or so is banished from town, citing what some past officer named a *Footloose* rule—aka some odd law, like *dancing is illegal in town limits*. A weird enough thing that has the person not wanting to bother with our backward settlement, a thought driven home by the wards. A couple of decades ago, someone made an official leather-bound book with a whole list of them.

But with the wards weak enough to let someone like Michael Dryer in, a silly law won't keep him out.

"Let me think on it," I mutter. "If I can't come up with a solution, I'll call everyone." Everyone meaning Mayor Nightson and the rest of The Council.

Samantha offers a nod and heads back to her desk. I stalk out to the main hall, needing space and quiet to think.

There must be a way to fix this.

If I don't find one, then Moira will find out how big this mess is, and I can easily see her blaming herself. That's something I've noticed about my selkie. She piles responsibility onto her shoulders. And I don't think she'll stop even if the weight threatens to crush her.

I have a theory for the failed protection spells, but I pray to the gods I'm wrong. If I'm not, then that means the twisted magic of plot 236 is what weakened the wards. Which means Moira putting off the cleansing might have left the town vulnerable.

I don't hold the hesitation against her anymore. Moira has a reason for why that land needs to be preserved. Just because I don't know what the reason is, it doesn't mean it's not important. The selkie's unwillingness to share simply means she doesn't trust me enough.

Which is my fault.

So, right now, I'm going to fix this mess for Folk Haven and for Moira. Then, I'm going to prove to my selkie that I'm worth trusting. But as I stand in the middle of the echoing space that makes up the entryway of Folk Haven's Town Hall, my brain is as void of ideas as the room.

"Damn it," I mutter, glaring at the marble under my feet.

"Heard you arrested someone."

I jump back at the sound of the voice, which came far closer than someone should've gotten without me hearing. The younger Shelly witch stands to my left, her hands tucked into the pockets of worn overalls, her black cat she claims is a cursed man sitting at her feet.

"What are you doing here?" When a growl coats my question, I try to calm myself further. "And how'd you get in?"

Amethyst points over her shoulder. "The front door was unlocked. Sorry if I scared you. I like to get close to woodland creatures, and they run away if you're too loud. I learned to be quiet." The young witch glances between me and the door to the police station, her gaze more focused than in The Council meeting. "The man you arrested, he's in there?"

"I can't discuss information like that with a civilian." Sighing, I press my fingers against my aching head, in no mood to deal with a curious onlooker.

"I don't need the details. The bartender already told me why he was arrested." She twiddles her fingers with the ends of her copper-colored braids, the pigtail style making her appear almost childlike, though I could swear she is at least mid-twenties. "As a potential citizen of Folk Haven, I want to know how these cases are handled. For safety's sake."

Fair point, though the distraction grates on my nerves. Maybe I can answer a few quick queries and get her to leave.

"As a potential threat to mythical citizens, he will be removed from Folk Haven tomorrow and forbidden to return." I use my official council member voice, hoping it lends authority to the proclamation.

"What if he comes back?"

Damn it. "He'll be arrested."

"And removed again. And then he'll come back. Or he'll send someone else. How do you plan to get him to stay away?"

I open my mouth, hoping a satisfactory answer will come

out. But nothing does. This is the question that has me out here, pacing the halls.

After my silence stretches, the witch reclaims the conversation. "When we arrived, crossed the border into Folk Haven, Morgana and I felt the wards. They're weak. Which is understandable for a place this large. Wards were meant for rooms or homes. Not towns." Amethyst steps forward, holding my eyes with her intensely green ones. "I am the solution."

The statement rings through the hall, raising chills on the back of my neck. I realize then that my reaction isn't only to her proclamation. My nerve endings buzz from the press of her power.

Not because Amethyst is working a spell on me. Instead, she's pulling back the curtain enough for me to see how easily she could.

"What can you do?" *Whatever it is, we need her on our side.*

"I can help. He'll never want to come back."

Witches have a whole spectrum of abilities based off their bloodlines and training. Her help could mean almost anything. My mother's version of help would most likely involve slipping him a fast-working poison, coaxed from one of the carefully cultivated blooms in her deadly garden.

"He can't go missing or be injured." But I wouldn't mind after all the times he's called Moira a bitch.

"I'll leave him unharmed." Amethyst twists a ring on her finger, the silver band holding a small amber stone. The simple piece of jewelry almost too much decoration for her casual appearance.

No matter how homespun her style, I won't be fooled into thinking she's offering charity.

"How much?"

Witches never work for free. My mother taught me that.

"Consider this a demonstration." Amethyst shrugs. "If you

like what you see, then The Council already knows what my sister and I want. That is the payment for any future services."

It's a mark of how desperate I am that I agree, praying to the gods that this isn't a mistake. As I lead Amethyst into the police station, Samantha rises from her chair, confusion wrinkling her face. The mermaid jumps back when the black cat leaps onto her desk.

"What's going on?"

"Hi, Samantha," Amethyst murmurs instead of explaining as she heads toward the cell.

The police chief and I follow.

A few steps from the bars, the witch pauses and turns, pointing a finger at me. "You can only share this with the mayor and The Council." Her finger drifts over to Samantha. "You can tell no one."

Amethyst doesn't wait for our responses, which leads me to believe she doesn't think our agreement is necessary.

Then, the young witch wraps her hands around the bars.

"Wait—" Samantha moves just as the asshole lunges forward and grabs at the young woman, a hungry gleam in his eye.

"Hello," Amethyst says in a low, smooth-as-butter-tone, and his face goes slack.

That's when I realize he doesn't have ahold of her. Amethyst was the one to grab his wrists, and she holds them tight now, a mysterious red powder coating her palms.

The police chief pauses her rescue attempt, arms still outstretched. "Are you okay?"

The witch nods, not taking her eyes off the human. "Tell me your name."

"Michael Fredrick Dryer." The prisoner speaks with a robotic tone, the lack of animation eerie.

"Michael, you've had a bad time in Folk Haven. You want to leave as soon as possible." Her tone has a hypnotic quality.

"I do," he says.

"If your family finds out what happened here, they won't want to know you anymore."

"They won't want to know me," Michael agrees.

Chills skitter over my skin, but I'm distracted from the display by the sounds of voices out in the hall. Loud, angry ones. Samantha and I share a look.

"I'll go check it out," I offer.

She nods.

Jogging into the main hall, I close the police station door behind me and curse myself for not asking Samantha to lock the front door after Amethyst revealed it was still open.

The other assholes from the bar stride toward me, rage and privilege a noxious, thick cloud around them.

"Where is he?" one spits.

Then, they all start shouting, demanding to see their friend. I plant myself in front of the entrance to the precinct, giving the witch time to work.

"You can come see him in the morning," I say over their raised voices, my deep tone booming.

Some step back, but one sneers and tries to shove past. His human strength barely bothers me, and I stand, unmovable, the next best thing to a brick wall. The guy stumbles away, scowling through his confusion.

"Fuck this. I'm calling a lawyer." He pulls out his cell.

Gods, more outsiders coming to this town will only make things worse.

Just as I'm considering snatching the device from his hands and snapping it in half, Samantha opens the door behind me.

"What's going on?" the police chief asks.

"We want to see ..." The man starts off bellowing but then must notice the hand she has rested on her holster. "We want to see our friend," he says at a normal volume.

Samantha grips my shoulder, guiding me to the side, and I

let her move me. "You can have five minutes, but he's staying overnight for being drunk and disorderly."

The men sulk into the room and then rush back to the cell. Amethyst doesn't have her hands on Michael anymore. Instead, she reclines in a chair in the opposite corner of the room, her cat by her side. The animal's stare tracks the humans with an eerie focus.

"Man, we're gonna get you out of here." One of the asshole's friends bangs on the iron bars, like he can Hulk his way through them.

That might be a fun failure to watch.

"I'll call your dad—" another starts.

"No!" Michael waves his hands to shut up his helpful posse. "Don't call him. He'll cut me off if he finds out about this. If I stay overnight, I'm not getting charged." His voice is noticeably soberer, which has me glancing at Amethyst.

She offers a distracted smile and then stares at the ceiling.

"Tomorrow morning, I'm getting out of here, and then I want to leave this shitty little town in the dust. Got it? Don't call anyone. Just come pick me up tomorrow."

They go back and forth for a bit, but eventually, the group agrees not to contact lawyers or parents. They file out, muttering curses as they go. Michael lies on the bench, and by all accounts, he passes out.

Samantha and I stare at Amethyst, neither of us knowing exactly what to say.

Thank you.

Holy shit, did you fry his brain?

How often do you use this power?

The witch stands slowly, moving as if her body aches like a runner's after a long marathon, and though she wears a pleasant expression on her face, dark circles pool under her eyes.

"Don't freak out." Amethyst holds up her hands, now free of

red powder. "My focus is persuasion. And I'm good. But I avoid using this unless I need to protect myself or something I care about." She straightens further, a grimace marring her freckled face. "I'd care a whole lot more about Folk Haven if my sister's library was here."

"I thought you both wanted it," I say, thinking back on the presentation they gave to The Council.

Morgana spoke more, but we all believed the library was a joint venture.

Amethyst tilts her head from side to side, spine cracking with the movement. "She wants it. I want her to have what she wants. Plus, it's a good idea." The witch offers a halfhearted salute and shuffles toward the exit. "I'll see you around."

After she steps through the door, the cat follows, pausing at the threshold. The creature turns intelligent eyes on the two of us, lets out a menacing growl, and then continues on his way.

"Well, that's a game changer." The police chief stares at the slumbering prisoner.

I'm distracted, stuck on the selfless nature of Amethyst's offer. And how her willingness to help reminds me of a certain selkie. "You'll keep her powers to yourself?" I ask.

The mermaid snorts. "After that display? She looks innocent, but that witch is a force to be reckoned with. As long as she's not going around, enchanting the people of Folk Haven, she can keep her secrets."

I nod and make my own exit, planning to set up a call with the other council members before our next meeting. They all need to know the new offer on the table. But now that the harasser is taken care of, I have other priorities. Which is why when I retrieve my phone from my pocket, I text the only council member I'm actually interested in seeing.

A smirk curls my lips when I finish my message. But the satisfaction dissolves when I realize I have a missed call from one of my constituents. He left a voice mail, and I'm reluctant to listen, wanting to put my responsibilities off until morning.

But this monster is not one to be ignored.

"Oh, glorious Council Member Abadi." The voice mocks my title with a flippant tone. "If you would be so gracious as to visit my abode, I have something to show you. Hurry, before I lose it." A pause. "Or kill it."

I mutter a string of curses as I jog to my car.

25

———

SEV

Do you plan on com—

Before I can finish my text, the creature in my arms flails in a wild attempt to get free. It fails, but one of its sharp limbs strikes my phone, sending the device flying from my hand to land with a resolute crack on the hardwood floor.

This night keeps taking unpredictable turns.

When I went for a midnight swim in Lake Galen, I had little hope of finding the quarry I'd been seeking for weeks. But here I am, target located and in my hold. Unfortunately, I'm still nude from my swim, and I'm not liking the chances of my testicles coming out unscathed from this encounter. Not when my enemy has inch-long claws.

"Well, that was ungentlemanly of you." No longer struggling to tap out a message, I put my entire focus on restraining my captive. "You really are quite ugly. And that is coming from me. Many have claimed I am a nightmare in my other form. I have sent entire villages fleeing in fear."

The thing screeches, although I'm not sure how it retains

177

vocal cords. The being seems fashioned from bones with only the barest paper flesh covering its form. No muscles or fat. Just angles and menace.

"I don't suppose you plan to cover the cost of my replacement phone? Not that I need your assistance. I am impressively wealthy."

The creature lets out another wail, unwilling or unable to form words through the sharp, long teeth protruding from its mouth.

I make a note to myself to order a new phone. The devices are quite useful. Despite the general destruction humans have enacted over the millennia, the mortals have crafted a collection of wonderful inventions. Handheld computers. The internet. Battery-operated toothbrushes.

The sound of expensive tires drifts to me over the clicking of my captive's jaw.

So, he did come.

Moving farther into my ornate dining room, I drag my find with me, keeping it subdued all the while. At least, attempting to. Spindly, long legs kick out, overturning a ten-thousand-dollar vase. The price plummets when the porcelain hits the ground, shattering easier than my phone screen.

I wrap my arms tighter around the creature, considering if I should simply snap its legs.

"Sev?" A shiver goes through my body as my wards alert me to the new arrival. "I got your message. Are you all right?"

Just as I open my mouth to respond, the creature in my arms throws back what approximates as an elbow, catching me just below the ribs. A shout born more of surprise than pain coughs out, and I work to adjust my grip again.

The feel of eyes on me has me glancing to the doorway, and I spy Levi Abadi. The monster's eyes widen.

"Oh good. You've arrived." I manage a casual tone, even as the bony creature thrashes in my grip. "I found your thief. No need to thank me. Not at the moment anyway. However, I might ask you to assist in the restraining. For not having muscle, the bastard is surprisingly strong."

In the man's favor, he doesn't hesitate. Levi circles my dining table and immediately adds his strong hold to mine. Which finally gives me the opportunity to let go.

"Where are you going?" Levi shouts while avoiding snapping teeth.

"To get a solution." I stroll through a doorway, aiming for the stairs.

Levi should be grateful I'm not immediately shoving him and my discovery out the door. I found The Council's thief for them. He should be overjoyed. *I'm* certainly happy to know the governing body of Folk Haven no longer has a reason to turn their noses toward my business.

They all thought I was behind the attempted robbery of Calder MacNamara's pelt. The idea is insulting.

I would never have my name attached to such shoddy work. If I wanted a selkie skin, no one would be able to stop me. Maybe one day, I'll decide to claim one, but run-of-the-mill mythical items hold no appeal for me.

The plush rug of my bedroom caresses my bare feet as I stroll to my closet and select a silken crimson robe. I don't go around displaying my gods-blessed body for free.

Once my magnificent member is tucked behind the fabric, I push aside shelving on hidden tracks and press my palm against a lock screen. A door made of solid steel swings open. Automatic lights gently illuminate the hidden room, spotlights shining down on the pedestals. Normally, I take my time to admire my many treasures. But Levi, while maintaining a political power greater than mine, has only a fraction of my physical strength. He's never bested me in a wrestling match, which we partake in on a monthly basis. No doubt the creature will break free of his hold if I take too long.

And then I would have a known thief in my house.

I won't stand for the competition or the insult of those twig fingers grasping at my precious collection.

"Where did I put you? Oh, yes." Stepping around a display with a set of golden cuffs, I find the small bird carving. A crane. The wooden image warms in my hand as I hold it close. I slip it into my robe pocket as I shut the treasure room door and make my way back to the dining room.

Levi is struggling as much as I expected, his normally golden skin flushing red.

"Hold it," I remind him.

"I am!"

"Here we are." When I present the crane, displaying the figurine so the council member can clearly see the object of power, I'm briefly transported back to the moment I finally located the artifact. Four years of scouring the waters surrounding Xisha Islands, all to get my hands on this. "Do you know how many sunken ships I had to search through to find this?" The weight of the water crushing at times. "You need to be extremely careful in those situations. The current, you see, can pull away anything you find if you don't keep a proper hold."

"I don't need a treasure-hunting lesson." Levi grunts as the creature lands a hit. "Just use whatever your toy is to calm this guy down."

Toy. If he only knew.

I lunge forward, pressing the crane against the papery skin of the captive, and shout a word in a language not used for close to a millennium. Power tears out of me through the arti-fact, demanding payment for use. A shock wave rattles my house, but the magic only affects the thing in Levi's arms.

Which we quickly discover is not a living creature when a shower of starched white bones falls to the floor. The pieces are all that's left of the captive.

"What happened?" Levi stares around the room, searching for the creature.

Holding up the carving, I offer a wry grin. "I commanded the creepy-crawly to take its true form. It would seem that our failed thief was nothing more than fish bones." Immediately, I have my suspicions of what bound the thing to a semblance of life. "A spell." I pluck up a bone and sniff. "The Council was wrong to point fingers our way. This is not the work of monsters. Could be a witch. More likely a sorcerer. I found the thief near the grave."

"The grave?" Levi's discomfort rings in his deep voice.

"*His* grave. *Le Collectionneur*." Normally, I wouldn't have swum near the location, but I had a sense I would find my prey there. "Never met the piece of scum. I was deep in the Amazon when he built his little zoo."

I exchange my bone for a larger one and drag my tongue across the surface.

A metallic taste teases my senses.

"What are you doing?" The council member's face takes on a greenish tinge.

"Sorcerer spells taste like copper," I explain. "I detect a note. It's faint. Could be because it was an old creation, made by *him*, only recently awakened. Or"—I gesture with the carved talisman, the crimson sleeve of my robe billowing with the grand wave—"this erased most traces of the spell."

Levi sinks into one of the chairs at my table. "What is that anyway?"

"A tool of The Winged One."

And because I'm suddenly feeling generous, I relate the story behind the crane. A tale of a human musician loved by a dragon and how her devotion and strength saved the mythic with the assistance of a god.

"Would've thought you preferred tragedies," Levi mutters when I end on their happily ever after.

A sharp laugh cuts at my throat. "I've lived over two hundred years on this hellscape humans have made of their home. The whole world is a tragedy. Those stories are old and common."

"So, you're a do-gooder now?"

Is that hope in his voice?

"Hardly." I have no qualms of being the villain in another's story to achieve my own happiness. "But do you not wonder, my monster brethren, if we might get an impossible love like the musician and her dragon? Are we—mutated creations the gods never planned—allowed mates? In all my years, all my travels, my partner has never appeared to me."

And because I have lived more than two centuries, I easily conceal the sharp ache in my chest that accompanies that confession.

Levi is not so skilled, pain tracing deep lines in his face.

"You want it, too, don't you?" I scoop up a handful of fish bones and let them trickle through my fingers like water. "That's why I thought you would like the story. The Winged One allowed the dragon to regain his human form decades before he should have been able to. The tale shows nothing is immutable." One bone remains in my grasp. *I'll keep this one.* "The gods change their minds."

Suddenly, I need to be alone. Levi's presence, while less irritating than most, scrapes at my skin.

"This has been grand, my liege." I affect a mocking bow and straighten with all my emotions hidden behind stone features. "Now, kindly fuck off."

As I exit the room, I train my ears to track his movements. Once I'm in my bedroom, both sound and my wards inform me he's left. I speak the spell to fully activate my protections, and tension eases from my body to know I am alone.

Then, an ache like sorrow fills my gut. I reenter my treasure chamber, replacing the crane carving before strolling farther into the room. The area is large, the ceiling extending two stories with glass skylights that illuminate my collection during the day. The panes have heavy warding as well.

Reaching the end of the middle aisle, I come to the ornate chairs I commissioned from Dimitri Novac, a dragon who once lived in Folk Haven. The seats match perfectly, formed from iron, with thorny metal vines acting as decoration, linking the two together. With a flourish of my robe, I settle in the one on the left and gaze out at my many treasures, drawing comfort in the vast number before me.

I don't glance to the side. As long as my eyes stare straight ahead, I can pretend I've found the one treasure I crave above all.

My mate.

26

MOIRA

LEVI: If you don't come to the spa, you still owe me.

Days later, and the high-handed nature of the text still bothers me. But I'm here, in the newly paved parking lot of Haven's Relaxation.

What if I get too close to Levi and beg him to stick his hand up my skirt again?

The fear is ridiculous. And I wore pants.

Still, I brace myself as I walk through the automatic doors, entering the monster's domain and expecting an immediate sexy ambush. Not that he'll jump out at me, naked. But he might.

I've only seen Levi's dick in monster form, and that was glorious. Is it just as wonderful when he's a man?

This is bad. My mind is already undressing him. I should turn around and leave.

"Moira!"

I start at the sound of my name but breathe a sigh of relief when I realize the tone was too high and friendly to be Levi.

Behind the front desk stands Titan, former captain of the Folk Haven High debate club, which I know because I spend Thursday afternoons during the school year as a volunteer moderator.

"Titan!" I share their grin as I stroll up to the prominent wood desk the monster is posted at. "I didn't know you worked here."

They nod, and my eyes can't help admiring the tight electric-blue curls that contrast beautifully with their dark skin. Anyone unaware of Titan's parentage would assume the teen uses dye to manage the vibrant color. But with a merman father and forest sprite mother, Titan's hair has always grown blue from some strange twist of mythical genes.

They almost certainly have other abilities, but I've erred on the side of politeness and never asked. Not like when I drunkenly demanded Levi shift into his other form for me.

I keep my mind from entering a guilty spiral at that memory by asking Titan about their post-graduation plans.

"I'm going to Ramla. Full ride is hard to pass up. Plus, Mr. Abadi hired me for this cushy gig and said we can adjust my shifts to fit my classes come fall. Isn't he great?" The monster's eyes shine with hero worship for my fellow council member and the man I struggle to not fantasize about on an hourly basis.

"Oh yeah. So great." *Don't imagine him shirtless.* "Still interested in opening that flower shop?"

While some teenagers doodled their crush's name in hearts, Titan was busier, sketching out the logo for their dream business. Apparently, their mother has a gods-blessed garden. I bet the place is a lot more appealing than Violetta's dangerous nursery.

"That's the plan. I'm studying business, minor in marketing. Mr. Abadi said he could mentor me for some real-world experience."

Bubbles of happiness fill my chest to hear this young town member already planning on becoming an integral part of Folk Haven. A lot of the students in the debate club talked about going to school in other states. Getting away. I understand the impulse to leave—how a place you've lived in your whole life can become stifling. But I also know we're building something important here. A safe place that needs to last for generations.

Kids like Titan are this town's future.

"Well, you can never have too many mentors. You still have my number. Call me anytime you want to get coffee. And make sure to stop by the new bookstore Neri Onassis is opening."

Titan smirks. "Come on. You think I haven't already reserved a permanent spot in that bookshop? That's going to be my second home." We share a grin as they hand over a clipboard. "Mr. Abadi let me know you'd be one of our preview visitors. You're going to need to sign these liability forms and let us know if you have any medical issues that our employees should be aware of while seeing to all your relaxation needs." The monster's voice stays friendly but takes on a professional tone that I can't help feeling proud of. "The last sheet is our list of services. You just check off the ones you want." They lean forward a touch. "The starred ones are the treatments Mr. Abadi recommended for you specifically."

My intestines twist into a riot of excitement and annoyance.

"Thank you." I stroll to the nearby seating area and settle on a simple yet comfortable padded bench.

The whole waiting room looks just as I described. Large glass windows display a beautiful view of Lake Galen. Dark wooden beams span the high ceiling, contrasting nicely with light-colored walls that hold simple art prints. Breathing seems easier in the open, serene space. The floor beneath my heels is textured wood with an occasional plush rug to break up the expanse and give a touch of warmth to a room that could become cold.

Levi worked magic here.

Reading through the forms, I come to the sheet with services listed. A petty part of me wants to completely ignore his little stars and pick all the opposite services. But when I see *salt bath soak* listed, I give up on that maneuver.

Soon after I return the clipboard to Titan, another mythic approaches, leading me deeper into Levi's brainchild.

Three hours later, I've been scrubbed, massaged, covered in fancy goos, and made into a puddle of goo myself that had to be poured into this delicious private salt bath. Behind me, a frosted glass door leads back to the rest of the spa. In front of me, a window shows off a glittering view of Lake Galen. Somehow better than the one in the reception area. As I gaze out over the calm waters, I let the ocean-like bath caress my skin and wish my mind could find the same state of relaxation as my body.

Part of my attention replays how amazing this spa is. The services are wonderful, the staff—many of whom I know—are friendly and skilled, and the entire atmosphere demands visitors forget all their worries.

But I couldn't let go of my stress when around every corner, I expected Levi to appear.

When he didn't, I tried to convince myself the sinking sensation in my gut was satisfaction. Not disappointment.

I can't figure out what to do about the monster. He makes me forget myself. My responsibilities. Urges me to be selfish.

I never should've stayed the night at the ocean. It was irresponsible. And, gods, when was the last time I brought up my great-grandaunt's pelt? I know the retrieval was never a task my family demanded of me, but I'm sure they would if they knew I had a chance to get it back.

Self-centered. The voice in my head sounds different than my own with a tinge of Scottish drawl.

I'm a traitor. More interested in the pleasure of Levi's touch than fulfilling my duties to this town and my family.

"Relaxed yet?" The deep voice sounds so loud in the previously quiet room that I yelp and splash to the other side of the small pool before realizing who the new arrival is.

Levi Abadi.

27

———

MOIRA

LUST ROARS through my body when I drag my gaze over Levi's muscular form as he leans his shoulder against the tiled wall. Damn him for looking so handsome in his perfectly tailored slacks and button-down. The monster appears ready to attend a council meeting while I'm sitting in what's essentially a large soup pot, wearing a bikini. Good thing I decided against soaking in the nude.

Was that a good choice though?

Smoothing all reaction off my face, I answer as if we were both dressed in business casual. "Who can relax when our town's wards are failing and there are sorcerer creatures stealing selkie skins?"

Levi's smooth golden skin wrinkles with a grimace. "That's a morbid perspective." He tucks his hands in the pockets of his perfectly ironed slacks. "I thought our call ended on a productive note, if not necessarily a positive one."

The day after the bar incident, The Council had an impromptu conference call. Apparently, the night hadn't ended when I went home to sort out my messy emotions. Levi was left to deal with a potential shitshow. First, he'd had to follow through with the drunken human. Although, needing to tie up that loose end might have been a blessing in disguise now that we have Amethyst offering her persuasion skills to help the town. But her powers won't fix the wards. Still, Selena assured us that all spells have expiration dates, and the two protection witches living in Folk Haven should be able to address the issue. As long as they are properly compensated, of course.

There goes The Council's portion of the Gauntlet profits.

The biggest shock of the call came last.

"A few months back, Council Member MacNamara brought a threat to our attention. An unknown creature that attempted to steal her brother's selkie skin," Levi said, and I almost snapped my phone in half, my body going so rigid at his words. *"One of mine found and caught it. I saw the creature with my own eyes."*

"You trapped the monster?" Juan's demand rolled through the line, voicing a hope I shared.

"The thing was not a monster." Levi's voice hardened on the response. *"It was a spell. Animated bones. The magic broke while we were attempting to restrain the creation. I'm unfamiliar with spell work, but the monster who captured the being claimed it was the work of sorcery. I have the bones still. Council Member Evermore, if you could—"*

"You dare suggest I work with that twisted magic?" Selena hissed.

"No." I could hear the bite and repressed growl in Levi's voice. *"I'm merely offering the evidence to be examined by the one among us most knowledgeable in magic."*

"Who found the thing?" Georgiana asked.

There was a pause, and then with reluctance coloring his answer, Levi spoke the name. "Sev."

Sev. A long-lived monster we were all aware of but did not deal with. I'd met the man once when I sold him a plot of land. He was ... odd. His manner was playful one moment, cold the next. He seemed from a different century, which I guessed he was. I'd never been able to sense another mythic's abilities, but power had practically spilled off Sev's shoulders like a regal cape.

Hearing that Sev had captured our mystery beast gave me pause. From the silence on the phone line, I wasn't the only one.

"Look," Levi pressed on, "I would have brought it to you all whole if I could. The best I can offer are the bones, which Sev claims"—he cleared his throat—"taste of sorcery."

"I'll examine them," Selena agreed.

A day later, she confirmed that a spell had been worked on them, but there was no indication of the age of the spell.

It could have been cast a few months ago. Or a few decades.

Guilt pinched at me when she explained a pocket of evil magic could reanimate dormant spells. In other words, plot 236 might have been the reason a creature had almost stolen my brother's selkie pelt.

Am I any different than the leviathan?

I scowl at my salt bath. Yes, I *am* different. I never would have let the tainted magic persist if I had known it would bring thieves back to life.

"You know, I could have gotten a lot of work done today." I try to sound unaffected, annoyed even, as I direct the subject away from the ill effects of my stubbornness. *So what if I made sure to schedule all my appointments on other days and stayed a few hours later last evening to finish up my paperwork early?*

Levi moves to crouch at the edge of the pool, grinning as I glare at him. "You did get a lot of work done." He reaches a finger into the pool, as if testing the temperature. "You worked on yourself."

"I don't need to work on myself," I growl, not liking the insinuation that he finds me lacking.

"I beg to differ." His dark eyes meet mine, a hint of hunger in his gaze. "You're a novice at self-care."

A response refuses to appear when I open my mouth, so I snap my lips shut.

Levi is the opposite of Hamish, and the realization hits me like an ocean wave to the gut. The selkie spent half our relationship telling me I was being selfish by spending too much time at my job and the other half telling me I was too eager and demanding in the bedroom.

But here's this monster, encouraging me to just ... take care of myself.

I don't know how to process the discovery, which is probably why my maturity level takes a dive. When Levi's deliciously plump lips curl in a smirk, I can't help what my body does. With a sweep of my arm, I send a wave of salt water his way, drenching the monster in his nice clothes.

"Oops." A flush heats my cheeks as I bite the corner of my mouth.

What will he do?

Levi blinks, water droplets hanging from his lashes. Then, he barks out a laugh, and a tension in my chest eases. With a few quick movements, he shucks off his shoes and socks, setting them to the side, and then rolls up the legs of his pants to his knees. Next thing I know, he's dipping his feet in my bath.

And I don't mind.

Floating across the short expanse, I rest my arms on the lip of the pool and prop my chin on their pillow, gazing up at the damp monster.

"What's the verdict?" His gaze traces over my submerged body. He must see the way goose bumps form under his attention.

"All your staff members are monsters." Hopefully, the subject will distract him from staring.

Levi nods. "You noticed."

About the time I sat down for my facial, I realized the connection between the familiar faces.

He tilts a brow. "I see that as a good thing."

I agree. "They're all wonderful. The place is a paradise. Everyone who comes will leave cleansed from head to toe. Inside and out." I sigh and push past my pride. "I'm sorry for putting your business at risk by pushing for a witch cleansing." My jaw threatens to lock up, but I force out the next words. "The move was selfish."

Levi makes a noncommittal noise as he stares out at the lake. "You know, I don't think it was."

My body tenses, threatening to undo all the hard work of his staff.

Levi keeps talking, not noticing or ignoring my reaction. "I don't think you do many things for yourself, Moira MacNamara." He offers me a teasing smile. "Which is why I'm glad you came today. Tell me, what was your favorite part? Other than the salt bath, of course." He leans down and flicks a playful splash of water at me that I easily dodge.

Letting myself float to the middle of the tub, I give myself a few feet of distance to organize my thoughts. "The honey body wrap was interesting. I'll have to tell Heath about that. He'll either immediately sign up for one or disparage you for using the honey on bodies instead of baked goods."

The bear shifter who co-owns Coffee & Claws places pastries at the same level of deities.

"And the manicure was nice." I hold up my perfectly shaped nails, now coated in a shimmering aqua green. The staff recommended I get the manicure last, but I wanted to end this day in a big pool of salt water. And the customer is always right. "Never had one before."

Levi's eyes track my hands. "Lovely. And what color did you get for your toes?"

I scoff. "Sorry, but I drew the line at pampering my feet. That's just too far."

"What?" Levi's tone draws my attention to his shocked face. "She of the four-inch heels doesn't see a reason to take care of her feet?"

"I take care of them!" I protest. "I wash them."

He groans and then stands. "Wait here."

Like I planned on getting out of this tub before my entire body is a prune?

The monster returns in a matter of minutes, clutching a small bottle.

"Are you going to paint my toes?" The disbelief rings through the humid tiled room.

Levi resumes his seat on the edge of the pool and waves me closer. When I don't move, he huffs out a breath. "No, I'm not going to paint them. I'm going to massage them. Come here."

Reluctantly, I encourage the water to drift me toward him. My power to manipulate the liquid around me is minuscule, but occasionally, I find a use for the ability. "They worked on my feet during the full-body massage." Although I'd told them not to bother.

Levi rolls up his sleeves instead of responding.

"I don't want to get out of the water," I complain, knowing I sound like a pouty child.

His smirk agrees. "You don't have to. I assume a selkie can keep herself afloat if she wants."

"Of course." Slightly offended he had to ask.

"Then, float in front of me and give me your foot."

I roll my eyes at the demand in his tone but comply in the end, coaxing the water to hold me level. I bite my lip, worried I'll giggle at what I'm sure will be a torturously ticklish touch. But then a set of strong fingers grips my sole, and two thumbs dig deep into my heel, eradicating a knot I tried not to acknowledge.

I moan. Embarrassingly loud and overtly sexual. And I don't care.

With my head tilted back, water presses against my ears, and I only hear the faint trace of Levi's chuckle. But I don't care about that either. He can laugh at me all he wants if his talented fingers keep moving. Pressing. Digging in deeper.

Gods, has an orgasm ever come from a foot massage?

Because my nose is still above the surface, I catch a familiar scent. Wildly refreshing and invigorating.

"Is that eucalyptus?"

I pop my head out of the water, which causes my butt to sink. A quick prod with my powers keeps me afloat while I watch Levi pour out droplets from the small bottle onto his palms. When he rubs his hands together, the scent grows strong, and I refuse to acknowledge how much it looks like he's applying lube.

The monster pauses. "You said you liked it. At the B & B."

"I did. I do." I can't believe he remembers that randomly blurted comment.

"Am I okay to continue?" His brows rise, hands held up.

Nodding, I lie back in the water. Then, his touch comes, cool and slick and firm.

My concentration wavers, and I sink.

A second later, I come up spluttering, briefly forgetting that I can hold my breath underwater for hours.

Levi grimaces. "That bad?"

"What? No. I—I guess I relaxed too much." I stroke to the side of the pool. "I changed my mind. I'll get out for this." When I climb out of the water, rivers stream off me, puddling on the floor, including around the butt of the monster's pants. "People are going to think you peed yourself." I keep the evil joy off my face as I settle on the tiles beside him and place my foot in his lap, wetting his crotch too.

"I'm the boss. They'll keep their opinions to themselves."

He grins as he tracks a hungry gaze over my body, attention catching on my hard nipples pressing against the damp material of my suit.

But he doesn't make a move. Just goes back to the ecstasy-inducing foot massage.

He digs his knuckles into my arches. Stretches each one of my toes. Caresses the delicate muscles of my ankles.

"Where did you learn how to do this?" My question comes breathy, and I try to keep from imagining him sliding his hands up my calves, then my thighs, then into me.

"There are schools for massage therapy. I figured with my calming power, I'm naturally set up to work in this industry."

Levi finds just the right spot, and I gasp and groan. We both ignore the growing tent in his pants.

"When I decided to open Haven's Relaxation, I offered to sponsor any monster who wanted to train to be a masseuse. Or esthetician. Also nail technician. That's how I came by most my staff."

The idea makes my heart clench. No wonder the monsters elected Levi as their council representative. He's constantly taking steps to give them opportunities in the mythical world where so-called "pure" mythics would pass them over.

Their exclusion is an issue The Council should be addressing. But most members would dismiss actions about antidiscrimination against monsters. No doubt Levi felt he had to make changes on his own.

The way he cares for his people only makes me want him more.

Selfishly maybe. But I'm having trouble talking myself out of getting closer to him. Of opening to the generous, caring mythic. I want to wrap myself in his strong, comforting aura. I want to share my secrets with him.

Could I? Would he believe me? Would he understand?

Grabbing on to the last thread of control I have, I retract my foot from his lap. "I need to go."

"Do you?" Levi asks, voice low as he stares down at his empty hands, fingers flexing, as if missing their grip on me.

"Are you free for lunch tomorrow?"

His head whips up, and I'd have to be obtuse not to see the hope in his eyes. "For you, yes."

Covering myself in the thick terry-cloth robe provided by the spa, I camouflage the shiver that runs through me at his words. There are questions that hang between us. I can't help thinking that I've misinterpreted his actions in some way.

Ever since Hamish, I can't find it in me to trust my instincts about romantic relationships. If I leave our communication up to subtle cues and words unsaid, I'll never be sure of what Levi feels for me. What he wants us to be.

If there's any hope, I need to find a way to be completely honest. To make myself vulnerable.

My battered heart cringes at the idea, but I don't let myself retreat. Not fully.

"Meet me next door at noon." Tying the belt with definitive movements, I commit to my decision. "I'll tell you why I worked to save plot 236."

28

———

MOIRA

LEVI IS PROMPT. More than. He shows up before me, leaning against the side of his car as I pull up the gravel drive to plot 236. The monster dressed for the heat in shorts and a V-neck, dark sunglasses shading his eyes.

Whether he's professional or casual or butt naked in sea monster form, sitting in a Jacuzzi tub, I want this man in all versions. But I'm selfish like that. The question is, can I be selfish without causing a mess around me?

Levi strolls toward me when I park the car. His steps are purposeful. Almost hungry. In a panic, I quickly hop out of my car, grab the picnic basket from the passenger seat, and shove it into his chest as a barrier.

"I packed lunch!" I announce in a tone that sounds like a soccer mom in charge of snack time. *Why do I always lose my cool, professional demeanor around this man?*

Then, Levi leans in to press a brief kiss to my cheek, the scent of him rolling over me like a fast-moving thunderstorm. "Thank you."

Oh, that's why.

But right now, I need to focus on my main purpose.

Being honest about the history I have with plot 236.

"Come on." Reaching down, I twine my fingers with his strong, warm ones, trying to ignore memories of all the talented skills his have.

I lead him to the end of the drive and then into the woods. The lack of sticky, twisted magic has me grinning wide. All that's left is the soft buzz of power I've always felt here.

I wonder ...

"Do you feel anything?" I glance at Levi, where he follows a step behind me, still connected through our linked hands. His brows dip, and I clarify. "Here. Do you feel any magic here?"

Glancing around, as if he might see glimmering swirls of it in the air, the monster finally shakes his head. "I think the cleansing spell worked."

"I know. I'm talking about something different. Like ... like a hum. Pleasant. Or not bad, I guess."

Levi's brows wrinkle in concentration, but eventually, he shakes his head, expression apologetic. "I'm sorry. I don't."

"That's okay." I sigh.

Over the years, I've brought each of my family members here and asked them. No one could sense it. Same with a few friends. I guess it was too much to hope that Levi would be an outlier.

"Let's keep going."

As we delve farther into the woods, birdsong and the buzz of insects surround us. The shade from the trees helps cut down on the heat of the day, but the humidity still clings to my skin. When I hear the far-off roar of a Jet Ski, I know we're approaching our destination, and I angle north. My fingers reach out to brush certain trees as we pass, and I say a silent hello to these old friends. They hold memories so strong that I can almost hear the decades-old laughter from them. These trunks were there. In one rotation of their inner rings lies the lightest imprint of that day.

At the brush of a cool breeze on my face, I hurry forward, tugging Levi along with me. "Here."

We step around a towering pine and approach one of the many small streams that feed Lake Galen. This one is more robust than most, widening to around eight feet after a heavy rain. Now, I could easily hop over the width, but I head downstream toward a massive flat rock that partially juts into the water, forcing the flow around its unyielding body.

The mass is plenty large enough for two people to sit, and the wind off the mountain-fed stream refreshes the air.

"Time for our picnic." I accept the basket from Levi, ignoring his curious gaze for the moment, hoping that at the end of this, he understands my actions. If he doesn't ... well then, he wouldn't be the first.

I pull an old blanket from the basket, spread the fabric out, and then unpack the food.

"I can't believe you made me lunch." The monster accepts the sandwich I hand him.

"Well, as much as I'd like to take credit, this is my dad's handiwork. He's the chef in the family." I kick off my shoes and settle cross-legged on the blanket, biting into my turkey and cheese. After I swallow, I ask, "Have you met him?"

Levi chews on his own mouthful, bobbing his head in a satisfied nod. He snags a bottle of water from the basket and takes a gulp before answering. "Crossed paths a few times. I've rented a boat from your family's business, and he was at the counter. Seems like a nice guy."

"Yeah, he's great." I debate on asking about his father, but I'm worried it'll turn into an argument, and then I'll be too pissed off to open up.

Sorry, Blair. I swear I won't let the issue of your pelt go.

"I lucked out with Mom and Dad." I work my way through

my sandwich as I talk. "Other than expecting me to watch over my brothers, they gave me a lot of freedom when I was a kid." Sentence, bite, swallow. Sentence, bite, swallow. "I rode over every inch of Folk Haven on my bike. But for some reason, this plot of land was my favorite."

Levi stays quiet, his entire focus on me as he eats.

"One day was different. I showed up here, to this rock"—I pat the stone at my side—"and someone was already sitting here." I brush the crumbs off my hands and lap and then lean back, letting the memory of that day consume my mind as I close my eyes. "She looked to be around my age. Maybe a few years older. I never asked her name, and she never asked mine. We were just two kids who stumbled across each other. For the rest of the day, we ran around the woods together, playing make-believe games, climbing trees, swimming in the lake."

Every moment stays crystal clear in my memory. The crunch of the leaves under our running feet, the happy shout of her voice, the splash of the water when we jumped into Galen, fully clothed. And while we played, there were other presences around us, as if a large group of children were gathered. But those were just ghosts at the edge of my vision. She was the solid one, remaining in my mind to this day. In my heart.

"When the sun started to set, we ended up back here, lying down so we could watch the sky change colors." The moment was peaceful. In the back of my mind, I knew I should go home, but I couldn't leave her. Not yet. "She told me her family owned this land. She asked me to watch over it when she went away. Keep it safe until she came back."

"Let me guess." Levi's wry voice tugs on my attention. "You made a blood vow?"

My lips curl, but I shake my head. "I likely would have if I'd known about them at the time. But no. I made a simple promise. We parted ways, and I never saw her again." I blink my eyes open, staring at the canopy above us. "She was a monster. She had these beautiful black wings. Like a siren but not quite. And at times, her eyes would go full white." Tilting my chin down, I meet Levi's intense stare. "The day was innocent for the most part. But there was something in our exchange that shook me to my core."

"For the most part?" he repeats the phrase I wish I hadn't let slip out.

Heaving a sigh, I stare over his shoulder, watching the sparkle of sunlight flash off the wings of birds as they alight from limb to limb.

"I stayed out much later than I normally did. I always made a point to be home in time for dinner. My dad was frantic when I rode up on my bike. My mom was at the hospital with Seamus. Apparently, he had been so worried I was lost that he ran off into the woods to find me, tripped and fell down a hill, and broke his arm." Just the memory of that cast on my brother's little arm has me cringing.

"That wasn't your fault." Levi's presence grows stronger as he leans toward me. "You made a mistake, but you were a kid."

I shrug, still not ready to let myself off the hook, even decades later. "When my parents asked why I was late, I told them about the girl. They asked around town, but no one knew who I was talking about. Eventually, my parents decided she was imaginary. That I'd made her up. I tried to find out on my own, but no one knew who owned this land, or they wouldn't tell nine-year-old me.

"When I first got hired by my old boss, I searched through the records. All I could find attached to this plot was a lawyer's office in Atlanta, and they wouldn't disclose the owner. Confidentiality and all that." When I offer Levi a hopeless smile, he keeps quiet, sensing I'm not done. So, I let the words continue to spill out of me. "Owen was the only one who believed me. Of course, he was four, too young to realize he could decide not to believe me if he wanted. But he did, and he'd always ask me for the Forest Girl story. That's what he called her. It was nice, being able to tell someone who didn't think I was making it up." I snort. "Sometimes, when he's really drunk, he still asks me to tell the story again."

We're quiet for a moment, the sounds of the woods and the gurgle of the stream filling the air between us.

"The promise you made to her—that's why you wanted to avoid a burning?"

I bob my head. "Yes, but more than that." I lean toward him, trying to find the words. "I knew then—and I still know now—that there's power here. Tied to everything she touched. But maybe it wasn't her touch. There was a lot going on around us that day I don't think I comprehended." Watching Levi's brows dip, I fight against the same frustration I felt whenever trying to talk to a person other than Owen about this topic. "Gods, I wish I could describe it better than that." My fingers splay out in front of me, and I'm sure I can sense a thrumming energy in the air. But no one else feels it. "What I wouldn't give to have clear answers. Then, I could make up a PowerPoint to present to The Council. But all I have is this feeling. This knowledge. She was here. She's important. Someday, she's coming back." Spreading my arms wide, I try to encompass the wildness surrounding us. "This all needs to be here when she does."

Levi stretches his legs out in front of him, crossing his ankles and leaning back on his hands. "What did she look like?"

Pulling in a calming breath, I bring Forest Girl's image to the front of my mind. "Long black hair. Tan skin. Maybe Latina. Hazel eyes when they weren't solid white. Black wings, like I said before."

His expression is thoughtful. "I don't know her, but I haven't met every monster."

My breath stutters in my lungs. "You're talking like she was real."

Levi gives me his unflinching stare, digging past a protective barrier I wasn't aware I'd slowly constructed over the years.

"You say she's real. She's real."

My throat closes for a moment, and I turn my head toward the cool breeze of the stream to combat the heat racing through my body. He doesn't know what his trust, his belief in me, means.

She's real.

I've known that. But I just wanted the world—or at least more than my goofball of a brother—to believe me.

In this moment, I want to launch myself at Levi. Wrap myself around his lean body and devour every delicious inch of him. But the collateral damage of my selfish acts plays through my mind. Seamus in the hospital. Bad people drawn to Folk Haven, causing mischief. Committing crimes.

I don't want to cause strife by grabbing at something I want without considering the consequences. So, I hold off from touching Levi, sitting up straight, as if I were in my lumbar-supporting office chair rather than a rock in the middle of the woods. And I dive into the hard topic.

"You put space between us." At my statement, he jerks his head toward me, and I press on, "I know I was being too aggressive that night at the beach. Pushing you about shifting for me and then draping myself over you." Shame radiates heat through my body, and I pray to The Cold One for another cool breeze off the stream.

"You sleeping on the floor ... I get it. You wanted to set some boundaries. That makes complete sense. I didn't take the time to consider feelings. How you might not want to be touched when you're in your other form. Or how being with me would cause you more grief and gossip than you already must deal with, just existing as a monster in Folk Haven." Frowning, I dig my fingers into the back of my neck to stave off a stress headache.

"I know we argue, and at one point, I considered you my enemy. But I don't anymore. And I don't *want* to cause you more trouble. Though it seems like I do most times." I give him a smile, knowing it's more like a grimace. "Telling me to back off is valid, and I won't hold it against you."

"What?" The man looks like I just told him I want to live in a tree and eat only a diet of dried moss.

I try again. "We're attracted to each other. That's undeniable. But I get why you would hesitate at the idea of being with me."

Levi would probably receive dirty looks from some townspeople even if he dated another monster. The bigots seem to want monsters to become monks rather than procreating and producing another mysterious offspring with untested powers. And there's also Levi's constituents to think about. How would they react to him dating a selkie?

"We'd never be able to keep our relationship entirely private. Two council members have never dated before. There would be blowback, and most would hit you. Your family doesn't have deep roots in the town, and there's the ingrained prejudice against monsters. Plus, you're trying to build up good favor for your new business." I force my voice to be steady as a quiver threatens to trip me up. "I'm saying that I understand I make life harder for you. And I don't blame you for having mixed feelings about me."

Gods, that hurt. But after all this flirting and back-and-forth, the words needed to be said.

Levi holds my gaze with his, and when he speaks, the low growl of the words reverberates through my bones. "Anyone who tells me I can't be with you can go take a long breath at the deepest part of Galen for all the fucks I give."

If public opinion isn't what pushed him away, then that leaves only one option as far as I can tell.

"Then, it was because I was too aggressive? That's why you

slept on the floor?" I demand, tired of coming up with my own answers for the question, needing him to give me the truth.

Levi's brows inch up. "The only reason I didn't hold you in my arms that night was because I didn't want you to push me away in the morning."

"Why would I ..." My brain brings the night back to me, which I remember in full despite the alcohol consumption. His hesitancy to change in front of me and him hiding his sexual organs at first.

"We live in the same world," Levi murmurs, staring off into the trees. "One where my kind is reviled. I thought I'd wake up and see regret, maybe fear, on your face. I wanted to give you space."

Give me *space?* Disbelief slows my comprehension, but when his confession finally settles, I rise to my knees, looming over him.

"Are you telling me," I growl with pent-up frustration, "that the reason I didn't get to gaze out at the ocean while you fucked me from behind is because you thought I would be *scared* of you?"

Levi's attention flies back to me as I move forward, mounting his lap. His hair is a collection of cool silk against my fingers, and I tug on the strands in a small revenge, loving the sound of his gasp and the way his pupils dilate. Heavy hands cup my ass, pressing the linen of my shorts into my flesh as he grips me the way he did that night, only without claws this time.

I don't need to turn down the level of my desire for him. He wants my passion.

"You," I hiss, my lips less than an inch from his, letting my need fuel aggressiveness that apparently doesn't bother this mythic, "owe me a beach vacation. A long one. Where I orgasm multiple times with salt on my skin and your cock sliding deep."

"Hell, Moira." He pants my name. "You want me that way?"

My heart aches at the vulnerable statement. Levi Abadi's confident demeanor hides a soft core I will rip the world apart to protect. My fingers ease in his hair, only to slide down and circle his neck.

"You're lucky I want you like that," I whisper against his mouth, my fierce lust rising. "Or else I might've killed you by now."

Then, I take him, tasting lightning on my tongue as I lick past his lips while my hips roll in time with each luxurious swipe. The monster groans, and I feast on the decadent sound. Between our bodies, his cock hardens, and, gods, I long for that delicious length to sink into me.

Levi Abadi wants me. Which means I can be selfish with him.

"Give me your power," I whisper between kisses. "Make me feel good."

The monster grunts, and a second later, a glorious sensation spills through my body. Like I'm back in that salt bath after a strong set of hands worked me over. *His* hands.

My clit pulses, and I'm so close. Gods, I haven't come from dry-humping someone's lap since that time I hooked up with Sonya in high school. But damn if Levi isn't about to get me there.

"You going to come for me, my little selkie?" he grunts the question as I press a hungry kiss to the pounding pulse in his neck. "Use my body. I'm all for you. Every part of me is yours."

And it's that. The realization that he's mine sets off the delicious, repetitive clenching inside me.

"Yes," I moan out. Then, I suck in a breath for another demand. "More."

29

LEVI

As Moira falls apart in my arms, I hold her to me. And when that demand leaves her lips, I'm ready to obey.

"More."

"Anything," I promise before tasting her lips again. "Anything you want, I'll give it to you."

A desperate edge colors my words. One mistake, born from my insecurity, could have stolen this from me. Erased any chance I had with this woman. I almost fucked up my opportunity of claiming perfection.

Not that Moira is without flaws. Her complete disregard for her own wants is something I plan to dissuade her of. But us, together like this? I've never felt closer to nirvana.

"There are condoms in the picnic basket," my selkie informs me, blinking the lingering haze of her orgasm out of her eyes. Well, that's no good. I'm ready to blur her concentration with another round of pleasure.

Only a stray thought pops into my head and out of my mouth. "Did your dad pack the condoms too?"

"No!" Moira snorts out an inelegant sound, shoving her fist against her mouth to cut the noise off, but then she dissolves into a round of laughter that forces a few stray tears out of the corners of her eyes.

I revel in the beauty of her completely at ease.

She should be like this more often. Relaxed yet demanding. Taking what she wants instead of focusing solely on the needs of everyone but herself.

Luckily, I'll be around to remind her. Or maybe to coax her if she's reluctant.

Keeping an arm tight on her waist, I lean over, grabbing the basket and dropping the wicker container at my side. Scrounging through the contents, I discover the foil packets, holding one up with a raised eyebrow and teasing smile.

Moira snatches it, devilish smirk in place. "A woman should always be prepared."

"Let me guess. Your dagger is in there too."

My selkie shrugs. "Never know when you need to cut something at a picnic."

Then, she squeaks when I tip her back. But I'm gentle as I settle her on the blanket, my hands dragging over the curves of her body to hook in the waistband of her linen shorts. They slide off easily, revealing a bare pussy underneath.

"Prepared, you say?" The question comes out strangled, and the woman spears me with a grin.

"*Optimistic* might be a better word."

Starving is the only one I can think of, which is why I dive in, tracing my tongue through the damp results of her recent orgasm. She's the ocean on my lips, and I pin her hips down as she writhes.

"Levi." Moira's voice is a plea, and then a strong foot presses into my chest, forcing me away from my treat. An animalistic growl of protest leaves my throat, but the brown eyes I meet are equally as fierce.

"Strip," she demands. "Now."

I might never be in charge in this pairing, but I'm okay with that. Standing above her, I whip my shirt over my head and then take a more cautious approach with my fly, a prominent erection demanding I be careful with my zipper. The problem is, my dick keeps giving needy twitches as I gaze down on my woman as she peels her loose top off. A lace bra cups her generous breasts, the material taking the job my hands want. Luckily, Moira is quick to bow her back, reaching underneath herself to unclasp the hooks and fling the sheer garment away.

Bare, at my feet.

Mate. The word presses through my skull in a resounding wave. *Is it merely that I want the title? Or is this how it happens for monsters? We discover our one, and the gods tell us by infusing our beings with a sense of rightness mixed with longing?*

Was I even meant to have a mate?

I tell myself the label isn't what matters. Her, here with me, hand stretched up, beckoning me closer—that's what's important.

The moment I slide off my briefs, Moira sits up, taking my cock in hand. I lock my knees to keep from falling to them. Her warm hand with her adorable painted nails strokes leisurely, driving all thoughts from my mind. Then, a new pressure rolls from the head to the base as she sheathes my member in a condom.

Now, I do drop down, kneeling between her legs. If I were an animal, I'd crush her beneath me, pounding away with a wild fury. But I have enough sense to grasp her hand and her waist and pull her up to straddle my lap. My selkie is precious and deserves more than a bruising rut against hard stone. Sliding my palm to her ass, I hold her high enough to ease the tip of myself past her lush entrance.

"Gods, Levi. Fuck me!"

The hairband that kept her hair pulled back has disappeared, and the wild curls frame her ferocious eyes. Those aqua-green nails dig into the skin of my shoulders, and I love the bite. Slowly, I ease her down onto my cock, inch by inch, until she's panting out curses and I'm clenching my teeth to keep from spilling too early.

Moira hooks her fingers behind my neck and then leans back the full length of her arms. I watch, hypnotized, as she rolls her hips in a figure-eight pattern, massaging my dick with every shift of her inner muscles. I palm her breasts, thumbs dragging over her nipples before I slide my touch lower, over the curls on her mound, until I locate the hard nub of her clit. Moira jerks at the contact, losing her rhythm but clenching around me all the same.

"This," she moans, thrusting against me, her tits bouncing with each move. "Every day, I want this."

Every day. Long term. The rest of our lives.

The promise only makes me harder.

But she's not done.

"I want you in every way. Every position. Every form. Gods, when you spark in your monster shape, I swear I feel the energy inside me. I need you to let me have you like that. I want you to wrap yourself around me when you're inside me."

The erotic monologue drags at the awareness of my other form. Not only does she tolerate that part of me, but she also craves it. When the cloudy presence pushes at my mind, I let myself sink into it, and suddenly, my body is shifting as I stay buried inside her.

Hopefully, the latex isn't affected.

"Oh!" Moira wraps her arms tighter around my neck and slings her legs around my waist as we rise a good six feet off the ground, held aloft by the strength of my tail. Her gaze meets mine, eyes wide. "Oh gods." Her lids flutter when I give an experimental thrust. "Yes," she groans, and that's when she comes a second time, warmth and tightness milking me.

Holding her close, breathing in her cold ocean scent, I rock my body in and out of her slick grip, awed by the content smile that spreads over her face. I'm still thrusting when she recovers enough to cup my face and stare deep into my eyes.

"You're mine, Levi. My monster."

My entire monstrous form jerks, powerful currents of ecstasy pulsing through me as I come harder than I ever have. When the initial wave passes and I'm left with twitches of pleasure, I sink back to the picnic blanket, slowly shifting back to my human shape. Collapsing, I lie, spent, Moira sprawled across my heaving chest.

Every molecule of the world around me glimmers with such a glorious sensation that I wonder if I'm finally experiencing the magic my selkie finds in this place. Every inch of my being thrums with an undeniable power I've never experienced before.

But that could easily be from the woman I'm using as a blanket.

At the gentle brush of her lips on my chest, I replay the words that sent me over the edge.

"You're mine, Levi. My monster."

I'm not her only monster, though I don't hold any jealousy toward Forest Girl.

But I do know that I'll use every resource at my disposal to protect this land and help Moira fulfill her promise to the dark-winged monster.

30

MOIRA

A FULL DAY LATER, my body is still buzzing from the multiple orgasms Levi coaxed out of me. The thought of the way he worshipped every inch of my skin has me wanting to make a U-turn and drive out to his house to demand a few more.

But my office and work wait for me.

"Responsibilities, blah. Who wants those?" I mutter to myself as I grin like a ghoul at my dashboard.

Normally, the answer is *me*. I'm duty first, me last. But a certain leviathan has been tricking me into putting myself first.

And the world isn't ending.

Funny how, not long ago, I was cursing Levi Abadi's name.

Now, all I want to do is moan it.

I chuckle to myself as I parallel park in the street in front of my office and climb out into the muggy morning. Main Street is quiet this early on Sunday, but things will pick up in a couple of hours. After slinging my purse over my shoulder, I stroll toward the front door of Folk Haven Realty. When I'm a foot away, I realize something is wrong.

The door is ajar. The handle is bent at a weird angle, and the lock hangs out of its normally secure home.

My dagger is in my hand before the truth registers. *Someone broke into my work.*

My hand reaches to shove the door wide, but I stop myself. While mythic-on-mythic violence is rare in Folk Haven, there are creatures here that would laugh at my dagger, as if I were wielding a toothpick as a weapon. Trying to be smart, I slip my free hand back in my bag and pull out my cell.

Carl answers the precinct phone after the first ring, and the officer instructs me not to go inside before he arrives on the scene. As much as standing idle grates my nerves, I follow his orders. Still, I stand ready in case someone waltzes out, posed to cut the piece of shit who shoved their way into my space, uninvited.

Since my office is only a couple of blocks over from Town Hall, Carl pulls up in record time.

"Stand clear." He gestures me to back up a few steps, unholstering his weapon. "I'm going to check the space." Then, he shoulders the door open and disappears inside.

A minute later, a truck pulls up, and Samantha hops out in civilian clothes. I spare a regret that she has to work on what is obviously her day off. The police force has gotten more action in the last week than usual.

"Carl called me," she explains as the merman steps out of the building.

His holstered weapon answers my first question before he says anything.

"All clear, but the place is a mess."

"Fuck," I whisper under my breath.

Samantha gestures me toward the door. "Don't touch anything just yet but try to see if items are obviously missing. I'll call the wolves and get someone to scent the place."

I nod a quick thanks before stepping through the door into

chaos.

My cushy sofas are torn to pieces, their stuffing strewn around the room in a mockery of snow. The paintings done by a local talented harpy are sliced to ribbons, as if someone repeatedly plunged a knife into the canvas. My custom-crafted coffee table depicting Lake Galen is flipped over, one of the legs broken off.

I want to pick it up and check if the top is still intact, but I keep my hands off possible evidence.

When I move on to my office, the white debris shifts from sofa filling to papers. All my files lie in disarray across the floor. Never have I been so grateful that all the records on mythics are not only coded, but also kept at Wolf Trust Bank. Sometimes, I do bring the files to my office for work, but I always return them at the end of the day. In the past, I've wondered if I was going over the top with my security.

Now, I know the extra measures were imperative.

Another item I always take home with me is my laptop. My once-sleek desktop screen lies smashed on the floor. The destruction might be infuriating, but I haven't lost any digital data.

Wanting answers to this mystery, I pull my laptop out of my bag and set it on the one clear corner of my desk. In moments, I have the security video from last night cued up. The camera covers my waiting area and is motion activated. I long since shut off the notification capability because I kept getting a buzz on my phone every time a person arrived, or I came and went, or if someone walked by on the street just outside the office window. Now, files get saved to a cloud drive, and I can check them if I need.

But damn, I wish I'd caught these bastards red-handed.

Still, apparently since my office wasn't rigged with an alarm, the intruders assumed I had no security measures. I immediately recognize three of the men who broke into my office.

"Gods, those assholes again?" Samantha comes up behind me, watching over my shoulder. "I should've made them leave town with their friend."

The black-and-white video shows the men from the bar, the companions of the guy I made a fool of for grabbing that siren without her consent.

"Guess they found out who I was," I mutter, watching as the biggest one flips the coffee table and silently laughs in the screen.

"Damn it. I said your name, didn't I? When I showed up at the bar." Samantha's face flushes red with shame.

"Don't do that. Don't blame yourself." Seeing Samantha feel guilt over this immature act pisses me off on her behalf. "Greeting me by name did not give these assholes permission to harass me."

She sighs hard through her nose and then scans the room. "Anything missing that you can tell?"

"I don't think so. But look at this." I rewind the video to when the camera first started recording. The door jerks open, and the men pile in.

"Is that a fourth guy?" Samantha leans closer to the screen.

"Yeah."

In the crowd of rowdy vandals, the fourth is a shadow, dressed in all black with a hat pulled low to cover his face. He walks straight across the room to my office door, fiddles with the lock while the other three are causing mayhem, and then disappears into my office.

"Do you have a camera in here?"

"No. I didn't want even low-quality recordings of the documents I work with or the conversations I have."

Samantha nods in understanding, and we watch the rest of the video in silence. When the guy in black leaves, he moves just as quickly as the first time. The camera never sees his face.

Still, I'm almost positive I know who he is.

31

———

LEVI

MOIRA MENTIONED she was heading into the office early to get some work done, and since Coffee & Claws doesn't open until eight on Sundays, I figured I'd grab her a cup. Any excuse to see her. Maybe steal a kiss. Or if she has time for a longer break, maybe a quick fuck on her desk.

But I don't make it to the coffee shop. My fantasies evaporate at the sight of a cop car outside of Folk Haven Realty.

I park half up on the curb and barely remember to shut off the engine before sprinting up to Carl, who hovers just outside the door.

"What happened?" I'm not waiting around for an answer, about to rush inside when the officer grabs my arm.

"Break-in. No one is hurt. Place was empty when it happened. Looks like it was the friends of that guy making trouble at Local Brew. Revenge or something. But Fred is in there now, scenting the place," Carl explains, naming one of the Folk Haven werewolves.

A small amount of my panic eases, as I know Moira wasn't

working when whatever this was happened, but I can't fully calm down until I see her with my own eyes.

"Moira?" I ask.

"She's at the station with the chief. Giving her official statement." Carl barely gets the last word out before I sprint back the way I came and slide behind the wheel of my car.

I'm lucky all the police are busy because I speed the few blocks that separate me from my selkie.

I discover her sitting in the same chair Amethyst lounged in a few nights ago. *Should I have pushed the witch to use her magic on all the men that night? Could she have done it?*

"Levi?" Moira says my name in confusion as I stalk across the room toward her, scooping her out of the chair and scanning every inch of her with my eyes.

"Are you okay?" The question rasps from my throat, worry tearing it raw.

"Yes, yes. I'm fine. Did you go by my office?" She smooths a hand over my chest, no doubt feeling my racing heart. "I was about to text you. I just wanted to finish up with Samantha first."

When I glance to the side, the police chief gives a half-wave and then returns to typing whatever notes she was taking.

"You know who did this?" Somehow, I keep my voice calm and level, though I want to scale the tallest building in this tiny town and roar my fury for the perpetrators to hear.

Moira rolls her eyes as her lips twist in a grimace. "The friends of that guy from the bar."

"Easy enough to figure out who they are," Samantha interjects. "They posted group photos of their fishing trip on social media. They're all tagged."

Moira and I look at the officer's computer screen and see the four scumbags grinning, all of them holding up a dead fish.

A sudden urge rises in me—to impart those vacant, gaping looks on the men instead.

"This'll actually be an easier situation than the harassment case," the officer explains. "Since we have clear video footage, I can pass it to the local authorities in Atlanta ..."

Samantha keeps talking, but the words turn into white noise. All I can focus on are their faces.

Such entitled arrogance.

Are they content with destroying Moira's carefully constructed business, or will they be back to cause more harm?

What if Moira had decided to stop by her office last night instead of this morning? What would they have done to her if they'd found her there?

"Levi?" My selkie's strong voice calls me back, and my eyes retrace her whole unharmed body again.

Every inch of me aches for every inch of her. The soft, unruly curls framing her face, though she tried to restrain them with a hair clip. The bracing scent of the cool ocean that always surrounds her. The warmth of her pale skin under my palms.

"If you keep zoning out on me, I'm going to return *Till Death Do Us Part* to the library before you learn who the actual murderer is." She smirks up at me, naming the mystery novel we listened to on our trip.

A word pummels my body, stronger than the echoing shout of *mate.*

Love.

I love this woman. This selkie. This snarky, demanding being of perfection.

"Don't do that," I murmur, pulling Moira in and pressing my lips to her forehead, needing a taste of her to know she's here and she's unhurt.

I would do horrendous things to keep my love safe. As I cradle her against my chest, I envision plunging a clawed hand through the rib cages of those humans to tear out their beating hearts and watching the ignorant light die in their eyes. The fantasy is so real that I can feel the warmth of their blood seeping through my fingers.

If the world wants a monster, then I'll be one. For her.

Of course, Moira deserves better. I let my hold fall away. She steps back and gives my chest an affectionate pat that I want to lean into.

"It'll all be okay. But I'm adding security to the agenda for the next council meeting. Too many things are slipping through the cracks, and with plot 236 cleansed, we need to make sure there aren't any other lingering problems."

"Yes." My voice comes out robotic, but it's the only way I can keep my snarling rage undercover. "That makes sense."

Maybe those men are out on the lake even now. I can attack from below, tearing a hole in the bottom of their boat, and revel in their panic as they sink. And when they've convinced themselves they can swim to shore, I'll rise from the water as the terrifying creature I am. They might struggle, but I'll only enjoy it more as I drag them to the deepest part of Lake Galen. Let their bodies rot next to the bones of The Collector. Another human who thought he could mistreat mythics without consequences.

"... and then I could still get work done. What do you say?" Moira stares up at me, waiting for an answer to a question I didn't fully hear because my mind was too busy, plotting violent acts.

"Uh, yeah. Sounds good." *I can't let her see me like this. These vile thoughts shouldn't touch her.* I move toward the door, needing to put distance between us.

"Where are you going?" her tempting voice asks.

"A drive," I mutter.

But another truer answer growls in my mind.

A hunt.

32

———

MOIRA

Heat rises off the hot metal of my car as I pause beside it and try to figure out what happened. One minute, Levi was agreeing to walk with me over to Coffee & Claws, so I could still get some work done today. Then, a second later, he sprinted out the door, claiming he was going for a drive. When I came outside, there was no sign of him.

The sidewalk I stare at beneath my feet has no answers for me.

My phone buzzes in my purse, and I snatch it up, disappointed to see Samantha's name rather than Levi's. The mermaid must not realize I'm still right outside Town Hall.

"Hey," I answer. "You find something?"

"Apparently, they were renting Jethro's guest cabin." The police chief names a man who was married to a bobcat shifter before she passed away a couple of years ago. He's a kind man, and he won't be happy to hear his renters were causing trouble in town. "They checked out yesterday evening. Guess you were their last stop on the way out of town."

"Shitty good-bye, if you ask me."

Samantha lets out a dry chuckle. "I'm just glad I won't have to lock up Levi for multiple homicide."

"What?" The question snaps out of me, a protective instinct launching to the forefront.

The mermaid is quiet for a stretch, and then her voice comes across the line, lower this time, as if we're having a private conversation. "Look, it's obvious—at least to me—you two are together. Congrats and all that."

At her words, my muscles tense and then ease. I realize I don't mind we've been discovered. In fact, I'm ready for the whole town to know Levi is mine.

The police chief keeps talking. "Someone threatened you. Imagine it the other way. If someone had threatened Levi. I'm sure even the most mild-mannered selkie would work themselves up into a lather. And Levi Abadi is no selkie."

The truth of her assessment washes through me in a rush, and I'm left with a sudden jittery need to be … somewhere.

Damn The Finned One's games, I don't know where Levi went.

"Got it. Thanks for the heads-up."

Once I'm off the phone with Samantha, I call Levi. Voice mail greets me after a handful of rings. Not sure what to say, I hang up and slide behind the wheel of my Subaru to set off through town.

Where would he go?

The obvious answer is after the assholes who broke into my office. But I highly doubt Samantha called and gave him that location. She knows that could easily turn into a bloodbath.

Would he do it?

I don't know.

My fault. The words itch at my skin like a bad habit, ready for me to fall back into my cycle of self-blame.

"No," I say out loud as I roll to a stop at one of the few traffic lights in Folk Haven. Whatever Levi does in response to this situation is not my fault. There's no reason to pile blame on myself.

That doesn't mean I'm going to turn away and pretend nothing is happening. His actions are his, but I know if he follows through on any revenge acts he comes up with, he'll only end up hurt. Probably not physically, seeing as how he's a massive sea monster. But because he'll come down from whatever rage wave he's surfing and use his actions to prove he truly is a monster. A being that the world should fear.

I refuse to let the man I love go through that kind of pain if I can stop it.

The realization I feel so deeply for him should rock me. Instead, the knowledge settles easily in my consciousness. I can dig into that more when I have time to meditate on the new discovery. Right now, I need to find the slippery sea monster.

In case Levi did somehow learn where the men were staying, I swing by Jethro's house. No sign of Levi's car at the cabin, so I keep driving, trying his phone again without answer. My next stop is his house. There aren't any lights on, but he could easily be brooding in the dark. The garage door is closed, so I can't tell if his car is here.

Stalking up to the front door, I bang my fist against the black-painted wood. Seconds tick by without a response. I try peering through the glass but only get a foggy view. Probably spelled against this very thing.

I'm suddenly annoyed I don't have a key. *I should have a key to the house of the man I love.* One of the many things I'll talk to him about whenever I find his scaly ass. Lingering on his front step, I dial his phone and once again get his voice mail.

"Let's get something straight," I growl into the receiver. "I'm only putting up with this avoidance bullshit *one* time. You try this again, and I'll ..." I search my mind for the perfect threat, finally landing on one. "I'll tell Heath you think his bear claws are dry."

The bear shifter is notoriously arrogant about his baking skills.

"That's right. I'll tell him you think they're overcooked and under-glazed. You'll never eat a pastry in this town again." I end the call.

Not sure where to go next, I follow the curve of the highway to one of the four bridges that cross Lake Galen. This one leads me straight into witch territory, which gives me an idea.

Still no sign of Levi's car when I pull up to his mother's cottage. When no one answers my knock, I almost depart but pause when I hear clanking in the backyard. Circling around the house, I discover the witch carting a wheelbarrow full of mulch through rows and rows of vibrant plants.

"Violetta."

She turns at the sound of her name, a sharp smile cutting across her lips. The middle-aged woman has a timeless beauty, even when she's wearing muddy overalls and has leaves in her hair. A Morticia Addams kind of vibe, only willing to get dirty.

"Moira." Violetta lowers the wheelbarrow, settling the stubby legs on the ground. "Don't touch any of the plants if you value your limbs. And your life." Her giggle is so sweet that it's evil.

But I didn't need her warning. The yard is bursting with a riot of strange, colorful blooms. More like what one might find in a rainforest rather than a garden in Georgia. No doubt the witch chose plants like herself—deceptively gorgeous, secretly poisonous.

I cross my arms over my chest and glance down to make sure my feet are firmly on the stepping-stone path.

"What has you wandering my way again?" Violetta pats her work gloves together, letting dirt rain from the stiff fabric. "Have some more twisted magic for me?"

I scowl at her. "*For* you? I hope you're not saying you somehow collected that magic."

Gods, that would be an embarrassing start to a whole new bundle of trouble. I really don't want to set The Council against Levi's mom.

For the first time, I watch Violetta's creepily cheerful mask crack, revealing an even scarier expression of icy rage.

"I would never sully myself with the leavings of a *sorcerer*." She spits the last word.

My body screams at me to retreat in the face of her fury. But I am a leader in this town, and I will not be cowed by a witchy tantrum from the woman I plan to make my mother-in-law.

"Good," I say, my response terse.

Violetta's face sinks back into an overly innocent smile. "Why are you here then?"

"I'm looking for Levi. Have you seen him today?"

"No." She picks up a shovel and starts spreading the moist soil among her plants. "Should I have? I've never been able to keep track of that boy. His father filled him with wildness."

Holding on to my calm demeanor, I fight back the urge to correct her. Levi isn't some unruly creature. He's a highly responsible man who cares deeply for his people. For me.

"I'm worried about him. He found out a group of men broke into my business. I think he's going to do something he regrets." *If he can find them.*

Could he be driving to Atlanta even now? Does Samantha have the ability to track his phone?

If I can't find him, I'll ask. But I have a sense he's still within the boundaries of Folk Haven. For now.

Violetta affects an overly theatrical sigh. "Of course he'll do something dramatic. He's a monster." She shakes her head, a pitying expression on her beautiful face. "You can't change their violent nature. You either love them or you don't. But they'll always be beasts."

My teeth protest as I grit down hard, fighting the hot response on my tongue. I hate her dismissive take on Levi's potentially volatile emotional state. What was it like, growing up with those sentiments spoken to you as if they were unalterable truths? No wonder Levi is so hard on himself.

Realizing I won't get the help I need here, I turn to leave, pausing for a final comment.

"You're lucky Levi loves *you* as you are." I throw the words at her like darts meant to penetrate thick skin. "This garden"—I wave at the collection of dangerous plants—"seems pretty monstrous to me."

The witch's cackle comes just before a cryptic comment. "Impertinent selkie. Why is it always selkies? Like father, like son."

My curiosity begs me to turn back and interrogate her. *Does she know about my great-grandaunt Blair?*

But finding Levi is more important, so I leave without answers.

The next place I check is Haven's Relaxation, wondering if he might be holed up in his office. But the parking lot is empty, and the doors are locked. With a frustrated growl, I stalk down to the small dock the spa has jutting out into Galen. Another unanswered phone call has me wanting to chuck my cell across the shimmering surface like a skipping stone.

Instead, I tuck it in my back pocket and crouch down to plunge my hands into the cool water, trying to calm and clear my mind.

Any progress I made evaporates when I realize a watery face is staring up at me. With a yelp, I jerk back, my butt landing hard on the sun-warmed wood.

"Moira?" a clear voice asks.

Creepy. But also, I live in a town of mythical creatures. This isn't the strangest thing I've seen in my life. For gods' sake, I fucked a sea monster yesterday.

Peeking over the edge of the dock, I stare down into a feminine face formed on the surface of the lake.

"I'm sorry," I say. "Have we met?"

The liquid visage chuckles. "Not yet. I'm Satine. Levi's friend."

Ah. I've heard the name before. Mainly from the folks who make snide comments about inter-mythic relationships. They gossip how Satine is a half-dragon, half-undine, which resulted in a monster without a human form. As if her existence is proof the gods curse those kinds of couples. Some talk like Satine is a being to be feared. As far as I know, she lives a quiet life on the monster section of the lake and doesn't bother anyone.

A shimmering, see-through arm extends from the lake, offering a wave in greeting that I copy.

"Can I help you with something?" Even though Satine is not technically my constituent, I'm not about to dismiss her.

"Are you looking for Levi?"

At the sound of his name, my heart jumps, and I lean farther over the dock's edge. "Yes! Have you seen him?"

I get the impression the monster is nodding her head.

"He's moping on the property next door. During our last chess match, he couldn't shut up about you, so my best guess is, you two had a lovers' quarrel?" The last word ticks up at the end, leaving it sounding like a question.

Suddenly, I get the urge to open up. Maybe because this almost feels like talking to the lake rather than a stranger. "Not exactly. There was a group of out-of-towners who were pissed off at me and destroyed my office. I think Levi took it as a threat against me, and now, he wants to enact some kind of violent revenge."

Although, if he's moping, maybe I have it wrong.

Satine lets out a watery sigh. "Levi tries to be the best monster he can be. But sometimes, his brain tells him the only way to do that is to not be a monster at all." The mythic shifts and rises until her full, iridescent body stands on the lake surface. A risk in broad daylight, but there are no boats in sight now. "Some of us don't have a human face to hide behind. That might seem like the short straw, but it also means we have to find a way to connect with what we have." She gestures at her semi-translucent form. "Levi though, he's still split in two." Satine slowly sinks, melting into Lake Galen. Before her head connects with the water, she speaks again. "Also, his mom is a judgmental bitch."

I snort, moving to stand. A *thank you* sits on my lips, but the phrase sounds empty in my head. I don't want to dismiss Satine. Instead, I find myself wanting to get to know her better. She's Levi's friend and an embodiment of how Folk Haven isn't serving mythics as well as we could.

"My dad makes a big family breakfast every Monday and the morning after the dark moon," I say. "You should come by."

The only response is a splash of water before the lake surface clears of the monster's face. I'll take that as a maybe.

For a stretch, I stare over at the thick woods that mark the beginning of plot 236. As much as I want to rush over and find the man I've been searching for all morning, I force myself to walk in the opposite direction. Back in my car, I aim my wheels toward home.

33

LEVI

I DON'T KNOW how long I sit on Moira's stone. Time is hard to keep track of under the thick canopy of trees.

When I first left Town Hall, I went back to Moira's office without any sort of plan other than my drive to find the men and hurt them. But my nose is only slightly better than a human's. I'm no shifter wolf, able to track down someone with barely a trace left behind. Fred, a local werewolf, was coming out of the building as I arrived.

"Where are they?" I demanded.

Carl glanced from me to the wolf and back down to his notepad. "The chief radioed that they're already out of town."

The brief separation from my prey gave me enough willpower to pull myself back. To drive to a secluded place instead of on the road out of town.

Now, I hide away in this forest that my selkie loves so much and try to remember why gutting those humans might not be the best choice.

The violence won't help Moira. I don't need to eviscerate them.

But, gods, I want to. Bloody images of revenge play through my mind on a loop. Lopping off limbs. Reveling in their screams. Knowing they'd never be foolish enough to come after my selkie again even if I left them in fit enough form to do so.

Every time I've almost convinced myself to get off this perch and go after them, an image floats to the top of my rage storm. The look in Moira's eyes when she held me inside her on this spot yesterday. When she called me hers, even as I wore the visage that would terrify the rest of the world.

Would she still see me the same way if I tore those humans apart?

More vengeful ideas flicker through my brain, and a small part of me worries the evil I'm cooking up will somehow coax the toxic magic back to this place.

But the presence that arrives is not the sticky film left over by that hated sorcerer.

Instead, I'm surrounded by the scent of the sea.

She's here. I close my eyes in pleasurable agony.

"Only a monster would have destroyed this place," I admit as I listen to Moira's footsteps disturbing leaves and cracking twigs as she approaches.

One more shame I bow under. My mother is a cleansing witch, and I still pushed for fire. I demanded we burn all this down. Quick and brutal. No wonder Moira started off hating me. Just a matter of time before she realizes her initial instinct was right.

A sudden weight in my lap forces my eyes open. I glance down and discover I'm holding a luxurious piece of fabric. Soft and heavy, shimmering with magic. Awe slams through me when I finally realize what the item is. Then, terror follows with fast footsteps.

I jump to my feet, turning to find Moira watching me.

"I—I can't hold this." With gentle but desperate hands, I hold the cloak out to her. "Take it back."

But the stubborn woman doesn't, planting her fists on her hips instead. "It's my pelt. I can give it to whomever I want to."

"*Give* it to me?" The question chokes me.

A smile teases at the corner of her mouth. "Not forever. Just for a little bit. I thought you'd like to see it. Pretty, right? And warm. Not that you need it on a day like today. But in the winter? I'm always wanting to use it as a blanket. But then poof!" She mimes explosions with her hands. "I'd turn into a big seal. *You* can wrap yourself in it though."

"Moira." I can't understand how she'd joke about something like this. "You need to get this away from me. Now. You can't trust me with it. I-I'll tear it or something."

"No, you won't." She sinks down on the rock, crossing her legs and patting the space beside her. "Come on. Take a load off."

Hesitating at first, I finally move as though I were cradling a volatile bomb, carefully lowering myself beside her and then attempting to pass the selkie hide her way. But Moira piles the second skin back in my lap. Then, she leans into me and strokes her hand over the material.

"This is the most precious item I possess." She's solemn now. "And I trust you to hold it."

"Why?" My vulnerable disbelief spills into my voice.

Moira takes on the same tone she uses in council meetings when presenting an idea she'll end up fighting tooth and nail for. Part instructive, part steel.

"*Monster* is not inherently bad." Her fingers brush my knuckles, the gesture reassuring. "The moment someone decided it would be applied to a group of mythics based solely off their parentage, the way people reacted to the word should have changed. But it didn't. So, your whole life, mythics have called you monster, using the same tone as they'd say *garbage* or *murderer*." Moira sits back enough to meet my eyes, forcing me to take in everything she's saying. "I can see you fighting the invisible words attached to the label. You know monsters are the same as other mythical beings. Everyone making good and bad decisions as they live their lives like anybody else."

The truth pounds against my skull like a headache.

"You're never so understanding with yourself," Moira says.

I want to battle against that conclusion. She's convinced herself I'm an improperly labeled innocent.

"Moira." Her name threads with a growl from my chest, needy and warning. "I want to find those men who broke into your office. I want to hunt them like animals. Hurt them in unimaginable ways." *Be the monster that everyone knows I am.*

I flinch as a scoff bursts from her throat.

"That has nothing to do with you being a monster." She plants a hand on my chest and drags a slow path up to cup the back of my neck. "That's you being a mate."

A shudder ripples through my body. I'm not sure if I want to run from the selkie or dig my claws into her flesh to mark her as mine forever. The tormenting woman leans closer, her mouth inches from mine.

"If those men had broken into your spa"—her breath brushes against my lips—"that beautiful space you crafted, and tore it apart, I'd want to do some damage in return. And if they laid hands on you"—she strokes loving fingers down my cheek—"I would take their hands."

"Fuck," I sigh out the curse, letting myself accept how much her bloody words incite my lust.

Moira protects what's hers. And I'm in that group.

Still, I can't help a petulant mutter. "What if I'm corrupting you?"

My selkie grins, wide enough to show all her teeth, making the expression almost threatening. "Maybe all mythics have some violence in us. What do you expect when we constantly need to hide a part of ourselves to keep the world from hunting us?"

When she shifts forward, I feel the soft press of her kiss against my jaw. "Certain things are bound to bring that violence to the surface. Like a threat." She nips at my neck, and I shiver. "Or love."

All the air leaves me then. "What was that?"

Her tongue flicks the lobe of my ear. "I love you."

I turn my head and capture her teasing mouth. Between kisses, I return the word. Tenfold. Moira MacNamara can have no doubt that I am deeply in love with her. I'm about to prove it with my body when my mind kicks in enough for me to not be a totally selfish being.

"I'm sorry I ran off earlier." I cup her cheeks in my hands. "You wanted to go to the coffee shop and work."

Moira shrugs, her brown eyes warming. "I got to say hi to a few people while I hunted you down." She eases into my lap, settling on top of her pelt. "Apparently, when you play chess, you talk about me. A lot."

I groan, dropping my forehead to hers. "You ran into Satine."

"Yep. She's invited to Monday breakfast. So are you, by the way."

Blinking, I pull up a calendar in my head. "That's tomorrow."

"You got it. Hope you're ready for my rowdy, large family."

The surprising thing is, I am. I've met all the MacNamaras individually while living in Folk Haven, but I don't remember ever mingling with them.

Am I going to be accepted by Moira's people?

"Do you think they'll want to be around me? What with your great-grandaunt's skin still missing?"

The light dims a touch in her face, but she doesn't stop smiling. "That's not your fault. Which is the same thing I'll tell them. And believe me, I'm the hardest one to please in our family. You'll have an easy go of it."

"Okay." I decide to believe Moira because I'm not running away from her again.

"Besides"—she eases her fingers into my hair, scraping her nails along my skull, setting off a pleasure that threatens to roll my eyes back in my head—"there's the selkie mating myth."

"Hmm?" The questioning noise is all I can manage when she rocks against me.

"A selkie will know their mate when they are rescued." Moira speaks the words against my throat and then traces her tongue over my speeding pulse. "You rescued me from my fear in the Gauntlet. My heroic monster. My mate."

"I—" A groan separates my sentence as she bites my earlobe. "I never heard that before."

"Now, you know." Sitting up straight, Moira holds my gaze with hers. "You're mine. I plan to be very selfish with you."

The grin she wears has me wanting to kiss her until I forget my name.

But if I'm going to be a good mate, I need to support her in all ways.

"I am yours," I agree, diving in for a quick kiss. "You ready for me to fulfill my promise to escort you to the coffee shop?"

Moira tilts her head, and a smirk steals over her lips. She slides off my lap, taking her hide with her. A skillful wrist flick has the magical cloak spread across the rock we sit on. Moira promptly shoves me back onto the luxurious fabric.

"Work can wait." Her husky declaration might as well be a hand on my cock as she slings a leg over my hips.

"You're a temptress." A moan wrenches from my throat as her thighs embrace me.

"And you're as monstrous as I am, Levi Abadi. Which I'd say is the exact right amount."

34

———

MOIRA

AFTER I ONCE AGAIN TOOK MY monster on a rock in the woods, we decided to spend time with each other under a roof. Where there are less mosquitoes.

The small house I live in by myself sits on a larger plot owned by the MacNamara family. Even with my parents and brothers living so close, I normally have plenty of privacy. Which is why I'm shocked to find a collection of siblings and their partners lounging all over my deck furniture when I park in my gravel drive.

"Moira MacNamara, where the hell have you been?" Owen, the second youngest of our lot, stalks down the front steps. "I had to hear from Carl that your place was broken into, and then none of us could find you all day!"

The storm cloud shadowing my brother's normally good-natured personality throws me off-balance.

Where's this coming from?

If anyone is scolding someone in this family, it tends to be me.

235

Owen goes so far as to grab me by the shoulders and turn me around as he scans for injuries.

"Stop it." I slap his hands away.

"Did you find the assholes?" he demands. "Do we need some wet cement? I know a ghoul."

"Calm down. I don't have any bodies to get rid of. But if you keep acting like this, I might." I prod him in the chest, trying to ignore how mine goes soft, knowing my family worried about me. My phone rang a couple of times during the day, but when none of the names were Levi's, I ignored the calls.

More tires grind on the gravel, and I glance back to see the monster who distracted me all day pulling into my drive.

Owen immediately changes his tune. "*Oh.* I see. You having an all-day meeting with Council Member Abadi? You two get a lot of work done?"

My incorrigible brother waggles his eyebrows at me, and I consider feeding him a handful of plants from Violetta's garden.

My monster climbs out of his car and approaches with what I'm sure he thinks is a polite smile but looks more like a painfully hopeful grimace.

Time for him to meet the family.

Stepping forward, I slide my hand into Levi's, lacing our fingers together. Owen's eyes go rounder than inner tubes. I ignore his shock.

"Levi and I are mates," I announce loud enough for everyone hanging around the outside of my house to hear.

Owen's mouth drops open into a delighted grin.

"Shut up." I glare at him.

"I didn't say anything," he crows back.

"Then, shut your face up," I hiss and stalk past him, pulling Levi after me, feeling more like a teenager bringing a date home for the first time rather than a woman in her thirties about to start a lifelong commitment.

I blame Owen. I'm much more collected when I face my baby brother Calder and the second-oldest MacNamara sibling, Seamus. They've brought their respective mates, Delta and Neri, along.

"Hey, y'all"—I slip a possessive arm around my monster's waist—"welcome Levi to the family."

A small cheer goes up, and the four approach to congratulate us, Owen joining in on the celebration. Making a quick trip inside, I raid my kitchen, bringing out beers and snacks for the impromptu porch gathering.

When everyone settles down, Calder and Delta have the porch swing, Seamus and Neri are in Adirondack chairs, Owen is in the rocker Granny gave me, and I'm in Levi's arms, the two of us leaning back against the porch railing.

We spend some time going over the events of the morning, which, by now, feels like a week ago.

When we get to the end of the story, Owen is muttering curses under his breath, and I notice Seamus and Neri share a significant look. The blonde siren glances my way, meeting my eyes.

"We heard what happened already." She offers a half-smile. "Gossip spreads fast in Folk Haven."

I'm not surprised.

"In fact," Neri continues, "all of the sirens heard what happened. Including what you did for Nicki at the bar. We would've come over to check on you anyway"—she squeezes Seamus's hand, and he nods in agreement—"but the others sent me with a gift. A thank-you for helping a siren in need."

My brother leans forward. "They know about Great-Grandaunt Blair."

Shock flows through me, and I glance over my shoulder to meet eyes with Levi. His are hesitant but curious.

Will we finally get the answer to what happened with his father and my aunt?

"I have permission to sing you the story." She grins ruefully. "And then have Seamus translate."

Of course. Since Neri fell in love with Seamus, he's one of the few non-sirens who can remember their songs.

The woman opens her mouth, and out spills beautiful notes that bring tears to my eyes. But the next thing I know, I'm blinking away a fog that's formed over my brain, noticing Calder, Delta, and Owen wearing the same bemused expression that no doubt sits on my face.

Behind me, Levi clears his throat. "Lovely, I think. Almost positive I enjoyed every moment until I forgot it."

The siren chuckles and then turns to her mate. "Go ahead. You have a great singing voice."

Seamus's face flushes red. "I have to sing it? Can't I just tell them what happened?"

"Nope." Neri raises their joined hands to her mouth and presses a kiss to his knuckles. "I believe in you."

After a put-upon sigh, Seamus stares down at his lap and starts singing. Neri wasn't wrong. My brother has some decent pipes. But I soon forget who's singing when the words of the song register, and I get lost in the story.

Two creatures of the sea
Devoted friendship
Unbroken kinship
Leviathan and selkie
Forming waves with their play
Together always
Losing the days
Born from innocent gaze

The tale goes on, detailing how as the friends grew older, the leviathan fell in love with the selkie. However, the selkie did not feel the same deep romantic love. Not for the monster. Instead, she fell for a human woman.

My entire body braces for the tale to turn sad. To learn of Levi's father's anger and theft.

But that's not how it goes.

The leviathan accepted that he wouldn't ever have the selkie's heart in that way. And when Blair's family, my ancestors, were forced to leave their homeland or risk the hiding place for their pelts to be discovered, my great-aunt refused to join them on their immigration. She also refused to tell them why.

Many traditional mythics share a stilted mindset with traditional humans. That a mating's most important goal is to produce offspring.

Maybe that's why my family assumed someone had stolen her pelt. Blair no doubt thought it was easier to let them believe she was forced to stay because her selkie skin had been taken rather than share the nature of her mating and be scorned.

But she had no safe hiding place for her pelt anymore, which meant every trip on land to see her love was a risk.

So, the leviathan offered to guard her second skin for her. He did so for years, holding the piece of the woman he loved in his impenetrable sea cave as she left to be with another. Once a month, he would meet Blair on a rocky beach, and she'd don her pelt. For the night, the friends would swim together, and come morning, she would return to her human mate.

Then, one horrible night, my aunt and her lover were discovered. The humans condemned them for their love. They sentenced them to death.

The leviathan didn't find out until it was too late. His love, his best friend, was dead.

And all he had to remember her by was her selkie pelt.

A pressure against my skin draws me out of the story, and I

realize Levi's thumbs are tracing across my cheeks, collecting my tears.

"Your father was her friend," I whisper, awed and heart-broken at the terrible tale.

"And he kept her hide. Both of us were right, and both of us were wrong." His smile is all sadness. "That always seems to be the way of history."

Turning back to my brother, I realize he's stopped singing.

"What happened next?"

Seamus blinks. "Uh, well, the first part of the song repeats. But you've already heard that. So, that's everything." He looks to Neri. "Thank you. We never knew."

The siren grimaces. "I wish it could've been happier. Or that I could provide more detail." Her attention shifts to me, and she offers a defeated shrug. "Sirens don't know everything."

"It helps to know that Aunt Blair entrusted that piece of herself to him." The comment comes from Owen, and I turn to him with surprise. But I shouldn't be. This is all of our history. I guess I've just been more of a bulldog about it. Or bullheaded.

"He's living in his monster form." Levi's comment brings my attention back to him, and I turn in his arms in time to watch a grimace twist his lips. "I didn't want to say anything. Because the monster taboo is strong enough on its own." His eyes meet mine and then drop. "Him choosing to live that way—in some deep, unreachable part of the ocean—I thought people might see it as proof that we're more beast than anything."

Violetta's condemnation hides under his words.

As I move to wrap my arms around him, Delta's husky voice pipes up. "My father lived in dragon form up in the Arctic for forty years straight before I was born." The pale, dark-haired woman offers Levi an understanding smile. "So, no judgment here."

I could kiss the woman when I feel my monster's body relax.

"That's why you haven't been in touch with him?" I ask Levi.

He nods. "I should've told you. But I do plan to ask him about the skin whenever I hear he's back in human form. If he turns back."

That has me hugging my mate tight. "For now, it's enough to know the truth. Even though our aunt met a bad end, I'm still glad to know what it was." The truth hurts, but there's no one at fault other than the small-minded humans who committed the crime. At least they're long dead.

Not that they were the last the world holds.

Sliding my hold from Levi's back to his hands, I lace our fingers together. "And I'm glad there's nothing pushing us apart any longer. It's more important than ever that we make Folk Haven a safe place for our kind. Working together, I think we can make that happen."

Levi presses his forehead to mine, leaning in for a quick kiss. "I pity the mythics who try to stand in your way."

35

MOIRA

Five Months Later

Sea spray coats my skin as Levi sails us toward the sunset. He handles the massive sailboat with ease—a skill I learned his father taught him when he was a teenager. Now, my monster uses the knowledge to take us on our perfect honeymoon. A week of sailing between islands in the Caribbean. If I'd known this was the surprise trip, I wouldn't have waited five months to have our official mating ceremony.

Plenty of mythics, like my brothers and their partners, are perfectly content to acknowledge their mating to themselves and each other and then go forth, living life as a mated couple. However, Levi and I knew our pairing would be a greater upset in Folk Haven. Sure, my brothers both fell in love with mythics different than themselves, therefore disregarding the monster bigotry. But the more traditional townsfolk have been able to brush them off as eccentrics. Easily ignored.

Levi and I cannot be ignored. We are on The Council, each of us holding our seats for the next few years. We have political clout, a say on the future of our town, and we wanted to make clear that our union was not something we planned to keep behind closed doors.

I am a selkie who's in love with a monster, and I'm not ashamed of that fact.

Thus the massive wedding-like mating ceremony we held yesterday, where all mythics in town were invited to attend the reception held on the MacNamara property. Luckily, our family had a large enough plot of land to host everyone who was curious or outraged enough to attend.

We also decided to have a handfasting. The same as my parents had when my mythical mother fell in love with a human. That part of the ceremony was an intimate affair. Just family and close friends.

When I approached the aisle, ready to meet Levi at the edge of Lake Galen, Violetta stepped in my path. The witch presented me with a crown, woven from colorful flowers. I only eyed the creation briefly before confidently—at least on the outside—settling the arrangement onto my head. I figured if I broke out in a rash or collapsed from a paralyzing pollen, at least I wouldn't have backed down.

But nothing disconcerting happened other than Levi's mother offering a nod with a shrewd gaze and a toothy smile.

After the day Satine had helped me find Levi, I'd made it my mission to become friends with her. When she showed up to my parents' house for Monday breakfast in her winged, blue-scaled shape, I stuck by her side. In a matter of weeks, we had grown as close as she and Levi, though I know I'll never truly understand their shared struggle of living in a community where many consider them less than.

Still, when it came time to ask someone to tie the ribbon around our clasped palms at the mating ceremony, we agreed we wanted our friend to bind us together. Satine arrived in her water form and then took on her monster shape and dressed quickly behind a curtain, a besot bear shifter handing the woman a clever wrap dress that allowed her wings freedom. She met us on the shore and was careful of her claws as she twined the ribbon around our wrists.

"May the gods bless your union." Satine's proclamation was met with cheers.

The rest of the day was a blur of faces and congratulations and backhanded compliments. Georgiana in particular had a sharp fury in her eyes when she approached us at the party. I could only imagine how our partnering would read to her. The Council slipping away from her conservative approach. But I smiled and thanked her for coming, as I did with every other hater. Every outdated view was another wave that crashed around me as I stayed steady, next to my mate. We weathered all of it together.

"You ready to swim?" Levi calls the question out from behind the wheel, and I realize the sun has fully sunk below the horizon.

Soon, darkness will be fully upon us. An anonymity I've only ever experienced during the dark moon on Lake Galen. But in this ocean, we can spy for miles, and the water sits clear of ships.

Excitement buzzes against my nerve endings as I wobble on my newfound sea legs, walking from the bow back to where my mate lingers. Levi stands tall, windblown and handsome as the devil in his knit sweater. The air grows cool with the night, but my second skin will warm me.

"Yes." I'm already stripping off my clothes when I answer, high on the idea of finally immersing myself in the ocean while in my selkie form. When I'm fully naked, I reach for the durable locked chest we packed my pelt in.

But a strong set of hands stops me.

"A moment, my mate." Levi wraps his arms around my bare body, backing me up until I feel the cool railing against my lower back. "I want to taste you first."

He drops to his knees, slinging one of my legs over his shoulder to get direct access to his treat. Hot fingers spread my intimate lips, and the monster hums in happiness as he licks and sucks me into an orgasm I never expected would arrive so fast. Everything about this experience brings me pleasure, and I'm not sure if the salt on my cheeks comes from the splash of the waves or happy tears.

Levi stands, his lips glistening in the dim lights on the boat. He strips off his clothes. "I'll meet you in the waves." After a fierce kiss, he dives over the side.

Scrambling to unlock the chest, I'm not even a minute behind, groaning in delight at the melding of my two halves. I enter the water with a delicate splash and dive a hundred feet into the depths without stopping.

The sensation is glorious. The salt in the water makes my animal body buoyant, a sensation the baths at Haven's Relaxation only hinted at. When we're home, I'll have to book myself one of those rooms and sneak my pelt in with me.

Knowing that the water extends for hundreds of miles in all directions gives me a heady sense of freedom even though I remind myself not to stray too far from the boat while my mind still retains a grip on humanity.

A dark mass brushes past me, and I whirl around to discover a hulking tail slowly encircling me. I welcome the embrace of my mate, affectionately rubbing my thick hide against his smooth, starry scales. Levi glitters, even in this deep, dense darkness. A comforting light.

With barely a flick of my tail, I'm eye to eye with him.

I know my face is animalistic. Whiskers, snout, wide brown eyes.

Nonetheless, my monster grins at me as if I'm the most adorable sight.

Cute, he mouths, stroking a hand over my bald head.

I blow a stream of bubbles in his face before rocketing away. For hours, we play chase, dancing around each other in the massive playground of the ocean.

Eventually, we return to the boat, sprawling on the bow, naked and wet in our human forms.

As Levi settles between my splayed legs and slides his hard cock inside me, I gaze up at the starry night sky and thank the gods for my mate.

A sea monster fell in love with a selkie, this time with a happy ending.

EPILOGUE

Amethyst

Five Months Earlier

MOIRA WANTED the task done immediately, and Morgana wants her library, so here I am, stalking a human on a dark back road in rural Georgia.

Fun times.

At least I'm not alone. I glance down at the black form slinking beside me.

"I should've brought snacks."

Bee lets out a yowl of agreement. But the cat man is always hungry, so I'm not surprised.

At least this task is almost over. After days of trailing the man, he's finally settled in a spot that's perfect for me to work my persuasion magic on him. If the chase had gone on much longer, I might have asked Samantha to toss the guy in a cell, so I could get him still and away from curious eyes.

But now, I have Albert Durrand all to myself.

According to Moira, this man has been badgering her for weeks about property on the lake. He asks about pieces of land that he shouldn't know are on the market and aren't available to him. Because Mr. Durrand is a human.

After going through the long wait of discovering if Morgana could buy that house in winged territory, I could almost feel for the guy.

But Morgana and I wouldn't have broken into the selkie's office and fucked her shit up just because we might not get what we wanted.

The security footage of the attack on Folk Haven Realty shows there were four men on the tape, three with visible faces. Others assumed the fourth was that douche bag Michael, who'd tried to force a siren to sing for him.

But I had already persuaded that human to get the hell out of town.

Moira was the one to ID the fourth criminal. It was in the way he moved, she said.

Unfortunately, the werewolf who scented the scene couldn't corroborate her claim. He didn't smell the men. He didn't smell anything. As if the place were an empty, sterile room.

That set The Council on edge. It spoke of some kind of magic usage among beings who shouldn't be able to wield it. And even though the group obviously aren't all buddies, everyone took Moira at her word. There was unanimous agreement that Albert Durrand needed to be dealt with.

Hence, my mission now. To get rid of the man who is entirely too curious about our town.

When he was in Coffee & Claws the other day, I asked Bee to place a spell bag in the undercarriage of the human's car.

Asking Bee to do things is like ... well, like asking a cat to do things.

Except that he's a man. He seems more willing to help

when he's bored, which is often. Living life as a feline must be frustrating and tedious.

"In case I forgot to mention it lately, I'm still looking for a way to reverse whatever curse you're under." I meet his dark gaze as he climbs onto a branch that puts him closer to level with me. "I'd show you my notes if I could. I'm hoping putting the library together will help. You know Morgana is going to want assistance with cataloguing everything. I'll find the answer in one of the books we have, and if I don't, the library will draw more books. We'll find the answer there."

He blinks slowly at me. I hold my fist out, and after a moment, he taps his paw on top. Our basic way of me asking if he understands or agrees and his response of *yes*.

"Okay. Let's get this over with."

Bee hops down, and I move forward, following the draw of the spell bag. It's a dangerous item to use because I have to include a part of myself to connect to the bag and find it again. If the quarry discovered the bag, they'd have that piece of me.

I'd never use one to track another witch.

But with a human? Should be safe enough.

Through the trees, I make out the blocky shape of his beige sedan. The engine is off, but the interior light glows dimly, and I watch the man scribble in a notebook he has propped on his steering wheel.

Why would a human want to drive out into the middle of the woods at night to write?

For the past hour, I've merely been following the pull of the spell bag. Now, I do my best to orient myself based off my starting point.

Realization tightens an anxious strap around my ribs.

We're near the selkie's cove. And tonight is the night of the new moon.

That's too much of a coincidence. Tomorrow, I'll contact The Council and let them know Albert likely must have some knowledge of mythical kind. Maybe he's an academic, looking to study us. He wouldn't be the first professor to discover a lot of the myths are based on truths.

But he could be something more dangerous. A hunter. A sorcerer.

Right now, my priority is my job, which will hopefully keep us all safe from any nefarious plans he might have.

Using the dark of the night, I approach his car invisibly. I almost laugh when I see that the door to the backseat is unlocked. Creepy people rarely expect someone can creep better than they can.

In a smooth move, I pull the door open and slide behind the unsuspecting human.

"Wha—" He only has time to widen his eyes and get out half of that word before I press my palm, covered in red powder, against his neck. Albert stills, held in limbo by my magic.

That's the first skill I mastered. Compliance.

Dislike of this next bit slides through me, but I continue anyway. Capturing his stare in the rearview mirror, I let my consciousness sink into the mesh of emotions that flow through the human's brain.

My power isn't mind reading. I can't pick out words. The vision I have is of colored strands, twining together—some of them thrumming, some dormant. Morgana has described doing this, but the image is far more detailed, and the strands stretch toward her, wanting to be manipulated. I have to find mine. The only one I can influence.

There. A deep red that holds his desires.

Mentally, I reach forward to touch it, but then I see a gray thread wrapping around part of it. The gray somehow seems sticky and alive, as if it could creep toward me.

I keep my distance and start speaking. "Folk Haven is an uninteresting place. You'd be better off, going somewhere else.

Where there are secrets to be discovered. There are no secrets here other than normal small-town gossip."

"No secrets," Albert mutters to himself, voice zombie-like.

"In fact, it's quite unpleasant for you here. So humid. Too many bugs. And the water tastes bad."

The man grimaces, as if taking a sip of swamp muck.

Good.

"Any notes you took are useless. You don't want your note-book anymore. You want to give it to me." The exhaustion approaches. My free hand quivers as I accept the composition book he passes over his shoulder.

"Tomorrow"—I try not to let my voice stutter as I sense that sticky gray thread creeping closer to me—"you'll pack up and leave town. And you won't ever want to come back."

"Won't come back," he murmurs.

"Go to sleep now," I gasp, pulling back my hand just before that clinging presence reaches me.

The man's head falls against his window, snores rumbling from his nose.

With weak fingers, I search for the handle, finally shoving the door open and stumbling out of the car, the human's note-book clutched to my chest. Bee waits nearby, my spell bag in his mouth.

Thank the gods.

"Let's go."

At first, I move at a quick walk, but a strange urgency spurs me on, and my legs start to jog. Then, I'm sprinting, twigs whip-ping my face and roots trying to trip me. Finally, I stumble to a stop when water blocks my way.

Lake Galen.

I drop to my knees on the bank, tossing the notebook aside and shoving my hands into the water, letting the liquid clean away the sick sensation that came from touching that man. A pressure against my leg has me glancing down to find

Bee at my side, leaning his warm, small body against my thigh.

If he were a normal house cat, I'd scoop him up in my arms and bury my face in his fur to drive away this gross feeling. But that would be rude, knowing he's a man trapped.

"It's done," I tell Bee—or maybe myself.

The Council proposed that if I signed an agreement to use my skills for security of the town for three years, Morgana could purchase the house she wanted. "We're going to have our library. I'll find your answer."

And maybe somewhere in those grimoires, we'll find a protection spell strong enough to cover the whole town of Folk Haven, so I'll never have to touch a corrupt mind again.

Bee, for the first time since I found him wandering alone in the woods of Maine two years ago, starts to purr.

The End

Thank you so much for reading SWEARING AT A SEA MONSTER. I hope you enjoyed Moira and Levi's love story! Do you want to spend more time in the mythic-filled Folk Haven? Check out the following books for more small town, sexy, fated mates romances.

SEDUCED BY A SELKIE

Folk Haven Book 1

Delta Novac hates Folk Haven, and as soon as she's done cleaning out her father's mess of a house, she's giving the town her taillights. But after she dives into the lake to save a drowning man that's not actually in danger, she finds herself with a sweet and sexy selkie shadow ready to do anything to get her to stay.

SUCKER FOR A SIREN
Folk Haven Book 2

Seamus MacNamara refuses to believe in the selkie mating myth: that his one true partner will rescue him from great danger. So, when the adorably beautiful barista he has a secret crush on gives him the Heimlich, Seamus ends up insulting her instead offering heartfelt thanks. Now he just wants a chance to redeem himself...and he's willing to go down on his knees to earn her forgiveness.

If you enjoyed SWEARING AT A SEA MONSTER, please consider rating and reviewing the book. Reviews help other readers discover my books, which helps me make a living and funds my ability to write more mythical romances for you!

NEWSLETTER SIGN UP

Get another Folk Haven romance for FREE! Sign up for my newsletter to receive *A Selkie's Secret,* a novella that tells the story of Isla, a selkie, and Finn, the human she refuses to fall in love with...

Keep reading for a sneak peak of *Remembering a Witch*, the story of Fenella, a witch who sees visions of the past, and Graham, the ginger haired professor who looks alarmingly like a man who died hundreds of years ago...

257

REMEMBERING A WITCH

Fenella

When the deep rumble of a man's chuckle brushes past my ears, ducking behind the nearest large object isn't even a conscious decision.

I don't normally take cover at the sound of laughter. Only I've never heard this particular laugh anywhere other than my dreams. The familiar sound fills my mind with memories that don't belong to me.

As I press my back against the rough bark, I am transported away from the pristine university campus, finding myself surrounded by untamed woods.

Sunlight barely reaches the forest floor, filtering through the tall canopy, stingy about which surfaces the rays illuminate. Small bugs flit about, sparkling when they pass through the light. They add a soft hum to the whistle of the breeze between branches. But all these sights and sounds fall away, overshadowed by the man standing across the clearing from me.

His hair, the vibrant color of a ripe pumpkin, shimmers as if the strands were aflame. A friendly grin shows off a set of charmingly crooked teeth, which parts to let out another roll of chuckles.

I've always loved making Henry laugh.

No, not me, I remind myself.

Marbella made Henry laugh.

I am not Marbella. Henry is not the man I just heard.

They both died long ago.

I press my fingers against my closed eyelids as if that'll clear the phantom image from my mind. After a moment, the wild forest and the handsome man drift away. As the vision dissipates, I drag in a deep breath to calm my racing pulse.

This is what happens when I break with my routine.

I blink my eyes open and find everything is as it should be. The well-manicured, grassy expanse of lawn in the middle of the local university campus stretches out before me. Stray students meander along neatly paved sidewalks, many in shorts and tank tops on this beautiful, sunny day.

Unfortunately, I remain pressed against the tree.

"So, the man sounded like him," I mutter to myself. "That doesn't mean anything."

As I converse with myself, Daisy sits on her haunches, staring up at me. My surprise vision has interrupted her walk, but she is kind enough to wait patiently as I work through my shock.

I pull in another fortifying breath, planning to take a confident step away from my hiding place, spine straight, head held high.

My body betrays me. Instead, I end up pulling the brim of my floppy hat low over my face and peeking around the trunk.

The owner of the laughter is not hard to find. His flaming hair is a beacon, bright and familiar as Henry's.

I retreat. "By all the gods and goddesses, this can't be real. This can't be happening."

Twigs pluck at the back of my long floral dress as I crouch, as if making myself smaller might somehow lessen the magnitude of this situation. Breathing becomes difficult, air stuttering in and out of my lungs, my body forgetting exactly how to absorb oxygen. My mind, despite being well tuned into the magical currents of the world, never expected to meet Henry anywhere other than in my dreams.

He's not Henry, I remind myself.

Not any more than I'm Marbella.

Another memory rises to the surface, this one my own.

"You are the spitting image of her." My mother holds up a centuries-old painting beside my face, eyes flitting between the image and my teenage scowl with wonder in her expression.

The heirloom is barely larger than my palm. A portrait of my ancestor, Marbella Henwood. The strongest witch our family has ever laid claim to. A woman who died three hundred years ago.

Discovering I was the reincarnation of a long-ago dead woman has never sat well with me. What is a reincarnation anyway? My mother couldn't give me a good answer. Could never say with utter confidence that I was my own person rather than a copy of one from the past.

I've done my best to forget my odd heritage as I live my life how I see fit.

But my magic doesn't want me to ignore anything. The Henwoods are seers. Prone to visions. A pesky skill that showed up the same time I started using tampons. Dizzy spells would hit me hard moments before my mind fell back hundreds of years to watch short scenes from my ancestor's life.

So, Mom taught me to brew a tea filled with a particular combination of herbs that helped suppress unwanted magical interventions.

But at night, with my mind relaxed in sleep, every so often, Marbella's memories will slip into my dreams. Memories of Henry, the ginger-haired horse breeder she fell in love with.

A man who, it seems, has also been reincarnated.

Mom would claim his appearing here, on a campus in Roanoke, Virginia, where I just happened to be walking my dog, was an act of fate. She has always assured me that, with witches, there's no such thing as coincidences.

But what am I supposed to do with this knowledge?

Even growing up in a household filled with magic, I rejected the idea of my doppelgänger status.

Am I supposed to walk up to this stranger, stick out my hand, and say, "Hello. I'm Fenella Henwood. I've dreamed of you since I was a child. Probably because I'm descended from a line of witches, and I believe that you are the reincarnation of my ancestor's lover"?

In that moment, Daisy's patience runs out. Taking advantage of my distraction, she gives a quick tug, and the leash is out of my hands.

"No! Daisy, come!" My whispered command rushes out low and furious.

She ignores it, dancing away.

"Traitor!"

She wags her tail.

Unlike most dogs, who would use their newfound freedom to bolt, my dog sets out at an almost mockingly slow trot. I could catch up to her easily.

If only I left my hiding spot.

Dread settles in my chest as my furry companion heads straight for the Henry look-alike.

I groan, considering abandoning her out of spite.

If only I didn't love the silly pit bull so much.

One more breath, deep and centering, and I follow her.

I have to clutch my skirt, holding it up so the fabric won't tangle my legs, as I sprint after my dog. With my other hand pressing my hat to my head, I'm sure I look ridiculous. As if sensing my approach, Daisy picks up her pace, beelining for a pair of people, the not-Henry one of them.

The familiar man stands next to a blonde woman who spots Daisy trotting toward them. She lets out a squeak before attempting to hide behind not-Henry in the same way as I just used the tree.

I try not to roll my eyes. With Daisy's cropped ears and muscular body, I know most of the world sees her as the embodiment of aggression. But her lack of a killer instinct is the whole reason she got abandoned.

When I found Daisy in the animal shelter, I knew I couldn't leave without her. There was a force, a push and pull, that existed beyond my physical body. She sat still that day as I lay my palm on her soft head. The expression in her liquid brown eyes was more intelligent than I'd ever expected from any animal.

Finally, you found me, she seemed to say.

And I knew, beyond a doubt, she was my familiar. An animal companion brought to my side by the subtle hint of magic in my veins.

"I'm sorry! She's friendly!" I call out. The classic words of an irresponsible dog owner, but at least I didn't *mean* to let Daisy run loose.

To my surprise, the ginger-haired man crouches low and holds out a hand, inviting Daisy to sidle straight up to him. Happiness flutters through my chest at the sight, leaving me more breathless than my short sprint.

When I reach them, I'm panting. Unfortunately, with the familiar stranger crouching on the ground, I can't even use the wide brim of my hat to hide my face from him.

"I wasn't paying attention, and she pulled the leash out of my hand. I'm sorry," I breathe the words out with my exhale, watching the top of the man's head as he grins down at my dog.

"Don't worry about it. I ..." Whatever he was about to say trails off as he glances up and meets my gaze, surprise slackening his jaw.

Does he feel it too? A strange sense of knowing?

This close, I can see he has the same faded blue irises as Henry. But I also pick up the slight differences between the man of Marbella's memories and this flesh-and-blood figure before me. Not-Henry's carrot hair barely brushes the tops of his ears while original Henry let his locks fall to his shoulders. Not-Henry sports a tame beard, compared to the full growth of original Henry.

Still, underneath it all, the face is the same sharply angled shape.

"I'll see you at the faculty meeting tomorrow." The woman who hid from Daisy practically power-walks away, throwing nervous glances over her shoulder.

Not that my dog has any interest in giving chase. She's too busy getting her belly scratched.

Which brings my gaze to his hands. Long fingers, but this set seems almost soft without the scars of hard work Henry sported. I've stumbled upon an academic, clearly.

And I don't approve of the way my heart beats heavy in my rib cage as I watch not-Henry love on my dog.

The woman had the right idea. It's time to flee.

"Daisy, come here. Leave the nice man alone." I give a gentle tug on the leash, and my familiar lets out a pathetic groan.

"Have we met before?" Even as the man rises from his crouch, his eyes never leave my face.

Not sure exactly what the truth is, I offer a vague answer. "I'm not a student here. Just enjoy visiting the campus on nice days."

His head tilts, and some phantom pull in my chest begs me to step closer.

But I am my own person, and I shouldn't have to listen to magical urges if I don't want to.

Problem is, I'm too overwhelmed to sift out exactly which wants are mine and which belong to Marbella.

Distance. I need distance.

This time, when I give the leash a firmer tug, Daisy grunts and rolls to her feet, falling in step beside me as I do my best not to look like I'm running away.

"Wait!"

My body listens to him, even as my mind doubts that I should. There's a set of heavy footfalls, and the overwhelming presence of him comes up beside me.

"Do you mind if I walk with you?"

Keep reading Remembering a Witch...

ALSO BY LAUREN CONNOLLY

Paranormal

Folk Haven

A Selkie's Secret (Book 0.5)

Seduced by a Selkie (Book 1)

Sucker for a Siren (Book 2)

Swearing at a Sea Monster (Book 3)

Casual Magic

Fire Magic & Ice Cream (Book 1) – coming spring 2022

Seasonal Magic

Remembering a Witch (Book 1)

Wanting a Witch (Book 2)

Contemporary

Forget the Past

Rescue Me (Book 1)

Read Me (Book 2)

Resist Me (Book 3) – coming summer 2022

Standalone Novel

You Only Need One

ABOUT THE AUTHOR

Lauren Connolly is a Colorado Book Awards Finalist and an author of contemporary and paranormal romance stories. She's lived among mountains, next to lakes, and in imaginary worlds. Lauren can never seem to stay in one place for too long, but trust that wherever she's residing there is a dog who thinks he's a troll, twin cats hiding in the couch, and bookshelves bursting with the diverse stories written by the authors she loves.